KOKOMO-HOWARD COUNTY PUBLIC LIBRARY
www.KHCPL.org

3 9223 037934497

DI

DEC 2014

KHCPL SOUTH
1755 East Center Road
Kokomo, Indiana 46902-5393
765.453.4150
www.KHCPL.org

Kokomo-Howard County
PUBLIC LIBRARY

GRAVITY

D1125622

GRAVITY

KOKOMO-HOWARD COUNTY PUBLIC LIBRARY
KOKOMO, INDIANA

MELISSA WEST

This book is a work of fiction. Names, characters, places, and incidents are the product of the author's imagination or are used fictitiously. Any resemblance to actual events, locales, or persons, living or dead, is coincidental.

Copyright © 2012 by Melissa West. All rights reserved, including the right to reproduce, distribute, or transmit in any form or by any means. For information regarding subsidiary rights, please contact the Publisher.

Entangled Publishing, LLC
2614 South Timberline Road
Suite 109
Fort Collins, CO 80525
Visit our website at www.entangledpublishing.com.

Edited by Liz Pelletier and Heather Howland
Cover design by Heather Howland

Ebook ISBN   978-1-62061-092-3
Print ISBN   978-1-62061-091-6

Manufactured in the United States of America

First Edition November 2012

The author acknowledges the copyrighted or trademarked status and trademark owners of the following wordmarks mentioned in this work of fiction: Taser.

For Dad, my constant voice of reason. Thank you for pushing me to reach for the sky and forever catching me when I fall.

PROLOGUE

Year: 2133

The T-screen in our family room crackles just before President Cartier fills the screen. I wonder briefly if Lawrence is watching him, too, like the rest of America, or if he was given an advance showing. After all, the president is his grandfather. I remember the first time I met President Cartier. He was less gray then, less wrinkled. He was joking that Lawrence was too mature for a six-year-old and asked me to take him under my wing, teach him how to be young.

Now four years later, staring into the T-screen on one of the biggest nights of my life, I wish I had some of Lawrence's maturity. I wish I weren't so…afraid.

President Cartier smiles widely into the camera and begins his talk. It's prerecorded—the same talk given every year to each new group of ten-year-olds. I'm told they used to show the video in class on the first day of school, but so many children left crying that they felt doing it at home was better. I'm not so sure. Right now, it's eight o'clock in the evening, which means I have only four hours until they come—four hours to prepare.

"Ladies and gentlemen of our beloved nation," President Cartier begins. "Today marks the first day of your journey to adulthood. It is not to be taken lightly. But rest assured, your parents and older siblings sitting with you have endured this same talk. Time has not changed our process, which, in the very least, should bring you comfort."

He smiles again, this time in that condescending way that adults do. It's supposed to reassure us. It doesn't.

"Parents, please hand over your child's Taking patch."

Daddy holds out the tiny silver case to me, the silver catching the light from the composite crystal chandelier above us. I try to steady my hands as I sit it in my lap, my legs jumping ever so slightly.

"Now, boys and girls, please listen carefully to these instructions, as they will not be repeated."

The screen dims and an image appears of America just before the fall. A voice-over blasts from the T-screen, explaining all the things I already know. Power led to the most destructive war in our history—World War IV. The screen cuts to the full scope of the nuclear war, showing city after city, at first beautiful and strong, and then the bomb hits and there is nothing left but rubble and smoke and sadness. Our world, decimated and no longer able to thrive.

I lower my eyes from the screen, hoping Daddy doesn't notice. The commander doesn't appreciate weakness, even in his daughter, but it saddens me to think how far we fell. I lift my head again and focus back on the screen, anxiously awaiting the important part—the part where the Ancients attacked.

I watch as the screen changes to the alien crafts arriving in our skies, watch as more and more appear until they look like large flocks of birds. There are too many to count. Too many to defend against. We now know that they are older than us as a species, much older. Thousands of years older than the first known existence of man, though I've often wondered how they know. Did one of them tell us? Is it a guess? Regardless, that is how we now know them as the Ancients. What they were called before, I'm not sure. Though I can imagine the people of the time thought of something more appropriately frightening than *alien*.

"Please pay attention, Ari," Mom says, motioning to the screen.

I clear my throat and nod. I didn't realize I was staring at my patch case, hard in my hand. It's small. Maybe eight inches long and four wide. And inside…inside rests the single most frightening thing any of us has ever held. Our patch.

The screen cuts again to the signing of the Treaty of 2090. The five leaders of Earth with the Ancient leader, though there was no Ancient present that day, or at least not visible to us. I know little to nothing about what they actually are or what they looked like prior to our agreement. I know only what the current Ancient leader looks like and he *looks* human, though most say they aren't really like us. It's an illusion. Some say they're made of water. Some say plant. Others say they are no form at all, existing yet not—at least not in the way we do. I'm not sure. Still, there is an empty chair present at the table, as though the Ancient leader sits there, bored, waiting for the meeting to adjourn.

The screen zooms in on the treaty, to the six signatures that agree to our new role. From that moment on, we were no longer just human beings—we were hosts. We provide them with antibodies through the Taking so they can survive life on Earth, which is the only reason we're alive. Had their bodies responded to Earth as they had hoped, we would all be gone. Genocide of the human species. Instead, they needed us—and we needed them. Our planet was destroyed, and they alone possessed the ability to terraform Earth back to health. Could we have done it on our own? Yes, but not before millions died of dehydration or starvation. We needed an answer quickly. They needed a new planet. And so the treaty was signed and we agreed to follow their rules.

President Cartier returns, another fake smile on his face. "You now understand our history and the importance of what you are about to embark upon. Please remove your patches from their cases and let us go through the proper Taking protocol for this evening."

I slip my hand over my patch case and pop the lid open, exposing the tiny silver patch inside. It's as light as composite silk, as smooth as water. Two large oval pieces connected by a thin one-inch piece of cloth that goes over the bridge of your nose. I lift the patch into my hand and hear a nearly silent buzzing from it, as though it's alive—though I know that must be whatever Chemist technology is within it that allows the patch to immobilize us.

I run my thumb easily over the fabric. It doesn't look or feel so scary. Then President Cartier instructs us to put on our patches and I feel my body turn to stone. My eyes widen as they lift to the T-screen.

"Go on, dear," Mom says from beside me. She pats my knee easily and smiles brightly. "It's okay."

"I thought we did it at night?" I say, my voice small.

"We do. This is just a test. It allows you to feel the sensation with us around you. That way you are less afraid. Let me help." She takes the patch from my hand and starts for my face.

"Wait," I say, fighting to keep my voice steady. "What's going to happen? What will I see? How will I get it back off? What if I can't—"

"It's okay," she says again. Then she leans closer to me and I feel my breath catch. *I don't want to do this. Please don't make me do this.*

And then the smooth cloth slides over my eyes, blinding me. I relax for only a moment, then the patch suctions around my eyes as though laced into the bone, and I feel it against my temple, pressing, digging in. I want to pull it away. I scream out for Mom to help me and hear her say over and over that it's okay, everything's okay.

Briefly, I hear President Cartier's voice in the background. He explains the Taking, how our bodies don't feel the Ancients receiving our antibodies. How our daily supplements guarantee we have plenty. How our assigned Ancient will come into our room at midnight and how the Ancient will Take for thirty minutes before returning to Loge, their planet. The patch then deactivates, he says. I wonder why he's saying all of this so quickly and then I know.

As though someone turned off the sound, I can no longer

hear. I strain to find a sound in the silence, but there is nothing. And then I can no longer feel or smell. My lungs burn and for a moment I'm sure I'm being suffocated. I try to move my arms, to reach for Mom, but they won't budge. I try to scream out but no words come. Panic sears my mind, and then one by one my senses return. I feel Mom's hand gripping mine hard, hear President Cartier's voice in the background, but still I can't see or move.

I know I should be listening. I know I should try to remember what to do and how and when. But all I can think about is how in four hours I will have to do this all by myself, in the darkness of my room, waiting, blind and immobilized…as one of them comes for me.

If I could scream…I would.

CHAPTER 1

Seven Years Later

I stare out my window into the darkness, hoping to see them. But of course, that's stupid. It's only 11:53. They haven't even reached Mainland yet.

I'm supposed to be ready, patch secured, but I hate the patch. The way it suctions to my temples like it wants to crawl right into my brain, leaving me immobilized and blind, yet still able to hear, smell...*feel*.

I don't get why we have to wear them, but it's required. Their rule, not ours. Something about an encounter years ago. No one talks about it. No one talks about them at all. Odd considering they control so much of our lives. I haven't slept over at a friend's house since I was little. We can't miss the Taking. And I haven't gone to sleep before midnight since I was nine. I can't sleep during the Taking.

Each night I wait by my window, my curiosity almost too

much to stand, while I scan the trees hoping to see one of them emerge. I never have, likely never will. "The Ancients prefer discretion," Mom once told me. But I'm not sure it's that simple. Some say they stay hidden because they're so freakish we'd drop dead of fright. Others say they're too attractive, too tempting.

I prefer this theory.

The leaves rustle outside, a sound kind of like wind. They are here. They're unleashing from the trees this very moment, literally moving from their world to ours. The leaves move in rhythm when they emerge, beautiful and unsettling.

As I step away from the window, the first signs of nervousness crawl up my spine. I'm not afraid of them, or at least I'm not afraid of *mine*, though maybe I should be. I know next to nothing about it. I don't even know if it's a he or a she.

I remember the first time. I remember being unable to shake or flinch or show fear and wondering if I'd ever be able to move again. Losing sight was terrifying enough. But throw in being unable to move, while the rest of my senses—hearing, touch— were heightened… I'm not sure how I survived.

That night I was afraid, but that was seven years ago. Now… I'm not sure how I feel. While fear is part of it, if I'm honest, completely honest, there is something deeper than fear inside me for this thing that climbs in my window. I'm curious…too curious to be of any good.

My alarm clock beeps. 11:55 shines out in bright red, the date, October 10, 2140, below it.

I rummage through my nightstand and grab the silver case that holds my patch. Hurriedly, I pop the lid, preparing to slap it over my eyes, but jerk back.

It's empty.

I flip the drawer upside down. The contents scatter to the floor in a mess. Oh no, oh no, oh no! This isn't happening. I cover my mouth with my hands and force myself to draw a few breaths. I reach for the case, checking it again. Still empty. Of course it's still empty!

Beep. 11:56.

The tin roof of my house *ting*s as they step across it. Sort of like a smattering of rain or, better yet, hail. I press the side panel of my stainless steel bed. The hidden drawer slides open. But after another thirty seconds of searching, I'm still empty-handed. I need the patch. I need the patch. I need the patch.

My eyes scour the room and land on my closet, the last place it's likely to be, but I'm running out of options—and time. I hesitate, glancing around my room, and hear my alarm beep again.

11:58.

I rush to my closet keypad and jab in the code. The steel doors swing open to reveal my perfectly organized shoes and clothes and handbags—perks of being the Engineer commander's daughter. I search the floor, then yesterday's clothes pile, hoping the patch is buried inside. It's not. I scramble out of my closet and to my desk, kicking the chair out of the way.

My hands have just reached into the drawer when the final beep jars me.

11:59. It's time.

The keypad outside my window sings out with the familiar ten-digit code. I run to my bed and lie down, clenching my eyes shut. My heart beats wildly in my chest. I'm on the verge of hyperventilating. If I make it through tonight, I'll either be executed or dosed with memory serum. That's the human punishment, anyway, but how will the Ancients respond? What about *my* Ancient? There have been stories, old legends— disappearances. Which is why no one is stupid or reckless enough to lose the patch.

Except me.

Beep. Beep. Beep. 12:00.

The floor-to-ceiling window slides open, letting in a gentle breeze. An earthy smell, like pine or freshly mown grass, fills the room. Their smell. It creeps in, making only the tiniest of sounds, and then the springs of my bed creak. Warmth surrounds me and nervous sweat oozes from every gland in my body, but still I hold my eyes tight. My body tenses, a reflex of years of combat training preparing me to fight if necessary. I feel arms on either side of me, and then air as its body lifts and hovers above me, preparing for the Taking.

The heat intensifies. It bounces back and forth, back and forth. Our bodies make the connection. Now the waiting as the antibodies it needs are sucked from my body into its body.

Five minutes pass, then ten, maybe more. I've tried to count many times but lose track with each breath it releases upon me. Has it noticed I'm not wearing the patch? Surely so, but then wouldn't it say something—do something? I don't know. Chills run over my body, and I fight to push them away. I need to focus, think. And then it happens.

A single drop of liquid hits my lip, and reflexively I lick it away. My taste buds explode with flavor. A perfect mixture of sweet and sour, warm and cold. I've felt the droplets before but only ever a single drop. I hardly gave it notice. Another drop and another.

My eyes fly open and round out in shock.

It—*he*—hovers above me as light as air. A bright glow encircles him. His eyes are closed. A sweet smile rests on his perfect face. Another drop hits my cheek, and I glance up to see tiny teardrops slip from his eyes, as though the Taking is too overwhelming to handle.

I should move. I should speak. I should do *something*, but I can't look away. I want to reach out to him. Touch his face to see if he's real. Because he can't be…this can't be. Yet it is.

My Ancient is Jackson Locke.

Athletic. Smart. Arrogant. The kind of boy all the girls notice at school but few are comfortable enough to talk to. He leads in everything he does…and he's my great competition for top seed.

My mind replays every instance I can remember of seeing him. He looked so normal—*looks* so normal. But he's here. So he must be…

His eyes snap open and, startled, I jerk up in bed, slamming into him. He crashes down on top of me. "Hey!" I fight to get his giant six-foot body off me.

"Shhh. Are you crazy?"

"What are you doing here?" I ask, my voice shrill.

"Be quiet! We don't want to— Oh no." His head jerks to the window. "No faith, that's for sure," he mutters, and I shake my head in confusion. He isn't making any sense. I strain to listen, but I can't hear or see anything at all. Then I realize someone is coming. Another Ancient. I'd forgotten about Dad's and Mom's Ancients. They may have been in the house when I screamed. For the first time since losing my patch, fear grips my chest, coursing through my body like an electrical pulse.

Jackson's gaze falls on mine. "Ari…" he whispers. "I know how this looks and I can explain, I can, but not now. Tomorrow night."

His head jerks to the window again, and I feel his body tense against mine. I don't know what to say. I don't know what to think. All I know is that I'm in trouble, maybe even *we're* in trouble, yet all I can think about is the way he just said my name. Ari. Not with menace or sarcasm or jealousy, like I'm used to from everyone—including him, the few times we've faced each other at school. He says it like I'm more than just a girl who everyone recognizes but no one sees.

He looks back down at me. "Close your eyes," he whispers. "We have to finish the Taking."

I hesitate, not wanting to be so vulnerable, but eventually close my eyes. What choice do I have? Seconds tick by, then minutes. The heat returns. He's over me again. Then a soft tap sounds against the window.

Jackson lowers himself off the bed. I want to steal a peek, but fear forces me to stay still, eyes shut tight.

A conversation starts low, too low for me to hear. Sort of like a fly buzzing close to your ear. I ache to move closer, to hear what they're saying. Jackson's tone hardens.

"No," he says. "Same as usual. I'm done. Let's head back."

Another buzzing.

"She can't move," he says, which would be true if I were wearing the patch. But I'm not, which he knows. He's protecting me.

Buzzing.

"Yes, it's fine. I'm sure."

Why is he protecting me? Hosts are assigned. He has known me most of my life. The revelation sends my mind into turbo mode. He knew me all along yet has never given me a moment's notice in school. Do the Engineers know? Does Dad know?

My mind continues to contemplate everything I've always known and everything I've never guessed, until the sweet smell of his skin evaporates. The window slides open and clicks closed.

He's gone.

Everything that just happened is swarming my thoughts at once, but one thought rises above all the others...

I'm not sure I can wait until tomorrow night to find out what's going on.

CHAPTER 2

"Ari!"

I jerk up in bed, my eyes darting around for Jackson before I remember that he already left. I yank off the covers. What time is it? Time, time, come on, where are you? I stumble through the darkness until I find my alarm clock, which is facedown on the floor. 5:10. I spin around, cursing myself for not setting out training clothes last night.

I'm almost to my closet when my bedroom door slides open and my dad storms in. He's so tall his head barely clears the doorframe. As usual, he looks as though he wakes already dressed for the day—gelled dark brown hair, smooth shave—except that instead of his usual black collared shirt and slacks, he has on his training clothes. Uh oh. Since Dad is too rigid to be normal, he fully dresses for the day when he works in his home office during the hour before our training. The fact that he's already changed means I'm even later than I thought.

"Do you see the time?" he asks. "I expected you downstairs ten minutes ago. You know my schedule. I—"

"I know, I know, I'm sorry. My alarm didn't go off. I'm almost ready. Give me five minutes." I fumble with my closet keypad, entering the code wrong three times before I get it right.

Dad crosses his arms, oozing disappointment and annoyance. Heat rises on my neck and my palms grow clammy, like my body can't decide whether to be angry or embarrassed. "Fine, you have five minutes," he says. "But I expect you to take this seriously." He reaches for my nightstand. "I'll log your patch—"

"No!" I race to the nightstand and slam the drawer before he can pull out my patch case. The case that, once placed in our reader, will show my patch missing. I don't think the Ancients require executions anymore, but memory serum sucks. Every kid has been given it for accidentally forgetting the patch or not putting it on correctly…and none of us ever wants to get it again. No memories for twenty-four hours. A whole day gone, and that's precautionary. The whole thing leaves you feeling violated.

Dad cocks his head. "What are you doing?"

"Nothing," I say as I plant myself between him and the evidence.

"Your patch case. Now."

"I'll do it, Dad, really. You go set up." I fight the urge to cringe. I can't let him know I have an ulterior motive.

He hesitates but marches from the room. As soon as he leaves, I slump against my bed and draw a long breath. I feel like I've lied to him, even though I didn't say a single untrue word. With him gone, the events of last night flash through my mind like lightning, one after the other, each more confusing than the last.

Jackson Locke.

I think back to yesterday when Coach revealed he and I were the top two seeds. Jackson had nodded toward me and I to him, respectful. I tried not to watch him fight after that, but I couldn't help it. It's hard to avoid watching your biggest competition. I watched as he quickly beat his opponent and felt a tinge of jealousy. He made it look so easy. Now I know why.

I get dressed in a daze, throwing on the stretchy gray pants and tank Dad had designed for our training, and head downstairs. The case reader is visible from the bottom step, implanted in the wall, sort of like a safe except with a glass front. Mom and Dad already placed their cases inside. Each has a green light beside it, letting us know all is well…and no investigation will be commencing. I have no idea how the Ancients are assigned to us or, more likely, how we are assigned to them, considering they are the ones who require the patch and monitor the case readers. But it seems odd that of all the people in our city of Sydia, Jackson Locke is assigned to me.

The reader activates as I near. I press my thumb into the fingerprint scanner, causing the glass to slide open. A cold mist releases from the box and I wonder, not for the first time, what they do to the patches when analyzing them. I fiddle with the case in my hand, hoping the device won't detect the missing patch. Maybe I can tell Mom I lost it. No, she'll tell Dad, and even he won't be able to save me from this. I lift the case up and then lower my hand, up again, then drop it. Blast!

Finally after several seconds of staring, I drop my case in its slot and back away, my eyes clenched tight. I hear the glass close. Then something magical happens—it clicks off. I open one eye and see a green light beside my case. I can't help it. I have to check.

I press my thumb into the scanner, and once the glass lifts, grab the case and pop the lid, preparing to slam it back into its slot, but stop cold. My patch is there, silver and shiny and staring at me as innocent as ever. My mouth drops. How did it…? I shove the case back and rush from the scene before whatever just happened reverses and my patch goes missing again.

I think to last night. It wasn't there. I had dumped my case upside down. I checked everywhere in my bedroom. Yet…maybe it was a dream. And if I imagined that, then maybe I imagined Jackson, too. My mind replays his face, his eyes, the way his jaw looked so strong, confident. I didn't imagine it.

I need to tell Dad, but if I do I'll get interrogated and dosed with memory serum for sure. I release a long breath. I have to tell him but not yet. I need to question Jackson first.

I step over to our transfer door. The glass lifts, and once I'm inside, the elevator shoots down to one of the most advanced training rooms in the city. The four gray walls appear ordinary, but these walls are temp-treated, soundproof, and able to absorb a bullet without causing it to ricochet back. Dad structures the rest of the room according to our training schedule. Last year, there were four shooting stations. Now, the room is empty except for the combat mat positioned in the center. Dad is already on it, bouncing around as though he's still a trainee. Sometimes I think he wishes he still were one, which is why he pushes me so hard. Reliving it and all.

"I'm here," I say without looking at him.

"Put on your gear."

The air-conditioning blows through the air ducts in the ceiling. I shiver as I pass underneath one. He knows I hate being cold. I yank a pair of gloves from the weapons shelves against the left wall and walk back to the mat. I bounce for a second, finding my balance, and then slide on the gloves.

I tilt my head to the side until my neck cracks, an anxious response, Dad tells me, but I do it to remind myself that I'm tough. Dad waves me forward with his hands. He likes me to take the first jab, so he can tell me what I did wrong and then test my blocking ability by demonstrating on me. Any other day, I'd go along with it, but I don't have time for this today.

The sooner I finish training, the sooner I can get to Jackson.

I flip forward and switch kick, aiming for his face, but he grabs my foot, spinning me around so I land hard on the mat. I bounce up and jab, not letting him stop to demonstrate, and end up clipping his jaw. I cringe, unsure of what he'll say or do.

Dad nods in approval. "Nice work. Never give the opponent a chance to have the upper hand. Go again."

I punch once, twice, three times as Dad blocks each hit, while my mind drifts again to last night. Jackson is an Ancient. A boy from school is an Ancient. Even now, I can't wrap my mind around it.

The only Ancient I've ever seen is Zeus, their leader, during one of the televised addresses. And yeah, he looks human enough. I guess I assumed they looked human, but were actually something else, like they were projecting the human form. Some sort of illusion, like everyone says. But Jackson is very real. And if Ancients actually look and act just like humans, then maybe there are others at school. Maybe they are around us all the time, watching, analyzing—preparing to attack. And maybe that's the real reason we train so hard. I've often wondered why Engineers need so many Operatives. Of course we're told they maintain civil arrest throughout the country, though there are rarely uprisings, especially now that food shortage isn't an issue. We all know that we're training as a precautionary measure. It isn't something they hide. But still, I always assumed we trained in case they attacked, not because they were already here.

A shudder creeps down my back. I have to corner Jackson today. This isn't something I can keep from my dad for long.

"Are you listening to me? Where is your head today?"

"Sorry." I shake all thought from my mind, wishing I'd grabbed some coffee or at least an energy shot. Tomorrow I'll get up on time, but I know better than to ask for a break. I have ten more minutes to go, fifteen if I can't get my act together.

"Start the sequence," Dad says.

I bounce on the mat and tumble backward in a series of flips to give me the distance I need to do the sequence. Dad widens his stance, rotating his arms forward to get into position. He won't hit me—well, he never has—but this look, serious and deadly, always makes me think he will. It's no wonder he was top seed, top Operative, top everything. Part of it was because he wasn't a legacy like me, but I think it's also just who he is—driven, always a step ahead. Even though I'm the legacy, the one legally born to be commander, I'm not sure I'll ever have the determination he has.

I sigh, wishing I could fight someone—anyone—other than
Dad, and run across the mat, dive into the air, and then flip again
and again until I'm in front of him, in motion before my mind
can slow me down. I spin and kick. Throw punch after punch. My
teeth grit together.

I push harder and harder, Dad blocking each move, but I
refuse to give up. I shake the last of sleep from my body and
continue to fight without thought or worry, until Dad throws up
his right hand, his signal to stop.

He steps up, towering over me. "Good, but not good enough.
You need to close the fight in under five. To pass Op training,
you'll have to do it in under two. To live if you're in a *real* fight,
you'll need to know how to kill the enemy in less than a minute.
You have to respond faster, Ari. The Ancients will guess your
moves before you can think them. The key? Stop thinking so
much."

I glance at him, bewildered. "Under five? I clipped you.
Aren't you—" A zillion different words come to mind. What I
really want to say is *proud*, but I know better than to speak of
self-praise.

Dad watches me for a fleeting second, then exits the room
without another word.

I grab a towel from the weapons shelves, wipe my face, and
return my gloves, my mind reeling. Even if I weren't rattled
beyond measure, there's no way I could knock someone out in
under a minute, forget the enemy. I sigh. Well, I guess I'll figure it
out or get bruised up trying.

I walk back to the transfer door and step inside. It shoots

up, opening to the main level of our three-story house. I wave to Mom, who's watching some computerized cooking program on the T-screen in our sitting area. Thanks to World War IV, 95 percent of Sydia can't afford food. Our land was destroyed, toxic, so that nothing would grow. As part of the treaty, the Ancients cultivate our land, but they can't—or won't—sustain the entire planet. So our genius Chemists created food supplements. A single pill provides all the nutrition of an entire meal. The problem is that manufacturing them is expensive. Their solution? Charge ridiculous amounts for real food and use that money to cover the costs. So while no one starves now, the majority can't afford to even buy an apple, while the rest can have anything we wish. Mom's wishes are simple—cooking and the necessary tools to make it fun for her. But she still feels guilty, which is why she transferred from Composites to Nutritional Development. I think if I weren't so programmed to become an Engineer, I might have liked to try Chemist training. They do lots of good things.

My bedroom door slides open as I near. I take my time across the composite carpet. The softness surrounds my toes, and I wiggle them deeper into the carpet before reaching my closet. I weed through my clothes, choose my outfit for today, and then head to the shower. I need a plan, a way to question Jackson without anyone noticing. The last thing I need is for him to go all Ancient on me at school, exposing both of us. I need this to stay a secret—for now—until I can find out why he's here…and why he protected me. Twenty minutes later, I come down to a silent house. "Mom?" I call out.

"Here!" she shouts from the kitchen. I round the corner to see her already in her white Chemist coat and scrutinizing a tiny pill on the counter. She pulls a dropper from her pocket and dispenses a brown drop onto the pill. The liquid coats the encasing, changing it from white to a deep brown. She passes it over to me. "Do me a favor and taste this."

I recoil. It's not that I mind food pills. I take them every day even though my family can afford natural foods. But still, brown? I don't think so. "Thanks, but I'm not…hungry." I step as far from her outreached hand as possible.

"Oh, come on. I'm trying a new formula that infuses flavors into the pill. This one"—she smiles at the tiny dot in her hand—"is chocolate."

I eye the pill with suspicion. "Chocolate?" Her grin widens, so I relent and pluck the pill from her fingertips. "Are you—?"

"Just taste it already," she says, excitement in her voice.

I drop the pill into my mouth and instantly the taste of melting chocolate pours over my tongue. "Mmmm. How did you do that?"

"Chef's secret," she says before pulling a notes tablet from her other pocket and becoming absorbed with her findings. I watch her for a few moments, studying the intensity on her face, the smile that never leaves her when she's working. I wonder if I'll feel that way, love my work and all, or if I'll always look severe…like my other parent.

I grab a few breakfast supplements from the pantry and edge toward the front door without another glance from my mom. I reach the door and drape my keycard over my neck, which ensures my access to the tron, school, my locker, and anything or anywhere else I may need to go during the day. The door scanner flicks from red—no card—to green—good to go.

I set off down the street, trying not to run, refusing to think about what may—or may not—happen when I get there and see *him*.

I arrive at the tron just as the doors are about to close and rush onboard. Silver walls, silver seats, silver flooring. The entire thing is composite steel, with no hint of guilt at how cold it makes our ride, hence why I never sit on the top level. If the main level is cold, the top level is arctic.

The tron encircles and connects the four regions that comprise Sydia, our reborn American capital since a bomb decimated the previous one in the war. There are only three other well-established cities across America, one responsible for each section of the country—north, south, east, west. They're like mini governments, each reporting to Sydia, which handles both the entire country and the southern region. The rest of the nation is wasteland, livable yet unable to grow food or maintain natural water supplies. Everything the people in those areas need is filtered through their dominating city. It's like a business the way our government operates, but World War IV and its aftermath didn't leave the leaders of the time much of a choice. We needed strict survival methods and controlled authority. That's the only way we'll survive if the Ancients attack again.

I slide into the third seat and focus out the window at the reds and yellows and oranges of fall, trying to focus on my plan for cornering Jackson. Within moments, the tron kicks into motion, and I settle in for the short ride to school. We pass through more of the residential areas of Process Park, the upper-class region where I live. Here, the houses are three, sometimes four stories, with large front porches and immaculately manicured lawns. Wealth. That's what exists in Process Park. Wealth and expectation, which is why the school that Parliament insisted be shared by the two residential regions is positioned on Process land.

The tron reaches the school stop, and half a dozen of us exit onto the auto-walk, which leads into the main entrance. I glance to the left, to Landings Park, and swallow hard. It's desolate looking, but I guess that's expected of government-provided apartments. Building upon building, all stretching high into the sky, all slammed together so tightly a resident of one could jump through the window of another. A few kids walk down the main street toward school. They're dressed in government-provided clothes. Brown pants, white T-shirt, and optional brown jacket. I look down at my own outfit and feel a pang of guilt. Sometimes I wish—

"Ari Alexander!" I hear, then fast footsteps followed by, "Where in the 'verse did you get those boots?"

I spin around just as Gretchen, my best friend, bends down to take in my new composite leather ankle boots. I smile. If Mom's thing is cooking, Gretchen's is fashion. We scan our keycards at the door, and I half listen as she tells me about some new technology that allows you to change the height of your heel as needed. We are almost to our lockers, and I'm contemplating telling her about last night when my breath catches. Rounding the corner, completely at ease, is the Ancient himself.

Jackson.

CHAPTER 3

Jackson shakes the excess water from his damp head, flattens out his T-shirt, and throws on a government-provided brown jacket. The jacket wraps his body, tying at the side, exposing a small triangle of his white T-shirt. He waves to some giggling girl— probably a stupid freshman—and knocks knuckles with another Landings boy as he makes his way to Central Hall, the annex of our school. He never looks my way or even hints that he knows me. My teeth grind together as I watch him, each step like he's mocking me.

All along I've been jealous of him, of how quickly he moved up the rankings. I'm the future commander, my spot has always been known, but he's from Landings. Most of the top seeds have been children of Operatives, all from Prospect. Jackson had no previous training or help to get him to that spot. I admired him. And now I find out it was all a lie. He didn't succeed on merit; he succeeded because he's an Ancient.

"Hey, aren't you listening to me? I was— Ohhhhh!" Gretchen

follows my gaze. A wide smile stretches across her deep brown face.

I blink a few times and rub my right eye, faking an eyelash. "What?"

"Blast, Ari, when did you fall for Jackson?"

"Ugh! Like I would fall for an An—other." My eyes fleet to hers, but she's still smiling.

"Uh-huh, so why are you avoiding the question? Yeah, that's what I thought." She twiddles a transfer pen against her locker, the *ping* making it all that much harder for me to come up with a decent excuse.

"No. No, it isn't like that. I was just thinking that today I'll face him in F.T." I need to learn to lie better.

"Face who?" I spin around to see Lawrence Cartier, the third in our little group, coming toward us. He sweeps me into a tight hug and smiles over at Gretchen. "So…?"

Gretchen and I exchange glances. "So what?" she asks.

"Who were you talking about?"

"Oh, Ari faces Jackson in F.T. today. We were just talking strategy."

Law's face sours. "I don't get it. Why do the girls have to fight the guys? He's three times your size. It isn't—"

"It's fine," I say. "Size doesn't matter—you know that. Besides, I've been the best so far." Barely.

He bites back an argument, raking a hand through his shaggy brown hair. He has that hair girls would kill for, and it gets him almost as much attention as his large brown eyes and flawless olive skin. Girls notice him everywhere he goes. And maybe part of that is his future title, but I think it's his easygoing attitude combined with his innocent face, though maybe that's because I've known him forever. "Well, let's hope you're right," he says. "I'd hate to have to break his jaw."

I almost laugh. Even though Parliament trainees take mandatory combat classes, fighting was never Law's strongest skill. Thankfully, Gretchen pats his shoulder in that condescending way she does and says, "Nice thought, Lawrence, but we both know you better leave the fighting to our girl."

I smile uncomfortably. "We'll see how I do. We should get in there before the bell rings." I grab a few transfer pens and a notes tablet from my locker and follow Gretchen into the F.T. gym. Law waves to us as he heads to the library, a fitting place for Parliament trainees.

My next class is called Field Training or F.T. Once we hit high school, we were forced to decide our career paths, and all of us juniors are well into career training now, which means everyone who plans to become an Operative like Gretchen, Jackson, and me has to face off. Of course, not everyone will make it through true Op training. Dad likes to remind me of that fact when I'm struggling with one of our morning trainings.

The gym is two stories with the same bullet-absorbing silver walls of my training room at home, but this room can hold ten thousand people. It's huge, which to me seems crazy considering as far as I know only our Pre-Operatives class—twenty-five boys and girls—ever use it. I glance to the center of the gym. Stationed in the middle of the floor is a large, thick mat. Aerial boxing.

"Uh-oh," Gretchen says, nodding toward the mat. "You ready for this?"

"Of course," I say, but inside my nerves wind tight. I draw a breath, forcing myself to calm down as Gretchen and I head toward the girls' locker room to change into our training clothes. Like the ones I use at home, these are made of a formfitting, stretchy material, although these are black instead of gray. Girls can choose tank or regular sleeve tops to go with the pants. I reach for a tank and a pair of pants before heading to my training locker two rows away. I sit down on the steel bench in front of it and start to run through my moves in my head. I consider Jackson's size and strength, the various techniques I've seen him use during practice rounds, all of this making me glad that we're doing aerial boxing instead of floor combat. On the floor, it'd be next to impossible to outmatch him one-on-one without a weapon. Aerial boxing is different. It's all about speed and balance. Those who can control their bodies win. Those who can't face-plant on the mat. I've been in both positions, though I've never lost to a student.

When we exit the locker room, Coach Sanders, our seven-foot, balding instructor, is standing beside the aerial mat, legs braced and hands on his hips like we wasted his time dawdling in the locker rooms and he is irritated. Coach is an ex-Operative, as tough as they come, and with an impatience level that rivals Dad's. He's known to yell first, ask questions later. I pick up the pace and jog to the mat.

"You know your order," Coach says. "File into line with your opponent."

I scan the crowd to find Jackson sitting on the ground. As the two top seeds, we'll fight until the Engineers feel one of us is superior to the other. He spots me and winks. Fury lights up inside me, and I almost rush over and demand he answer my questions. How dare he act like he deserves to be here, like I don't know exactly what he is? He leaps up and struts over to me. "Ready to eat mat, Alexander?"

What's up with guys only using people's last names? I laugh and stretch my arms over my head, then stretch from side to side, resigning to keep up the charade. "Hmph, we'll see."

Jackson leans down to put himself at my eye level, a sly grin on his face. "Don't worry, I'll let you win."

"Alexander and Locke," Coach yells before I can respond. "You're up."

I glare at Jackson before walking off. Gretchen grabs my arm as I go and whispers, "He's tough. Fake a knockout if you have to."

I shoot her an annoyed look. I may be small, but I'm strong. "I've got this, Gretch," I say and then head to the weapons station for gloves.

I take my time finding the right gloves. Too big or too small and I'll be screwed. Finally, I slide into a pair and flex my hands. When I turn back, Jackson is on the mat, jumping around like he does this in his sleep. A tinge of worry seeps into my mind, but then he winks at me again. Ugh! I won't lose this fight. Blasted, arrogant Ancient. I'm going to lay him out flat.

I run forward and leap into the air, cutting flip after flip until I land in front of him. Coach laughs. "Good luck, Locke." And he presses the buzzer.

Everyone and everything is silent. My gaze holds on Jackson. I try not to notice the way his blond strands shadow his eyes or the way his body flexes as he prepares to strike. These aren't things to notice in an opponent—especially not now. I feel my breathing escalate, hear it release in short bursts. I attempt to close down my mind, but I'm wrecked with thoughts and worries.

He's a smart fighter. I can tell by the way his eyes never leave mine; he knows our eyes shift before our bodies do. And he's fit, but not just his upper body, like most guys. He knows the importance of our legs, how their strength determines our speed. That's when I realize he's not just an Ancient, he's a well-trained Ancient, and he's chosen to pretend to be from Landings instead of Prospect, which means he's not just a trained fighter. He's smart enough to blend in. Blend. Every possible scenario of what he is and what that means rips through my mind and I'm left with only one word—*danger*.

Suddenly, anger over the fact that he's been fighting for months now, all the while pretending to be human yet knowing he has the advantage as an Ancient, pits my stomach. I rush forward and jab just as Jackson spins away from the contact. He wraps his arms around my waist, tosses me to the mat, and pulls back his arm to punch. I leap up and his fist finds the mat. I flip backward and bounce around. I can't be on the defensive. I can't lose control. I pull my arms tight, adjust my focus, and force all fear from my mind.

I am the next commander.

I whip around, surprising Jackson with a kick in the gut. He stumbles back with a breathless laugh. "Oh, really?" he says. Then he's in my face. "Sorry, Alexander." And he punches me in the jaw.

My head snaps back, and my mouth fills with a metallic taste. I lick away the blood from my bottom lip and try to shake off the throbbing pain. Anger bubbles from my chest, and I lunge for him, kicking and swinging, unsure of anything but the force of my movements. I want to beat him. I'm going to beat him. I pull away and he stumbles again, shock written across his face. I fight the urge to spit at him and instead push him farther backward.

"Bring it," I scream, and then narrowing my eyes and lowering my voice, I whisper, "I'm not afraid of you."

The arrogance drips from his face, replaced by something more real. "You should be." And he flips forward. But my dad taught me well—I know the flip will alter the cushion around his brain just enough so when I slam my fist into his face, it will do more than cause blood; it will lay him out.

Jackson lands in front of me just as my fist connects with his temple. His balance wavers, his head bobs, and then as though in slow motion, his body falls to the mat.

For a second, I'm too surprised to move. We aren't supposed to use knockout moves in class, and I'm unsure whether to celebrate or apologize to Coach. But then Gretchen storms the mat, wrapping me in a tight hug.

Several of the other students clap and congratulate me. I allow a small giggle to release before glancing at Coach. He seems to be deciding whether to yell at me or congratulate me himself when Jackson stirs. He leans up on his elbows, and I stare down in amazement, a small welt the only sign that he was hit. He should be down for at least half a minute, not five seconds.

Blasted Ancient.

Coach looks as annoyed as me. "Well, if you can walk, get

off the mat," he says to Jackson. "O'Neil and Martin, you're up."

I consider helping Jackson to his feet but decide better of it, bounce off the mat, and pass my gloves over to Gretchen—she has my same hand size. "Good luck," I say to her. "You'll do great."

She smiles nervously, heading to her spot on the mat. Like Law, fighting isn't Gretchen's thing. She's the genius of our group, always the one with the highest test scores. Her having to fight almost feels wrong, but fighting is expected of us. We are training to become Operatives, after all.

Jackson walks up beside me, interrupting my worried thoughts. "Nice work," he says. "Surprisingly."

I sputter, prepared to really let him have it, when he motions to the mat. Lexis Martin, Gretchen's opponent, bends her knees and flexes her hands. She looks like she's preparing to snap Gretchen in two, and maybe she is. Everyone knows Lexis is a psycho. Built like a guy, total muscle, and with at least a foot on Gretchen. I try not to worry. Gretchen has had some advanced training like me, but not on the same level and not against someone like Lexis.

Gretchen jumps around on the mat, and Lexis follows. I shift my eyes from Gretchen to Lexis and back. Timing is everything, and one of them has to start. My palms itch from fear and nerves. Lexis lunges forward, sweeps Gretchen back, and decks her in the face.

Blood trickles from Gretchen's nose.

I take an unthinkable step forward when Jackson grabs my arm. I glare at him, but he's right. I can't intervene. Stepping in isn't considered brave on my part; it's considered selfish, reckless, even. Besides, Gretchen can handle this. She's—

Another blow and another. Her body falls back. Her head drops to the side. I suck in a sharp breath, my arms shaking from the tension. I lunge forward, then back, and forward again. Jackson's hand is still on my arm. Gretchen throws up her hands, signaling she's done. Coach calls the fight. The winner is supposed to step off the mat.

Instead, Lexis slams her fist into Gretchen again, and Gretchen collapses to the mat, gasping for breath. That's enough for me.

I wrench my arm free of Jackson's grasp and charge forward, diving into Lexis. She rolls over and I jump up, preparing to kick her in the face, when someone lifts me from behind. "Hey!" I scream and lash against the person encaging me.

Jackson sits me on the mat like I'm a child in a tantrum. He doesn't say anything, no one does. I know what I've done. Operatives are all about pride, and I've just risked Gretchen's.

Coach doesn't yell at me. Instead, he walks over to Gretchen, who is gushing blood. "She'll need the medic," he says to no one in particular.

"I'll go," I offer, even though he could buzz Dr. Tavis from here. Coach nods, and I head toward the medic station just outside the main gym doors. I don't notice that Jackson followed me until I reach for my keycard and feel his hand brush past mine. My skin tingles with awareness. He slides his card at the door and waits for me to go inside.

We walk down the short hall in silence, the air dense with our unspoken thoughts. It's the perfect opportunity for me to question him, but with Gretchen hurt I can't interrogate him the way I'd like. Something tells me he knows that. Finally, we reach the medic's counter at the end of the hall, relief flowing through me at the break in tension.

"We need healing gel, please," I say to Dr. Tavis, who is seated behind the small counter.

He furrows his gray eyebrows. "Another F.T. injury?" he asks, clearly getting tired of treating us all the time.

"Yes, but nothing serious. Just a flesh wound." Dr. Tavis nods, pulls out a tiny jar, and stuffs it in a clear coolant bag. The bag is so cold it burns against my skin, but I refuse to flinch. I grasp it and walk back out the door, Jackson following.

I'm about to turn around and ask the most important question on my mind—*Why are you here?*—when he says, "You were right to intervene."

I stop. "What?"

There is no one else in the hall. No one to wonder why we're talking. No one to see this moment of weakness in Jackson, a boy who defines himself by being mysterious and aloof. I spin around to face him, my words tumbling out before I can stop them. "No. There's no honor in what I did. No—"

"Pride?" He gives me a mock grin. "*You* define what makes you proud, not someone else, and definitely not rules that would have you watch your friend get beaten. There's no pride in that. You were right to step in. I would have."

I'm taken aback, feeling more and more awkward that we're having this conversation instead of the one we need to be having. I look into his eyes. They're a strange mix of blue and green, like

God couldn't decide what color to make them. "You're one to talk about honor."

He closes the distance so we're inches apart and whispers, "Tonight I'll explain. Just please, for now, trust me."

I study his face, which shows no signs of our fight, though I can feel my bottom lip swelling. I'm trained to trust no one, definitely not an Ancient. Yet I don't have a choice. I need answers…at least that's what I tell myself. "Just one question, then."

He waits.

"Why didn't you report me?"

He pauses, allowing his eyes to connect with mine, a slight smile on his face. "Who says I didn't?" I suck in a sharp breath and he laughs before turning to walk away.

I want to scream for him to explain, but more and more students are filtering into the hall. I have no choice. I have to wait until tonight.

When I get back to the gym, everyone's rushed off to next period except Gretchen, who is sitting up. Apparently Coach canceled the rest of the fights for the day. She gives me a weak grin, and I hand over the healing gel. "Want me to help?" I ask.

"Nah." She forces herself to stand up. "I'll see you in history."

I pack up her things and then grab my tablet and transfer pens. I'm about to leave when Coach shouts my name from across the gym. My stomach sinks. Here comes the bawling out I'd expected earlier.

I follow him into his small office and sit in one of the two metal chairs in front of his desk. I glance at the composite wood walls, the five framed pictures hanging haphazardly around the room, and then drop my gaze to my hands, intertwined in my lap.

I wonder if he called my dad. Maybe I'm being sent home. But surely what Lexis did was worse than my knockout, which didn't even *really* knock Jackson out.

"Do you know why I asked you here, Ari?" Coach finally asks.

I shake my head. "No, sir. I'm sorry about the knockout. I didn't…" I stop myself. I don't want to say I didn't mean to, because I did, and I'm not one to lie—well, not usually.

He laughs. "I'm surprised your father didn't tell you. I recommended you for early training."

"Early Op training?" I ask, sitting up taller in my chair. I thought only Dad could recommend early training, but he would never want to show favoritism by recommending his own daughter. He has never liked that being commander is my birthright. He'd rather I kill myself trying to advance, earn it the way he did. "Thank you, sir," I say. I fight to keep the excitement from my voice, and then doubt slips into my mind. Did he recommend me just because of Dad? Because of who I am instead of what I've done?

"Sir, the recommendation. I'm not sure I should accept."

Coach gives me a puzzled look. "Alexander, you're the best I've got. The best I've seen in years. You deserve this." He holds my gaze. "Don't doubt that."

I can tell by his expression that he's genuine. "So what does that mean, exactly? What do I do?" I ask, smiling.

He leans back in his chair, a giant grin on his face. "Well, you still have to complete testing, but you will participate in some early lessons with other Pre-Ops. I know you see a lot of this stuff already, but I think it would be beneficial for you to experience being an Operative from someone other than…"

"My dad."

His face turns serious. "Yes. You'll receive details later today. Congratulations."

I leave his office in a complete state of euphoria. Early Op training! And I did it without Dad's help. Sure, I'm the future commander, but I don't want to just go through the program. I want to be the best. I want to prove to Dad that I could do it whether I was guaranteed a spot or not. I don't want to give the other Operatives a reason to doubt me.

A bell rings through the hall, signaling the ten-second warning to get to class. I round the corner and slip into history just as the final bell rings, my mind traveling back to Jackson. He was a transfer student, something that rarely happens here. I remember all the girls going crazy when he first arrived—a new boy in Sydia. But he just seemed…lost. We never really spoke until one day in eighth grade English when he loaned me a transfer pen. I had forgotten mine, and it was a test day, which meant I would fail and be unable to make up the grade. I remember being on the verge of tears, and then Jackson slipped one of his pens onto my desk. He never looked at me or said anything at all, but I've never forgotten it. Just like last night, he protected me. He could have let me fail. It was nothing to him.

Now I'm left wondering how many times he's looked out for me over the years and I never knew it. The question is, why?

⟡

Class for the day finally ends. I stare out over the orchards behind our school. From the grassy hill above the field of trees, everything's visible. It's a warm day, full of giant white clouds dotting an expansive blue sky. This type of weather brings everyone out to stand among the rows and rows of trees after school, all of them bright green and full of perfectly ripe fruit thanks to the Ancients.

Ancients…

I scan the field for him, and instead spot a boy being chastised by Professor Vang, one of the Lit professors, likely for stealing fruit. The boy pulls an apple from under his shirt, then an orange, a pear, and before long, Professor Vang's exasperated and sends the boy back to the school for his punishment.

We're allowed to eat as much as we like while at school, but taking even a single piece of fruit off school property is considered stealing, punishable by law. Most kids abide by the rule, though I can't blame the ones who try for more. Food pills, while nutritionally adequate, don't provide the joy of real food. The excitement we get from biting into a juicy orange on a warm day. The comfort of warm soup in the dead of winter. Most of these kids rarely get that satisfaction, which is why I sit on the hill, never venturing into the orchards. Even though there's plenty, even though these orchards are really here for the Prospect kids like me, I can't bring myself to take a piece of fruit.

I start to look away when my gaze lands on Jackson. I study him, searching for something that differentiates him from the rest of us. He has stripped off his jacket, so he's wearing just a fitted white T-shirt and the brown government-provided pants. A small girl walks up to him and motions to the apple tree behind him. He plucks an apple from the tree and hands it to the little girl, who looks as though he's just made her entire day. For a second his eyes drift to mine, and then someone shouts his name from behind. It's Mackenzie Story. Gorgeous, blond, hate-worthy perfect Mackenzie Story.

Jackson smiles when he sees her. She runs to him, wrapping her arms around him. He laughs at something she says, then breaks free only to pull her back into a deep kiss. I look away, feeling the tiniest prick of envy in my chest. Not because I want him or wish I were her, but because I wish someone would kiss me like that, hold me like I was all that mattered in the world. Instead, I'm treated with delicacy, no one getting too close unless it's for combat training.

I lean on my elbows and tilt my head back until I feel the sun warm my face, soothing away the mixture of emotions moving through me. Doubt. Confusion. Excitement. Every element of my life is planned out, and for once, it feels nice to know something others don't. Jackson Locke is an Ancient. The curiosity is almost too much to stand—why is he on Earth? Are there others?

I'm about to get up when someone leans over me, casting a shadow on my face.

"Hello, sunshine."

"Hello, yourself." I squint in the sun, taking in Law's full profile. Without Gretchen around, he relaxes into his role, something that came so much easier to him than to me. Because Lawrence isn't just any boy. He's the president's son...and my future husband.

CHAPTER 4

"Ready to go?" Law reaches out to help me stand, his touch lingering. His smile is bright against his olive skin, and I find myself staring at him, wondering where the boy I'd grown up with went. He looks so mature, so ready for his future, not at all the kid who used to be afraid to go outside at night. No, now he's…I don't know, an adult.

I remember when our parents told us their plan a few months ago. How a union of the president and commander would strengthen the American people's faith in our system. Law nodded along as though the plan made perfect sense. To him, it was just another box to check off on his list of responsibilities. Career—check. Wife—check. We had always been best friends, so he knew me, was comfortable with me. But for me, it went against everything I had ever been taught about being an Operative. We're taught to think on our feet, be our own person.

How could Dad not see the irony of teaching me to think

on my own and then taking away one of the most important decisions of my life? It was wrong. It is wrong. And there is nothing I can do to change it.

He loosens his grip once I'm up, allowing our fingers to dangle together. He has that easiness, and I can't help but go along.

Law gives me a quizzical look just as my phone buzzes, saving me from an explanation. I touch the screen, and a message appears.

Come see me after school.

"Great," I say as I lock the phone and shove it back in my pocket.

"What is it?" Law asks.

I lift my eyes to his, shaking my head. "Dad. He wants me to come to his office." I grab my things and walk over to the far right side of the hill, Law falling in step beside me.

There's a path below that leads around to the auto-walks in front of the school. Near the bottom the drop is steep, and I'm about to just jump down that last section when Law stops me with his hand.

"Here, let me help," he says. His long legs clear the drop in an easy step, and he turns to hold his arms out to me.

I laugh. I'm in Pre-Op training and have received personal lessons from the commander. I can handle a stupid jump. I open my mouth to say as much, but then I see the seriousness in his eyes and realize it isn't that he thinks I can't do it; it's that he wants me to lean on him.

It's a strange thing for me to have someone wanting to take care of me that isn't my mom. Most assume I'm tough enough to handle myself, and I am, but still it's kind of nice.

I force a smile down at him and say, "Thanks," before taking hold of his outstretched hand and leaping into his arms. He catches me around my waist and eases me to the ground, keeping his hands relaxed at my hips. My breath catches as our bodies press together. It takes me a moment to meet his gaze, and when I do, I find myself flushing. I am so confused.

I just want everything to be the way it used to.

No Ancient Jackson. No husband Lawrence. No complications. I tell myself it'll get better. It has to get better.

Law clears his throat as he releases me. "I think I'll hang at your place for the address," he says. "Sound okay?"

I glance up, confused. "Are you skipping it tonight?" The address is a televised meeting of the four worldwide leaders with Zeus, the Ancient leader. They discuss the treaty, any issues, and then close with a reminder of our responsibility. It's basically the same thing every month, and Law always attends.

"Yeah, Mom wants me to watch body language. She said I'd learn more watching on the T-screen. And since your parents will be at the address like mine, I thought we could watch it together. You know, alone."

There it is—the word I dreaded the most.

I force myself to smile again, even though in my head I'm having a mini panic attack.

We reach the tron and separate, giving me a much-needed chance to think through how I'll get out of it. Law boards the south tron home, me the north to Dad's office. The tron holds for a few more people to board. I reach down for my training

GRAVITY

43

tablet and almost miss Jackson sliding in behind me. I freeze mid-motion. He never takes this tron.

My nerves kick up. I wonder if they've requested him for early Op training, too. He has the test scores for it and excels at combat training. But then Dad would have an Ancient on his team. I can't let that happen.

The tron announces the next stop, and then all doors close. We pass the croplands, also known as Life Park, full of fruit and vegetable fields that stay green all year round, like the orchards. Again, the Ancients. Most seem to think the Ancients are part plant or something and that's why they can travel between planets through the trees instead of just—

"You know," Jackson whispers, "you really shouldn't stare. It's rude."

"What? I'm not looking at you. I'm looking at the crops. Not that it's anything to you."

"Yes, but there are people out there. *Poor* people. Wouldn't want to be caught judging them."

"What are you—?"

"So what's up with you and Mr. President, anyway?"

I shake my head, locking my jaw to keep from screaming. How is this arrogant boy the same one who gave that little girl the apple or me the transfer pen all those years ago?

He laughs, deep and pure. The sort of sound that would make me smile if he were anyone else and if I didn't want to jab out his eyes right now. I start to respond when the intercom announces our arrival at Business Park. I exit the tron onto the auto-walk that lines the road, refusing to acknowledge the boy who follows me off.

There isn't a single tree—not a real one—anywhere in sight. Instead, composite trees decorate the open areas. But looking realistic isn't the point. The trees are there to soften what is considered the scariest place in the city. Few citizens come here beyond the Chemists, Engineers, and Parliament—the Trinity.

The Engineers aren't so bad. Though I guess I'm partial. Soon I'll become one. They maintain civil order, organize getting food and supplies out to the country, and ensure the Ancients keep to the treaty. The Chemists…well, most hate them. Their job is to create efficiencies in our world, or as Mom puts it, to steal the things we love little by little. It's an odd thing to say, considering she is one.

Parliament worships the Chemists, but they would—they're the government. What they do beyond bossing everyone around, I'm not sure, though I do know Parliament makes all the decisions, good or bad. Parliament is the only other section of the Trinity where leadership passes within a single family—the Cartiers—and Lawrence is the next in line.

The Engineer building comes into view, and then the larger Parliament building, followed by the Chemist building. The city developers didn't worry with fake plants here, only the three metallic buildings encircling the Pride Fountain—a giant water fountain filled with holographic water. It's a group of soldiers holding a flowing American flag. But that isn't the unsettling part. If you look into the depths of the fountain you'll see flashes of people trapped below the surface. Parliament claims the people represent our past enemies, but we all know better. The *people* aren't people at all. They symbolize the Ancients.

I focus back on the Engineer building, hoping to dislodge the guilt forming in my stomach. I hate keeping things from my dad. I tuck my hair behind my ear and catch Jackson walking up behind me. "It's called an auto-walk," I say, annoyed.

He smiles. "I prefer to control my speed."

I turn on him, spreading my stance so I don't fall. "What are you doing here?"

"I have an appointment."

"With who?"

"Who do you think?"

I stifle a gasp. Dad. No, he can't. Dad wouldn't see a Pre-Op, no way, unless I'm right and he's been requested for early training. I'm torn between fear and jealousy. "Not yet," I say. "We need to talk first. I have to know what you're doing. What *are* you doing?" I drop my voice and peek around to make sure we're alone.

Jackson doesn't break eye contact. "Ari, there's a lot going on. I can't explain now, not here. Tonight. Please just trust me."

"Trust you? You're about to see my dad, Jackson. Why? Why are you messing with him? Leave him alone. Leave us alone. Go back wherever you came from."

"I can't do that."

"Then don't expect me to trust you, and don't expect me to keep this a secret. I can't. I have to tell him." I rush forward, off the walk, when Jackson grabs my hand. I see a flash, and then I'm in the middle of a field. The land is burned black, the sky orange. There's nothing, no sounds, no movement…no one.

Jackson releases me, and I try not to stagger as the world rushes back. I suck in a sharp breath. "What was that?" No one had ever mentioned Ancients could project images or whatever that had been.

"You don't get it. This isn't a game. You have to trust me, or everyone you know will die."

I stumble back. "You can't—"

"It isn't me, and it's already done, already started. Everything changes today. I can't stop it." He looks past me, and I turn to see the guard to the Engineer building watching us. Jackson smiles at him. "Girls." He shrugs. "She forgot something at school."

The guard smiles back. I can't breathe.

I struggle to keep my hand still as I lift my keycard for the guard to scan. He waves me inside and the smell of machinery fills my nose. Any other day I would hypothesize about what they were working on, what new invention, but today I feel too sick to think about anything at all.

I step into the elevator and press the third floor button, but Jackson reaches in, stopping the closing doors. I grimace.

"I'm sorry I had to do that. I needed you to see what could happen. I know you don't trust me, and I don't blame you, but at least wait until I can explain." He bends down in front of me so we're eye to eye. "Can I count on you to keep this a secret? Just please—"

"All right," I say, knowing that it's my fear talking but feeling too gone to stop myself.

He relaxes against the elevator wall. "Thank you."

The door *beep*s and an announcer welcomes us to the executive suite. I rush through the doors and down the hall toward Dad's office, while soft footsteps sound from behind me.

I press the buzzer beside Dad's door. "It's Ari."

"Come in," Dad says.

I tighten my posture as I enter the room. Something about my dad makes me feel so inadequate in every way. It's like if I can stand straight, act like an adult, maybe he'll think of me as one.

"Sir," Jackson says from behind me.

Dad's eyes pass over Jackson, his demeanor projecting the distaste he feels for pretty much everyone.

"Can I help you with something, son?"

Jackson clears his throat. "Yes, sir. I'm Jackson Locke. I believe you requested to see me?"

But then the impossible happens. Dad removes his glasses, marches over to Jackson, and shakes his hand. "Yes, yes indeed. Your last statistical essay was genius. I've requested to have you transferred to my sector for early training."

My head jerks back and forth from Jackson to Dad. This can't be happening! I'm the one advancing to early training. Ancient Boy is now a genius, too? That's just great.

"Cybil," Dad calls.

A beep fills the room and then a voice. "Yes, sir?"

"I'm ready for you," Dad replies.

A petite woman with shiny black hair enters the room. I know all the Engineers and Operatives, yet I've never seen this woman before. I look from her to Dad, confused, but know better than to speak before spoken to, especially in front of his staff.

"Ari, meet Cybil, your new private trainer."

My mouth drops. "Private? I thought I was training with other Pre-Ops."

"You'll receive private lessons," Dad says. "You aren't ready for Op training. Not yet."

My heart sinks. Of course he would override Coach Sanders's request. I peek at Jackson, my entire body numb from embarrassment, but he doesn't return the look. Dad leads him out of the office without a second glance my way.

Cybil clears her throat and smiles at me.

"Are you new?" I ask.

"Me? No, I've assisted for years and was just promoted when your dad assigned me to your training."

I cringe. "Sorry."

"Nonsense. I'm excited to train you," she says with a smile. "Now let me show you around."

I follow her back down the main hall, wanting to tell her that I've already seen most of the Engineer building but not wanting to come across as rude. I expect her to stop at the elevator, when instead she walks to the end of the hall and to a floor-to-ceiling painting of President Randolf Cartier, Lawrence's grandfather, who died a few years ago. She slides her hand behind the right side of the frame and within a second, the painting swings open, exposing a hidden entryway.

Cybil motions me forward, and once we're both inside, turns on me. "Your father lied in his office," she says, her tone indifferent. I start to question what she means, but she raises her hand. "You're not receiving personal Op training. That was said for Locke's benefit. Your father wants you to experience more than that of an Operative. He wants you to learn his work, commander work. We'll meet daily after school."

Goose bumps rise across my body. "So when you say you've been an assistant, you mean…"

"Special Projects Assistant to the commander. I organize Engineer advancements, research, development, that sort of thing. I also monitor tracking."

"Tracking what?"

Cybil releases a curt laugh. "You'll see. Follow me."

She starts down a long hallway that looks like it should be part of the tron instead of the inside of a building—glaring metal walls with nothing but hiccups of black doors to break up the silver. The walkway is lined with lights on the floor and the ceiling. There is no one else in the hall, no sound coming from the doors. I release a breath and see the air puff in front of me.

Cybil reaches the fifth door and slides her keycard through the scanner stationed on the right side of the door. Inside, there are a thousand mini T-screens covering the back wall. Too many to count. Too many to focus on. And all of them are trained on people going about their lives. Working. Eating. Having sex. Ack. Okay, so the Engineers spy on us. I can't say I'm surprised.

Cybil walks over to the left side of the wall, where a male attendant with reddish hair and freckles sits, wearing the telltale black Engineer attire. She motions to me, and he nods as though my presence explains everything.

"Do you see this woman?" Cybil says as she clicks a screen and points to a blond lady getting onto the tron. "We suspect she's a Latent, a rogue Ancient hiding in our world. As you know, Ancients are only allowed to be on Earth during the Taking. The fact that they are here breaks the rules of the treaty."

"A rogue Ancient? How do you know?"

"It's tricky," she says. "Average people don't notice them. After all, there are tons of pretty people in the world. People with seemingly no imperfections, which is how they have existed for years—hidden among our beautiful." She redirects her attention to the screen, zooming in with her fingertips so every feature of the lady is in focus. "But they aren't like us. If you look closely you can see their skin is neither white nor brown, neither light nor dark. See," she says, tapping the screen, "it's almost golden. And their eyes…" She zooms farther and then taps the screens above and below the one with the lady. An older man appears in the top screen, a young female in the bottom. Cybil zooms in on their eyes. I have to stifle a gasp. They are all, all three, exactly like Jackson's. A strange combination of blue and green, changing, it seems, by what they wear, the color of the sky, their mood, who knows.

"Their eyes are all…"

"The same. We know," Cybil says. "But that isn't enough for us to take someone into questioning. We have to be sure. Recognizing an Ancient is recognizing that nothing about him or her can be easily classified. Nothing except movement, which is always premeditated. We don't notice the Ancients because they don't want us to notice them. And that is what makes them so dangerous."

"But you said they were rogue Ancients. Why don't you just contact Zeus about it?"

"We have, yet the number of Latents continues to rise. You're the future commander. Think like it. What do you think that suggests?" She crosses her arms, waiting.

There are Ancients living in our world, pretending to be human. Of course, I already knew that thanks to Jackson, but I had no idea the numbers were so high. Zeus wouldn't ignore our concerns unless...

"Zeus sent them to spy on us," I say. Jackson said it's already in motion. This must be what he meant. And this room shows thousands of Ancients, but there have to be more that are not yet discovered, like Jackson. My greatest fears from this morning may be true after all—they're watching us. But why or what they have planned I haven't a clue. Enough delaying; I need to question Jackson. The sooner I get home, the sooner I get answers.

Cybil dismisses me with the assignment to pay attention to those around me, but when I slide onto the tron, I find myself staring out the window, avoiding everyone. I don't want to start staring from person to person, checking for eye color, creeping everyone out. Instead, I try to think through how the Latents got here. They could stay after the Taking, I guess, but more than likely they come through one of the interplanetary ports. There are ten ports across the world, two here in America, all connecting to Loge—the Ancients' home planet. The Ancients control them, which would make for easy access of large numbers, but surely Earth's leaders watch the ports.

I focus out my window, trying to make sense of it, when my eye catches on the forest behind a series of houses. Trees. The trees act as hyperspaces between Loge and Earth, linking the two so that Ancients can travel easily between planets. So technically they could come at any time. But surely we monitor them on some level, though how could we possibly monitor every single tree? We couldn't. If they can cross over to Earth through any tree, at any time, there could be hundreds of thousands already here. The thought sends a shudder down my back.

The tron stops at Landings Park. Farther down the street are the rows of new composite steel apartments, but here, the old, rundown part of Landings, the buildings crumble in places, and it has the smell of burned wood. Of course, you'd never see a wooden building in Process. It seems stupid to me anyway to use wood to make a building or house when wood is so flammable. I guess the Chemists agreed and so they banned the use of wood ten years ago.

I glance out the window at a group of people huddled over a fiery metal bin. I wonder what they're doing and then realize — cooking. Landings is a food pill region, which means someone has found, stolen, or spent a month's salary on a piece of meat. A few more people walk up, then a group of kids, none of them older than five or six. The look of wasted taste buds envelops their small faces. I've seen the look before, especially around desserts.

I start to look away, saddened by the poverty our government allows, when something catches my eye. Adjacent to the fiery pit is a patch of trees, and clinging to a thick limb is a man. His golden skin contrasts against the brown of the tree. His brown hair moves with the wind. His expression looks focused, too focused. He watches the people for a fleeting second, and then he's on them, tossing children into the street, Taking one then another then another. I bang against the window. Everyone on the tron jumps up and rushes to the windows, all pointing and shouting, all horrified. My eyes dart down the aisle, and then back to the attack. I gasp. Every human lays lifeless on the ground—men, women, and children. There is no blood. The Ancient has leeched the life from these people.

Everything changes today, Jackson had said. He knew.

I race to the front of the tron. "Open the doors!" I scream at the attendant, but he just looks at me, confused. A few more passengers join me, all of us yelling at the attendant to do something. Finally he phones for emergency help, just as an explosion sounds from the site of the attack. Everyone darts back to the right side of the tron, but all we see is a thick cloud of smoke. The tron kicks back into motion, and we're ordered to take our seats, though no one does. Finally we reach Process, and everyone rushes off the tron. Several are already on their phones, recounting what happened, and I pull mine to do the same. First bringing up Dad's number and then switching to Mom's, I message *Attack at Landings, call for help. I'm okay. Almost home now.*

Ten minutes later, I'm home. I slide my keycard at my front door, activating Dad's home protection system. A red laser scans over me twice, and then the light on the alarm turns green. "Ari Alexander, welcome home," it says. I dash inside, looking frantically for my parents.

"Mom? Dad?" I yell.

"They aren't here," Lawrence says, walking in from the kitchen. He takes one look at me and wraps me in a hug. "Are you all right? I just heard about the attack." He loosens his embrace and motions to the T-screen in the sitting area off our kitchen.

I cover my mouth with my hands. They show the attack, and then what looks like a bomb dropping, followed by smoke. When the smoke clears, the ground is black, the trees decimated. I don't know how the building is still standing, but it is streaked in black.

My phone buzzes in my hand, and I click a message from Mom. *Are you okay? Are you at home?*

I type *yes* and drop my phone into my pocket. Lawrence hugs me closer, his warmth blanketing the chill in my spine. He starts to ask me more when the screen switches to the address. We both sit silently on the sofa in front of the T-screen, waiting to hear what they say about the attack.

President Cartier, Lawrence's mom, sits in the center of a long table. To her right and left are the three other worldwide leaders, and seated at the end of the table is Zeus Castello—the sole Ancient leader.

President Cartier is the smallest of the five, so petite she looks almost like a child in an adult's chair. Her brown hair curls in perfect waves, just like Lawrence's. Her olive skin shows her age, creasing in fine lines across her face, the heaviest lines around her eyes. To her right sits Alaster Krane, the European president, known for his stunning height and overpowering attitude. His skin and eyes and hair are as black as the night sky. Down the table to President Cartier's left are the African and Asian presidents. The African president is the only other female, and her skin is as fair as mine, but while I have nearly black hair, hers is fiery red. The Asian leader sits quietly. He's always quiet, as though he prefers to think more than speak, a quality I wish some of the other leaders would possess. His looks are perfectly symmetrical, and I imagine he was very beautiful when he was young.

Then my eyes drift to Zeus, my breath catching. He stares into the screen, ominous and powerful, like he knows so much more than any of the others. I've never met him, and I pray I never will. I study him as though I'm seeing him for the first time. Long white hair that must reach the center of his back. Eyes like a predator. He looks human, like Jackson and the other Latent Ancients, but now that I'm looking at him closely I realize that nothing about him is warm. From his expression, to his face, to his posture. Everything about Zeus oozes danger. I clear my throat to push back my fear.

They begin with the regular stuff—the laws of the treaty, discussion of amendments (there never are any), and a reminder of our responsibilities as humans. I almost scream for them to get to the attack. Law looks as tense as I feel.

Finally, President Cartier focuses on the main camera, her face solemn. "Today, there were four attacks across the world, one in each of the four governing territories. We believe the actions were that of a vigilante Ancient group. They have all been apprehended, returning our world to safe order." She turns to Zeus. "Mr. Castello, to your knowledge, can you guarantee there are no other threatening groups, and furthermore, do you agree to maintain our peaceful separation until coexistence can safely commence?"

"Vigilante Ancients?" Law asks, but I'm too shocked to respond. Because Zeus Castello has just walked off the stage.

The leaders jump up. One yells after him.

The screen cuts to black.

CHAPTER 5

Hours later, I'm alone in my room, left with my paranoid thoughts. Dad and Mom came home right after the address, both looking wrecked with worry. Dad went straight to his office and Mom, after asking me a zillion times if I'm okay and checking me for signs of stress, went straight to bed. I tried to listen by Dad's office for a while, hopeful he'd say something, anything to make sense of all this, but then he stormed out of his office, nearly barreling into me, and ordered me to go to bed.

I flip on my T-screen and wait for Gretchen or Law to sign on. Maybe they've heard something. A few messages appear from professors. At-home exercises from Coach Sanders. Each tiny note comes across as a virtual envelope and then disappears once I've read it. We're supposed to archive anything from school or the Trinity, but I'm too exhausted from the day to care.

I glance at the clock. 11:50. I need to prepare. I reach for the power-save button just as a message flitters across the screen. I sit back in my chair, watching as the note blinks from yellow to green, yellow to green. Across the letter, written in script, is the sender's name—Jackson Locke.

I hover my pointer over the letter and then say, "Open." It flips backward and a note appears.

> *I forgot to tell you—try not to scream.*
> *—J*

I stare at it, trying to analyze the words as though something more could come from them. I have no clue what he means. I click to discard the note, hesitate, and archive it instead.

My alarm beeps. 11:59. I lie down but don't worry about my patch. I didn't even check to see if it was in the case earlier. It's pointless now.

The window keypad *ping*s, and I force myself to draw a long, steady breath. *Relax-relax-relax-relax.* I repeat the mantra over and over, hoping the word processes into my subconscious, because inside I'm beyond vexed. Something tells me tonight will change everything.

Wind blows in through the now-open window, sending a mix of pine and honeysuckle into the room. Goose bumps form over my skin. I wait for Jackson to start the Taking, but the warmth never comes.

"Ari."

I ease my eyes open to see him sitting beside me. He looks so comfortable. He *always* looks comfortable, like nothing or no one could ever rattle him. I wish I were that way.

"What are you doing?" I ask.

"We need to talk first."

I sit up, pulling my knees to my chest, and wrap my arms tightly around them. "Fine, talk. Let's start with the attack. You knew didn't you? Why didn't you stop it? Those people...the children." I glance away to keep my eyes from brimming with tears.

"Yes, I knew." He drops his head. "And I already told you; I can't stop this. The attack was minor. It was a warning for things to come if Parliament continues to refuse coexistence."

"Refuse? That's always been part of the treaty. I thought—"

"No. Everything you've been told is a lie."

His words feel like a slap in the face, and I shake my head in disbelief. It's not possible. But the address...Zeus walked off the stage. Still, Dad wouldn't lie to me.

"He would and has. All the top leaders know."

I jump up. I hadn't said anything out loud. "Stop doing that. How are you doing that, anyway?"

Jackson shrugs, continuing to look at ease. "Sorry, I can't control it. I'm usually better at hiding it. All the RESs are equipped. It's a device implanted into our hearing system. It reads worry and stress in your tone and word choices, then transmits the reading into data."

"So you hear my thoughts?"

"No. It's more like an educated guess based upon your stress reading. I'm just better at it than most."

I freeze. My arms drop like noodles to my sides. "Most. Did you say 'most'? The rogue Ancients. They aren't rogue, are they? Zeus sent them, like he sent you. This isn't happening."

"Ari…"

"No, stop. Just stop." I pace the room, my mind a whirlwind of puzzle pieces that I can't make fit. There are more questions than I can focus enough to articulate, but one holds strong in my mind. I have to know. I pause in front of him, closer than I normally stand to anyone, but I want to be sure I hear his answer. "What do you want from me?"

For the first time, he looks away. He scratches his chin and rakes a hand through his hair. Then in a flash, he's beside me. He grabs my hand, and I'm sucked through a tunnel. I can't breathe. I can't breathe. "Jackson!" I scream. A hand clamps over my mouth.

"I asked you not to scream," he whispers.

The pressure locks over my chest and lungs. My eyes feel like they'll pop from their sockets. I bite his hand, but he holds tight. Then the pressure is gone, and I'm standing in an office, an office I recognize. Dad tells someone to come in. President Cartier enters followed by Zeus Castello. They look angry, but Dad, like Jackson, never appears rattled.

Dad scribbles a note and then peers up at them. "Thank you for coming," he says. "I've reviewed the information you provided, Mr. Castello. Unfortunately, our Chemists disagree. It is not yet time for coexistence. We will notify you when food supplies can support both species."

"Food supplies!" Zeus grabs hold of his chair. "*We* provide your food. We have kept our end of this agreement." His voice shakes and he stutters, "A-a-greement, the harmony of opinion, action, or character." His face relaxes, and he draws a deep breath before continuing. "Our kind, sir, became fully acclimated two months ago, yet you still refuse. What is your game, Commander?"

I glance nervously at Dad, but before I can hear his response I'm yanked back, the force pressing all the breath from my lungs. Bile climbs in my throat. Tears leak from my eyes. Then I'm stumbling backward onto the floor of my bedroom.

Several seconds pass before I open my eyes. Jackson is curled on the floor, white as paper and covered in sweat. His body spasms. I rush to him and check his pulse, which is racing in his veins. I run to my bathroom and soak a cloth with cold water. When I return, he's sitting up. I kneel beside him and press the cloth to his forehead and neck. "Are you all right?" I ask, then, realizing what I'm doing—or rather who I'm doing it for—drop the towel into his hand. He looks so much like a human that my instinct to help those in need must have caused me to move before I could think.

He nods. "Just…need…a second," he whispers. Neither of us speaks for a minute or two. Jackson opens his eyes and gazes into mine. "Thanks for this," he says, lifting the towel in his hand.

I pull away but stay seated on the floor. "What did you do to me?"

He draws a breath. "Recollective transmission. I showed you a memory that was shown to me. I knew that was the only way you'd believe me. I haven't transferred to a human before…well, since the last time." He smiles again. "It's exhausting. Your minds are more skeptical than ours. It requires more energy to implant the memory."

I think back to what I saw. "So you've acclimated to Earth?"

"Yes. Our bodies function very much like yours now. Our

antibody levels are strong. We're ready."

"And we're refusing to let you come here permanently."

"Yes. The memory I transferred happened four months ago. We've been told to continue the Taking until coexistence is agreed upon. But as you saw, negotiations have not gone well."

"But according to the treaty, failure to comply with coexistence will spark a—"

"War. Yes. We are a peaceful species, Ari, regardless of what you're told. Even Zeus doesn't want a war, but I can see this hardening him. He sent a formal ultimatum, which has gone unanswered. The attack today was nothing. A warning. He sent additional RESs a month ago. We're stationed at different areas, all given one goal—find out their strategy."

"And an RES is…?"

"Republic-Employed Spy."

Spy. So I was right. That explains the Operative thing. He's already an Operative…just not for humans, and he wants my help.

He leans closer to me. "Look, we don't want a war. We want to live in peace. Here. Coexisting. Just like we were promised when we first agreed to the treaty. We need information on the strategy, information that could be used to force your leaders to relent. But I can't do it alone. I need your help."

"Why me?"

"What can I say? I like you." He smiles.

I roll my eyes. "Be serious."

Jackson rakes a hand through his hair, showing his discomfort at the question. "You're smart, strong, and I can tell you don't necessarily agree with everything here."

"Look, you don't know me. You don't know what I think or feel, so don't—"

"Don't I? I've known you for seven years, Ari. I know you. Maybe better than you know yourself. And I need your help. I'm asking you, please. Help me prevent this war."

I place my head in my hands. I need to think. "Let me make sure I understand—you want me to lie to my dad, turn my back on my species, my people?" I glance through my hands. "Surely you get how crazy that sounds. I'm the future commander, Jackson. Do you really expect me to trust an Ancient over my own family?"

"No, but I hope you'll surprise me."

CHAPTER 6

The next morning I sit on Gretchen's bedroom floor while she surfs through dresses on her T-screen for the upcoming Trinity Masquerade Ball. It's a huge ordeal, celebrating the rebirth of Earth after World War IV. Everyone will be there, including the leaders from each of the governing countries around the world. After we signed the treaty, our leaders of the time quickly met and decided that part of what caused our past wars was the issue of differing governments. They created the Trinity and set up one in each of five regions—Asia, Africa, Australia, Europe, and the Americas. The Australian Trinity has since been dissolved, thanks to the last leader being unable to have children to continue the legacy of the founding Australian leader. That region is now controlled by the African Trinity.

The ball itself is usually all social, though I have to wonder with everything going on with the Ancients if it has always been a ruse to get the leaders all together.

Gretchen, Lawrence, and I usually go together, but this year,

Lawrence and I are expected to go as a couple. At first, I felt sick knowing that I would have to tell Gretchen that she couldn't come with us, that we'd have to meet her there. Remembering the conversation still makes me want to throw up. But with what all I've learned in the last twenty-four hours, I don't have the brainpower to worry about anything else.

I still don't understand why Jackson sought my help. Surely Lawrence—the future president—would have been a better choice. Regardless, he did and now I have to decide—help Jackson and prevent a war, or turn him over to Dad and possibly assist with the wipeout of humankind. Saying it in my mind like that makes the decision appear so easy, like whether to eat or breathe, basic life stuff.

It isn't easy. It's impossible.

Gretchen selects another category of dresses. The program pulls up a virtual version of her body and then crosschecks the perfect dress color, length, and shape, making sure not to duplicate any purchases in the last two years, then gives her fifty options. Each dress appears on the virtual Gretchen, and within a second she's clicking for the next to appear.

She no longer lets me choose mine by myself, and instead chooses one for me and then just calls me over to approve the purchase. Any other day, I might protest or at least be annoyed that I have to sit here while she shops, but right now I'm just thankful to be around normal people with normal problems. I want so badly to confide in her.

My training was canceled this morning. Mom and Dad were both gone when I woke up, handling the repercussions from the address last night. Already the news has reported protestors popping up across the city. President Cartier is supposed to speak tonight to reassure us—yet again—that everything is fine.

But it isn't fine.

"Hey, are you all right?" Gretchen says from her closet, now dressed in her fifth outfit for school.

"Yeah." I bite my lip. "Just thinking. What was up with Zeus last night?"

"No clue. Probably angry about something. I'm sure they've worked it out by now."

I hesitate. I want to tell her everything, to tell her they haven't worked it out. I want to ask her advice. I want someone else to come up with the answer of what to do. But I can't. I'm in this alone. "Yeah, you're probably right," I say, and she goes back to choosing her shoes.

I think about Gretchen, my best friend since forever, totally mollified by President Cartier's assurance that we're safe now. She doesn't know what's going to happen if I won't or can't help Jackson. But I can't help him.

My dad would disown me. Jackson has to understand.

Another round of excuses courses through my mind, then the memory of the burned land and orange sky finds its way to the surface and I feel sick and guilty all over again. Every time I think of why I can't help him, I see the Ancient attack or Zeus yelling at Dad. This is so much bigger than me. It's not my fight, not my place to second-guess Dad.

That is my logic as Gretchen and I walk into school. I wonder if Jackson will be waiting at my locker for his answer. I thought about it the entire ride to school. I can't help him. I'm preparing to tell him just that when I round the corner to my locker, but he isn't there. I breathe a sigh of relief, open my locker, and almost miss a letter falling from inside. It's paper, like paper-paper. Barely anyone uses paper anymore. I lean in closer to the letter and read:

> *If you're in, meet me at Parliament HQ's servants' entrance.*
> *8:00 p.m. Bring a flashlight.*
> *—J.*

Below the line is an arrow pointing to the right. I flip the letter over and nearly drop it to the ground. It's a copy of a letter signed by Zeus. At the top are the words PRIME TARGETS and below is a list of ten names. The first name is Grexic Alexander. I stifle a gasp. Dad is their main target. It's too much. I can't…

"Hey, what's that?" Gretchen asks, reaching around me for the letter.

I jerk back, shove the letter into my locker, and slam it shut. Thankfully she can't open it without my keycard. I flash her the most innocent smile I can manage. "Just a note from Dad. Top secret. You know how he is." I hold my breath as I wait for her response. That's what sucks about best friends—they know when you're lying.

She starts to ask more when I feel a tingling awareness at the back of my neck. Jackson steps up beside me. He stands close, too close. Close enough to divert Gretchen's attention from the letter to him.

"Hey, there," he says to me, his eyes filled with concern.

"Hey," I say, fighting to keep my voice steady.

"Will you be there?"

I look into his eyes, my mind replaying everything that has happened over the last twenty-four hours. I don't want to believe him, but there's too much evidence. The rising number of Latents. The attacks. Zeus walking off the stage. And it's only going to get worse. I can feel it deep in my gut, that horrible feeling we're all programmed with. It warns us, and right now mine is screaming at me to do something. I can't just hope this goes away. We have to stop it before it starts. I don't know if Jackson overestimates the Ancients or underestimates us, but I do know they have abilities and advanced technology far beyond anything we've even considered. Jackson said this wouldn't be a war; it'd be the complete wipeout of humankind. I won't let that happen.

"I'm in," I say. Then I turn to Gretchen, answering her question before she can ask it. "Early Op training stuff. Jackson was brought up early, too."

"That's great," she says, and I know she means it. Gretchen is nothing if not sincere.

I watch Jackson walk away and feel as though a weight has been lifted from my chest. I've made my decision, and I know, in my gut, it's the right thing to do. Now all I have to do is get home before my parents do, sneak into Dad's office, and steal his master key to Parliament headquarters.

Exactly three hours later and I'm pacing my house, jumping at the tiniest of sounds. I need Parliament's master key. I know exactly where the key is kept in Dad's office; I just need to quit stalling and get it over with. But if I'm caught, death would be a mild punishment.

I check my phone for the twelve zillionth time. It's nearing five thirty, which means by now my parents are en route home. I step around the stairs to the transfer door that leads to our training room. Dad's office is right beside that door, invisible to an average onlooker. He had it designed to blend seamlessly with the wall so only those he trusted most would be able to get inside.

Trust…I'm one of those people he trusts. And I'm about to betray him. My mind flashes to Dad's name on the target list. I have no choice. I will help Jackson find a way to stop this.

I rake my hand over the left side of where I know the door to be. A second passes, and then the door slides open. Inside, the office is eerily quiet. A large desk sits against the back wall, Dad's favorite chair behind it. Other than the desk, bookshelves line the right wall and a filing system, full of old Engineer records, lines the left. It seems obvious to house the master keys in the filing system, but this is Dad's office, which means nothing is as it seems.

I step over to the bookshelf closest to his desk and pull out the first book on the third row. Inside is a tiny keypad. I type in the code *5-12-12-14*, a combination of Mom's and my birthdays. A *click-click-click* sounds through the filing system as one by one the drawers and cabinets are unlocked.

I have just started for the third cabinet to the right when the front door announces my parents' arrival. I race forward and slide the cabinet open but can't remember which keycard is for

Parliament. Is it the gold one or the green one? I replay my dad's voice in my head. "The Engineers produce red, the Chemists grow green, and Parliament controls the…" I pull the gold keycard off its hook, close the cabinet door, and return Dad's secret book to the bookshelf.

I'm about to slide out the door just as my mom calls my name. I cringe. It sounds like she's in the kitchen. But what about Dad? I edge to the doorframe and peek out. Dad is in the foyer, reading a message or something on his phone. His head snaps up, and I lean away from view, my body tensing.

I strain my ears to listen for any movement. After several painful seconds, I hear Dad's heavy footsteps walk from the foyer to the kitchen. I release a long breath, edge to the door again, and peek out. It's clear. Yes! I slip out. The door shuts automatically behind me.

I tiptoe away from the door and around the stair rail in the foyer, almost giddy.

I did it. I—

"What are you doing?" Dad asks.

I turn slowly until I'm facing him. "Nothing. Why?"

"Where did you come from? I didn't see you down here earlier. Did you see her, Claire?" Mom joins Dad at the open doorway that leads into the kitchen.

"There you are," she says. "We were calling for you. Dinner is ready." She looks from Dad to me and back. "Grexic…stop it. She's not trying to sneak out. It's daylight outside. Kids don't sneak out during the day. Now come sit down before your food gets cold."

Dad relaxes his shoulders, but I can still see the questions in his eyes. He thinks I'm up to something. Perceptive as always. Thankfully, I put the keycard in my pocket before leaving his office.

I brush past him and into the kitchen. Mom made a roast, which is Dad's favorite, so maybe he'll lighten up. I sit down at the table and Mom sits beside me, Dad across from us. I want to ask about the attack or Zeus walking off the stage. Then I remember that President Cartier is supposed to speak tonight and hope that will facilitate the talk. "Aren't you going to turn on the T-screen?" I ask.

"Why would I do that?" Dad asks, stabbing a chunk of roast with his fork. "I already know what she's going to say, and frankly, I'm tired of hearing about it. I'd rather discuss your training. Cybil seems pleased with you."

"Well, I've only had the one meeting with her. Our training today was canceled." I stare at Dad, confused. He should've known Cybil canceled our training.

"Of course," Dad says, but I sense there's something he isn't telling me.

We spend the rest of dinner listening to Mom talk about her latest research—some variation on healing gel. I try to follow along, but I'm too focused on the time, which is ticking closer and closer to when I need to leave. Finally, Dad excuses himself to his office, giving me my chance. "I thought I might go to Gretchen's for a while," I say to Mom as she's leaving the kitchen. "Is that okay?"

Mom walks over and kisses my cheek. "Of course. Be home in an hour, though. You have school tomorrow."

I step out of my house and turn left, as though I'm going to Gretchen's house at the end of my street, but instead I cut across the main road and back up the sidewalk in the opposite direction, toward the tron. I pull my phone from my jacket and message Gretchen: *I'm at your house, okay?* I know she'll cover me. I just have to think up an excuse to tell her later. So with that handled, I lift the hood of my jacket over my head and slide into the first seat closest to the door.

There is practically no one on the tron at this hour—a few warehouse workers and that's it. I wait for the stop at Business Park, feeling my heart pound against my chest.

I try to clear my head as I edge around Pride Fountain, past the Engineer building and down the alley between it and Parliament headquarters. It's darker than dark here. There are no visible doors or entrances.

An average person might think the alley runs to a dead end. After all, there is nothing but a large cement wall at the end, connecting from one building to the other. But I know better. The cement wall accesses the below-ground auto-walk that goes from building to building. This way, Chemists, Engineers, and Parliament members can go among buildings without others seeing them. I've never been on that auto-walk, and as far as I know, it's restricted for lead personnel. Today, I won't need it.

I reach the end of the alley and find the opening in the walkway that I was looking for. In the dark of night, it appears to drop into nothing, but there is actually a series of steps that leads to the servants' entrance into the building. I pull out the flashlight I packed, flick it on, and shine it down into the opening, only to fall backward as the light flashes over a person standing by the door. "What are you doing?" I whisper. "You're lucky I didn't scream, ruining this before we even start."

Jackson laughs. "Nah. I trusted you."

"Well, move over. I've got the key."

"Like a master key?"

"Yeah, I took it from Dad's office. How else were we going to get in?"

Jackson shakes his head, evidently in awe. "I thought we'd do the normal thing—break in. But this works," he says as I swipe the card and hold the door for him to get inside. "This definitely works."

We ease down the hall, Jackson insisting on going first, until we reach the servants' elevator at the end. A scanner protrudes from the wall beside the elevator. I swipe the card, hoping the master keycard works for all the scanners in the building, and instantly the doors pop open. I guess so.

Once inside, Jackson pulls out a notes tablet and starts clicking through something I can't see. I lean closer until my arm touches his arm, my face inches from his. "What's that?" I whisper, unsure if we're supposed to be all spyish about this or not.

He turns, and I feel his breath on my cheek. He swallows hard. "It's a map of the security floor. We're going to duplicate a video chip."

The elevator *ping*s open before I can ask anything further. We step off into a dark hallway.

"Flashlight?" Jackson asks.

I click it on, shining a thin ray of light down the hall. He sneaks forward, but I grab his arm. "Wait, security cameras." I point at a two-inch silver triangle stuck to the ceiling.

He smiles. "No faith in me, huh? I had someone take care of that. We're invisible for the next fifteen minutes."

"How…?"

"Don't worry about it. The video library is down here." He motions to the right, and I follow close behind. We pass door after door. I wonder what lies within these walls. The truth about the Ancients? The truth about our history? I feel as though I'm walking through a morgue of secrets, as gross and decaying as the bodies at the medical one.

Jackson stops at a set of double doors and holds out his hand for the keycard. I hesitate. Stealing it was one thing, but handing the master key to an Ancient is on a whole different level. He must interpret my thoughts, because he steps back, giving me room to swipe the key myself.

A chilly breeze rushes from the room. We slip inside, and the door clicks shut behind us. My heart slams in my chest. We're here. I'm really doing this.

I flex my hands to keep them from shaking. The room is nothing but floor-to-ceiling cabinets, a thousand different drawers, and a single T-screen. Each drawer is labeled with a number and letter sequence that makes no sense to me, but Jackson goes directly to a drawer labeled CIV3. He pushes the door in, which should make it pop out, but it doesn't budge. He pulls on it and tries to wedge his keycard inside it, his face growing redder and redder. I glance around, wondering if the library has a locking system similar to the one in Dad's office.

I walk to the center of the room and peer around. Where

would they hide the keypad? No, they wouldn't use a keypad here. They would use a scanner. I study the room, the walls, the lights, each of the cabinets. Then it hits me. I turn back to the door. No one would think to scan the outside scanner once *inside* the room. Maybe…I step out and swipe the master keycard. Instantly, a series of clicks sounds through the room. "There," I say. "That's better. Now, can you tell me what we're looking for?"

Jackson stands, shaking his head. "Brilliant, Alexander. Really brilliant." He opens the drawer, exposing three rows of tiny squares. He pulls one out. "This is a video chip. The *C* stands for Chemist, meaning the building. *IV* is the floor and *3* the lab number. So this drawer holds the camera readings from that lab. Your dad took me through the Chemist lab yesterday. Lab 3 was blocked off, the glass in the door covered so no one could see inside. Why? There has to be a reason. I think it has to do with the war strategy, like maybe the Chemists are coming up with something. I don't know what. But I'm hoping this chip" —he holds it out to me— "will give us a clue."

"But why—"

"I'll explain later; we've only got a few more minutes." He loads the first chip into the T-screen. A lab. Chemists coming and going. But nothing unusual. He loads the next chip and the next, cycling through ten or more, all as boring as the first. I'm beginning to think it's not here when he inserts the next-to-last chip. A lab fills the screen, but this lab is nothing like the rest. It looks like a bomb went off in the room. Jackson and I both lean closer to the screen.

"Do you—"

"Shh," Jackson says. "Did you hear that?"

My ears strain, but I don't hear anything at all. I shake my head, my pulse racing. He shoves another chip into the T-screen and types a series of commands I don't recognize. REPLICATING flashes on the screen.

"Come on, come on," he whispers. Finally, both the chips pop out. Jackson returns the video chip to the drawer, grabs my hand, and yanks me from the room. He rounds a corner and presses against the wall. Several seconds pass. There's nothing. No sound. No light. Then a soft *click...click...click* echoes from the hall perpendicular to where we stand. It grows louder and louder, until I'm sure someone or something can hear my breathing or sense my fear.

I tug on Jackson's arm, but he shakes his head. We can't just stand here! I glance down the hall and back to Jackson, then the clicking stops.

"Go." Jackson urges me backward.

"Go where?" I whisper, glancing down the hall behind me. There's an emergency stairwell door at the very end, but we'd never make it without being seen. The clicking starts again.

"Go now!" he says. I race for the door, slam through it, and barrel down two flights of stairs before I stop to see where Jackson went. I look up, my heart pounding, to see him at the top of the stairs, watching the door. Thankfully, we were only on the third floor so the level I'm on should have an exit door to outside. I scan the open stairwell and sure enough, there's an exit sign above a door on my left. I glance back at Jackson, unsure whether I should run for it or wait for him. He tilts his head to listen, and I do the same. We wait in silence for what feels like an eternity, then Jackson leaps from the top of the third-level stairs down to the ground level where I'm standing, his face filled with excitement.

"We did it!" He lifts me into the air. "That was crazy. Amazing. I can't believe we weren't caught. I can't believe you came. That was so—"

"Hey! Put me down!" I wiggle out of his hold and then I hear movement at the top of the stairs and my blood turns to ice.

Jackson jerks around, angling me behind him.

"Hmph, you must have been pretty vexed to fondle a human," a voice calls from the third-level steps where Jackson had stood just moments before.

It takes a moment for my brain to process that the voice is Mackenzie Story's and that she just called me a human, which means she must be…

"Blast, Kenzie, where was the warning?" Jackson says. "I thought you were a guard or something." He pushes open the emergency exit door.

"Time's up," Mackenzie says. "Ari's parents are looking for her. She needs to get back." Even though she says my name, she doesn't look at me.

Jackson nods. "Ari, tell them you weren't feeling well. Apologize—"

"For what?"

He shoots me an annoyed look. "People don't ask questions when you admit you were wrong before they have to tell you."

"But what about the chip?"

Jackson steps into the alley, motioning for Mackenzie to

follow. "I'll be at your house, normal time, chip in hand. Sound good?"

I glance at the time on my phone and cringe. "Fine. See you later." And I turn and rush down the alley, hopping on the first tron I see, a more pressing fear on my mind.

My dad is going to kill me.

CHAPTER 7

I inch around the back of my house, hopeful that if I go in the back doors then my parents won't realize I've come home. I climb the steps to my back patio, swipe my keycard, and wait for the door to click open. Nothing happens. I swipe my key again and wait. Still nothing. I'm about to panic when the door opens from the other side. My entire body turns to stone.

I start cycling through excuses in my head. Dad won't let this go unless I have a full-proof reason for being late, but I don't even have a bad reason. I contemplate faking illness when I see Mom standing on the other side of the door. She presses a finger to her lips and urges me inside.

"Ari Elizabeth Alexander," she whispers, her tone hard, "we will talk about this in the morning, but as I don't want to be up half the night hearing you and your father fighting, I suggest you go on to bed. He's asleep. I'll tell him you came in earlier. I will not lie to him again. Understand?"

I nod, feeling sick down to my core. I never wanted her to lie for me. I'll have to be more careful from now on. I can't involve her. I can't involve anyone.

She walks around the stairs and turns right down the hallway to her and Dad's master suite. I wait until I hear her bedroom door close and then jolt into Dad's office, return his master key to Parliament, and take the stairs two at a time to get away from the danger zone.

I slip into my room, shaking my hands to stop them from trembling, and head to my bathroom to strip off my clothes, which somehow feel dirty even though I barely wore them. I splash water on my face and spin my hair into a messy knot on the top of my head.

My nerves are settling down, but still I'm too wired.

I stretch my arms over my head, close my eyes, and arch my back as I leave my bathroom to grab some pajamas from my closet. I have just stepped into my room when I hear the curtains sway by the window.

"Hey, I'm early," Jackson says as he slips through my window and turns around. We both freeze. "I— You—"

"Get out of here!" I dart back into the bathroom, but there's nothing in here but a hand towel and I've already dropped my old clothes in the laundry chute. This can't be happening. He did not just see me… I clear my throat and draw a long breath, forcing myself to calm down. I peek my head out of the bathroom. "I need some clothes. Can you…?" I point to my closet.

Jackson looks as flustered as I feel but manages to get into my closet and pull out some mismatched pajamas. He closes his eyes and hands me a red tank top and some fluorescent green silk pants. "I'm sorry, I had no idea. I didn't see anything. Well, maybe a little but—"

"Ugh! Just shut up! I'll be out in a second." I lean against the bathroom door. I am going to die. Right this second. Die. I throw on the clothes and storm out of my bathroom, my hands on my hips. "This is never to be brought up again, got it? You saw nothing. Nothing."

A smile plays at his lips. "Nothing."

I cross the room to sit in front of my T-screen. "Where's the chip? I'm guessing that's why you showed early, right?"

"Uh, yeah. Right." He sits down beside me, and we both stiffen. His shoulder rests against my shoulder, his thigh against my thigh. I have to remind myself to breathe, breathe, breathe, because all I can think about is how he just saw me naked. I run my hands over my face and try to press the thought from my mind, needing more than anything to change the subject.

"Don't be embarrassed," he says, studying my face.

"I'm not."

Jackson rolls his eyes. "You know, no one can be the job all the time. No one. Not even you. It's okay to show weakness. It doesn't make you—"

"Thanks, but I don't need a pep talk. And speaking of weakness, why do you cry during the Taking?" I ask. "Does everyone cry?" I know I sound insensitive, but I can't stand the focus on me. I don't need an evaluation into my mental well-being. I'm fine. At least before all of this craziness I was fine.

Jackson's eyebrow quirks up. "Cry? What the…?"

"Yeah, I saw you crying that first night. That's why I opened my eyes—a teardrop fell on me."

He shakes his head, laughing. "Not sure what you think you saw, but we don't cry."

"Don't be such a guy. You cried. It's fine. I'm just curious if everyone does or just you?"

"Aren't you listening? We don't—Ohhh. Xylem."

"What?"

"It was xylem," Jackson says. "Basically, it's like water inside the human body, what makes us Ancient instead of human. The xylem in our bodies activates during the Taking so we're able to pull the antibodies we need from you. It moves throughout our bodies, so I suppose that's what you felt. Xylem. It's our liquid evolution."

I try to process this. "What do you mean by liquid evolution?"

He releases a long breath, either considering how to explain or deciding if he wants to. "We haven't always looked like you, Ari. Like humans. We're not human. But xylem makes us look like you; it helps us duplicate your composition so we can survive here. It's inside us, sure, but it also *is* us. Does that make sense?"

I shake my head, lost. "No. So you really aren't…solid? You feel solid." I reach out to touch his hand, then jerk back, my cheeks burning. "So you're not on Earth all the time?" I ask, clearing my throat.

"No, we're definitely solid now. We aren't human, but our bodies are very human-like, thanks to the Taking—thanks to humans. But xylem still flows through us. And I stay here much of the time, but I have family and friends at home. I go back as often as I can."

The mention of Loge brings a recurring question in my mind

to the surface. "Jackson…what's the real reason that your kind wants to come here? I mean, I know what they tell us, but is that the truth?"

Jackson seems to contemplate how much to tell me. "Our version of the history is different than yours. Even though our bodies are comprised of xylem, we still need water, and the water supply on Loge has dwindled slowly for centuries. When World War IV collapsed Earth, your surviving leaders contacted us, as they had since the beginning of time. The Ancients have revitalized Earth after every major destruction, terraforming the planet back to health. But this time, we needed something in return—we needed a new planet. But we never attacked. We came here peacefully and asked if we could coexist once our bodies acclimated if we rebuilt the planet. Your leaders agreed and so the truce was made. Of course, everything has changed now."

"Because we aren't keeping our end of the truce. I wonder why."

"I don't know. But our numbers are growing here on Earth. Eventually this is going to get bad. I just hope we can stop it before it does."

"Speaking of numbers, what about Mackenzie? So she's an Ancient, too?"

"Yes. She was sent to assist me."

"Like making us invisible tonight."

He smiles. "Something like that."

I look down, picking at lint on my pants. "And you two are… involved or something?"

His eyebrows shoot up. "What? Kenzie and I? Noooo. She's a friend. The rest is just part of the role to help us blend in."

"Right." I clear my throat, embarrassed that I asked at all. It doesn't matter if they're together or not.

We fall silent for several seconds, then I look up at him, the question leaving my lips before I've thought it through. "Jackson, why are you doing this? Why do you care? I just don't understand."

He sits back in the chair, his eyes trained on mine. "How can I not care? One species shouldn't get to live over another. Why does death have to be the answer? It isn't how I'm made, Ari. Orders or not, I can't just sit back and let this happen. I'd never be able to live with myself if I did nothing. Zeus says the strategy will prevent a war, and I don't plan on stopping until I find it."

I let out a breath I didn't realize I was holding. "Do you have the chip?" I hold out my hand.

He pulls it from his pocket and inserts it into the T-screen. We wait for the video to begin. The destroyed lab fills the screen. But it doesn't look like a bomb went off as I'd thought before; it looks like a construction site. A giant, crumbling hole makes up the back wall. There are sheets and sheets of some clear material, leaning against the other walls, piled on the ground, everywhere. I'm not sure what the material is, but a few of the sheets are curled up at the corners. So it has the clarity of glass but the pliability of plastic. Definitely a Chemist invention.

"They're building something," Jackson says.

"Yeah, it looks like they're expanding the room, but what's up with the clear stuff?" I point to it.

He shakes his head. "I don't know."

We watch the rest of the video, but nothing changes and no one enters the room. I lean back in the chair, propping my left leg up in the seat. "What now?"

"You're training with Cybil now, right?" he asks.

"Yes, but—"

"Think you could sneak into the Chemist lab?"

I start to laugh, but he's serious. He wants me to sneak into the Chemist lab, the most restricted area in Sydia. I hesitate a second, then say, "I'll see what I can do. Cybil seems pretty cool. I should be able to get a little information out of her if nothing else."

"I'll keep my eye on it when I'm there, too. Maybe between the two of us we can—" He yanks the chip from my T-screen and turns around, his eyes locked on the door. "Did you hear that?" he whispers.

I shake my head, worry crawling through my mind. What if someone heard us? What if one of *them* heard us? Several seconds pass, and then Jackson jumps up and motions to my bed. "Get. In. Position," he mouths.

I move to my bed as quietly as possible and slump down until I'm lying flat. I glance up at Jackson to see him cupping his eyes with his hands and pointing to my nightstand. I reach over and pull my patch from its case, the silver reflecting in the light from my bedside lamp. It looks so innocent in my hands. I lay the patch over my eyes, and it suctions to my temples, surrounding my eyes as though sewn into my skin.

And then darkness finds me. My vision, my mind, my body— everything wrapped in nothingness. I feel nothing, hear nothing, sense nothing. My lungs stop working for the briefest second, and it's as if I've held my breath. No, like someone stole the very breath from my lungs. I have to fight off my body's natural instinct to panic at the lack of air supply, but then one by one I gain back my ability to breathe, to feel, to hear, to smell.

Jackson is already above me now. I smell his scent mere inches from my body. But before I have time to think about Jackson, I hear a soft shuffle outside my door, hardly audible, almost as silent as the wind.

Someone is out there. Not moving, not advancing—listening.

CHAPTER 8

I trudge into our training room the next morning at five, already in my training clothes, prepared to suffer so I can beat Dad this morning. I feel like death, look worse, and want nothing more than to crawl back into bed and continue my dream from last night, which may or may not have included a certain boy from another planet.

I glance around the room, but it's empty. Dad isn't here yet. That's never happened before. I take a few more steps into the room, and then decide to go back upstairs. Maybe he's canceling for today, confirming prayers can be answered.

The elevator opens to a completely silent house, same as earlier. I walk around to the kitchen. Empty. "Mom?" I call. No answer. Hmm. I guess they both went to work early. I edge back to the stairs, still feeling uneasy, when I hear my phone buzzing from upstairs. I dart to my room and pull it from my nightstand.

Emergency at work. We'll be home tonight. Love, Mom.

Okay…so no training today. Dad's been missing a lot lately. I consider going to Gretchen's, but I'm not in the mood for another fashion show. Plus it's way too early anyway. I've already decided just to go back to bed when I hear a soft tap at my window. I ease over and pull the curtains back. It's still dark out, the first signs of day not yet showing. I peer into the darkness and then *bam*, a fist collides with the glass right in front of my face. I jerk back, my heart pounding, to see Mackenzie staring back at me.

"Didn't know you were so jumpy," she says.

My mouth hangs open, my mind fuzzy on what to say. "What…?"

"Am I doing here? I came to give you a message. You may think this is some children's game, but there is a lot at stake if you can't keep your end of the bargain. There's no time for feelings, only action. Got it?" She looks at me as though I'm a kid who's just been caught doing something wrong.

I shake my head, completely lost. "Not sure what you mean, but feel free to get off my house."

"Yeah, sure you don't. I think I'll have a little present for you today. Don't be late." And then she slinks back into the trees and disappears.

The rest of the morning passes in a daze as my mind continues to replay what she said and what she could possibly mean by a present.

I step off the tron and onto the auto-walk to school, deep in thought until I feel someone's presence behind me. I peer around to see Jackson standing only a few feet away.

"Oh, hey," I say. I spent much of the night contemplating Jackson. Somehow everything I thought I knew about him is changing. I've known this boy for years, yet I feel like I'm just getting to know him—the real him.

"How was training this morning?" he asks.

"It was— Wait, how did you know I train in the mornings?"

He smiles genuinely, no hint of the arrogance I'm so used to seeing. "Lucky guess."

I turn back around, feeling a strange tingle in my stomach, and rush through the doors, refusing to look back.

I finally cave to take one peek over my shoulder, and I slam into someone. "Oh!"

"Hey," Law says. "You okay?" He pulls away from me, his eyes filled with concern.

My body tightens. "No, I mean, yes. Yes, I'm fine." I draw a breath, waiting to see if he saw me with Jackson. He kisses my cheek and drapes his arm around my shoulders, steering me toward our lockers. After a few seconds, I'm able to relax.

When we reach our lockers, we discover Gretchen, bouncing with excitement.

"Sooo…" Gretchen probes. "What did you think?"

"Think of what?"

"Your dress to the ball. Mine delivered this morning. It's so perfect. I can't wait for you to see it. Yours didn't come?"

I reach into my locker to grab a notes tablet. "No, we didn't order it yet, remember?"

She bites her lip like she's trying to keep herself from bursting.

I pull back from my locker and fix my gaze on her. "You didn't."

"I had to. Besides, I had your measurements, and it's you,

it's all you. I promise. You're going to love it and love me for ordering it."

I sigh, glancing down the hall to see students huddled in tiny groups every few yards, whispering and looking around nervously. "What's going on there?" I nod toward the groups.

"They're spreading the location for that fall party they do," Law says. "You remember. I heard someone say they're actually thinking of having it in the woods this year. Can you believe that?"

I can't. Ancients come from the trees, which means most humans are petrified of the woods that border Sydia. No one goes in there. There's always talk of deranged Ancients that stay on Earth all the time, prowling the woods, waiting for a human to enter so they can Take them to death. I can't believe anyone would be crazy enough to have a party there.

Not that I believe the stories.

My eyes shift down the hall and catch Jackson standing against his locker, watching us with a strange expression on his face, but then a group surrounds him, blocking him from view.

"What are you doing?" Gretchen says, peering behind her to see what caught my attention.

I shrug and she starts up with what shoes she'll wear with her dress and I smile down at her, relieved for the change of subject. But then my gaze drifts to Law. He tilts his head, his eyebrows threading together. He clears his throat. "Well, I should get going. See you tonight." He kisses my cheek again, and then he's gone.

The warning bell rings through the halls. One more minute and we'll be locked out of class. Gretchen and I speed down the hall to world literature, and just as we make the corner, I feel a pull in my stomach. Jackson is face-to-face with Mackenzie. Her blond hair flows down her back. They are smiling that sort of sickening smile of two people in a fresh relationship. I start to go past them when his eyes find mine.

"What are you gawking at, rich girl?" Mackenzie says. I guess this was her present. Thanks.

Gretchen fake laughs. "Give me a reason. I dare you."

I pull Gretchen to class before her feistiness overcomes her logic. We have Ops testing soon, and she can't afford a mark against her. Gretchen shoots me a concerned look as I sit down beside her and spread out my reading tablet and notes tablet and pens and anything else I can think of to distract me. Why did that bother me? He's nothing to me. It doesn't matter what he does. I release a long breath, confused by the weird feeling in my chest. Like anger—or hurt. But that's ridiculous.

"Okay, what's going on, Ari?" she asks. "First the locker thing, now this. What's up with you and Jackson? And don't say nothing."

"Seriously, nothing. We're just friends…sort of."

She starts to ask more when the classroom door slides open and Jackson walks in. He doesn't take world lit with Professor Kington. *He* takes the class from Marks three doors down.

He says something to Kington, and she motions to the back of the room. I stare at my desk and fiddle with the lamp affixed to the side for reading. It's an older turn-style. I work the dial between my fingers, but I can't get it to turn. Just then, Jackson passes me and slides his hand over mine, causing the lamp to fill with light. He sits down behind me, leans forward, and whispers low, "Sorry, had to defuse the rumor spreading about us."

About us. What? Does he mean himself and me? That's ridiculous. No, he must mean himself and Mackenzie. Either way, it doesn't matter. "Whatever," I say. "It's nothing to me."

"Right," he whispers, and I hear him lean back in his chair.

The tingly feeling resurfaces, and I shake my head to try to push it away. I slouch deep into my chair and try to ignore everyone around me. Gretchen shooting me questioning glances every few minutes. Jackson fidgeting in his seat behind me. It's all too much. So when the bell sounds for the end of class, I jump out of my seat and rush from the room as fast as possible.

"Wait up," Jackson calls before I can round the corner.

I cringe. Frankly, I don't want to discuss anything with him right now, and I'm preparing to say just that when another voice interrupts.

"What for?" Law says. I whip around to see him standing a few feet from Jackson, his expression menacing.

"Law…" I say.

"I wasn't talking to you," he says to me, but his eyes remain locked on Jackson. "What do you need to talk to her about?"

"That's between her and her God, and I'm pretty sure that's not you, bro." Jackson walks away and mutters, "Bet you wish you were."

Law lunges forward, but I hold him back. "Let it go," I say. "You know how he is."

"Why is he so interested in you all of a sudden?"

I shrug. "No clue. You heading to history?" I walk farther down the hall and wave for him to follow.

"Huh? Oh, no, that's why I stopped by. I have an early meeting, but do you want to do dinner after your training tonight?" We reach the cross section of the halls. Everyone can see us now. Law reaches for my hand. He glances over my shoulder and then kisses me. It's an easy kiss, as light as the wind, but the impact is immediate.

I jerk my head back, livid. "Feel better? I'm not some tree you need to mark." I storm off in the opposite direction without another word. Law calls after me, but I don't turn back. I can't believe him. My parents may have signed me away to Law, but I never agreed. He doesn't own me. He doesn't get to kiss me randomly just to prove he can.

I spend the rest of the day and the entire ride to Dad's office lost in my thoughts, and not all of them involve the strategy or the potential war.

I walk into the Engineer building and up to Cybil's office still in a daze, so distracted that I don't notice her enter the room until she drops a stack of books on her desk. She pulls out a chair for me and scatters the books. I glance down at the titles, all involving war heroes and military plans and psychological warfare.

"Why are we reviewing these?" I ask.

She flips open one of the books and slides it over. It's a photo of the world prior to World War IV. "Why did that war occur, Ari? Do you know?"

I think back to the history lesson last year on WWIV. A group of radicals sought world control. At first, most countries ignored the radicals. They, after all, provided debt relief for many of those countries. Eventually, the small group became a massive army, full of genius scientists and combat experts all across the world, hidden, waiting for their call to arms. We now know the plan began decades prior to the slaughter and, of course, the signs were all there. Strange political figures rose to power. The kind of people who should never step outside of a jail were now running the largest nations in the world. Fear crept into the minds of the smaller countries. Then the nukes dropped, destroying city after city in piles of rubble and smoke.

Before long, the radical leaders—known as the Octave— began to argue over who would rule once the dust settled. Their moment of weakness gave rise to the Rebels, a group of vigilantes that soon became the hope the rest of mankind needed. One by one the Octave fell and freedom reigned, though by then most of the world was destroyed. There was little cropland left, no electricity, and no way of getting anything. That's when we began to count on the smaller civilizations that had always lived off the food they grew or killed.

Humans regained strength, but we learned our lesson and formed the four worldwide sectors we have today.

I refocus on Cybil, replaying her question of why WWIV occurred. "Power," I say.

"Yes." She walks around her desk and points to a photo of people jumping for joy when the Octave fell. "And how did it end?"

"The Rebels outsmarted the Octave by taking them down one at a time."

"Right, and that brings us to our lesson for today. We are the Rebels, Ari. Humans. Now we just have to develop a plan to outsmart our Octave."

"Our Octave. Do you mean…?" I shift in my chair, making sure I'm able to see and hear what she says.

Cybil's face spreads into a devilish grin, her eyes shining bright. "That's exactly what I mean. From now on our training will involve Ancient analysis. What we feel they're capable of, what we know about them, everything."

It all makes sense—the refusal to coexist, the focus on combat training. We aren't just planning a weapon against them; we're planning to annihilate them. "So you're saying we plan to rebel against the Ancients. How?" I ask, hoping I don't sound too obvious.

She smiles again, tapping a finger to her head. "Our Chemists are geniuses, Ari. Trust me, we'll find a way."

For the rest of the training, we delve into past wars on Earth—Roman wars, Revolutionary wars, wars among nations, and wars against nations. There are so many it takes us the entire training just to record all of them and the timelines of each.

"Great work," Cybil says as the clock on the wall hits five. "Now for the fun part. I hope you don't mind if we extend training a bit today. Follow me." She steps out of her office and down the hall to the Chemist elevator. I stare after her, a mixture of nervousness and excitement kicking in.

Cybil scans her keycard over a tiny dot in the wall, causing it to flash from red to green and then open, exposing a steel elevator door. She slides her card through another scanner and prompts me to do the same. The scanner requests a clearance code for me, which she types in from memory. A moment later we're inside the elevator, zooming down several stories before it finally stops. The elevator opens to a long hallway with an auto-walk. After several yards, we reach a set of thick double doors, where Cybil scans her card again.

Inside is a series of ten labs, each with a large black number on the door. I inch forward, passing the first two, and then stop in front of the number three, my pulse racing. Lab three. I'm about to find out what happens here, getting us that much closer to discovering the strategy. Cybil reaches for the knob. This is it.

Except…it's not. The lab resembles every other lab I've ever scene. Crisp white walls, floors, and ceilings. Nothing appears out of order at all. I'm about to walk back to the door to double-check the number when Cybil types in a code on the wall keypad, causing the back wall to split open. My mouth drops. Hidden behind the main wall is a thick wall of glass. I inch closer and peer through it to a two-story room with the same white walls, floor, and ceiling as the lab. There's nothing inside. "What is that?" I ask, awe in my voice.

"It's a testing chamber," Cybil says. "The walls and ceiling are all temperature-treated. It's completely contained. Nothing can get in…or out." She smiles.

"Out? What would try to get out?"

"You'll see at our next training. For today, we'll go through here." She enters another code and the wall closes back, hiding the chamber. I start to leave the room, but Cybil calls after me. "This way." She nods at an open doorway to the far left.

The hallway is dark with nothing but a pale blue light at the end to guide us. I trip over my own feet and grab the walls for support. That's when I realize the hallway is no wider than my arms and no taller than a doorframe. Suddenly the air feels tight, and my breathing escalates. I hate confined spaces.

"It's horrible, isn't it?" she says.

My throat tightens. "Yes. Why can't we go another way?"

"This is the only way inside. Besides, we're here." She steps out of the hallway and into a nightmare. Containment chambers full of water line the walls. Inside the chambers are Ancients, all with the same golden skin and perfect features. But the room is filled with more than just bodies. Some chambers contain hands, others brains. Ancient body parts, I'm sure of it. Twenty or more tubes attach to each body or body part. The entire room is like some sick science project.

I edge closer to one of the chambers, a full body inside. The skin appears grayer close up, dead and lifeless. Her hair floats around the sides of her face and her eyes are closed. She's older, a grandmother maybe, though I have no idea how their aging works. I bite my lip to keep control. What have we done to her? I'm about to look away when her eyes snap open, and I stumble backward.

"She—she just opened her eyes!" I point at the chamber.

Cybil laughs. "Of course she did. The bodies are kept alive for analysis."

"But…so she's not…"

"Technically she's dead," Cybil says. "It's just an injection that allows the body to function post-mortem. Don't worry. She can't see you. Her eyes work, but they don't transmit information to her brain. Your father asked that we begin our study here."

It takes all my energy to keep my voice steady. "What sort of study?"

"Oh, mainly checking for changes and analyzing the reports. Nothing fun until we receive the live subjects."

"So the testing chamber back there…"

"Is for live Ancients, correct. How else will we discover how to kill them?"

CHAPTER 9

Two hours later, I knock on the door to Law's house. The all-brick estate home spans the size of three of mine, every element of it custom-built for the Cartiers. His house is set apart from the rest of Process by a gated driveway and thick, intricate fencing looping in metal swirls from the gate all the way around the house. Typically guests have to announce themselves at the gate, and then one of the staff will approve or deny admission. Gretchen and I are the exception. We used to come here all the time growing up, so Law taught us how to rig the gate open and sneak inside without bothering the staff.

Of course we used to call ahead to let him know we were coming. But I can't worry about that right now. I have to talk to him, to someone, and Jackson isn't an option right now. Besides, Law is our next president. He would want to know what we're doing. Then a horrible thought occurs to me — maybe he already does.

His door alarm has already announced me three times, yet no one has come to the door, even though he has a house full of staff. I knock again, this time a touch louder. I'm about to go around to the back when the door flies open.

"What— Ari?" Law says, his face shifting from anger to concern. "Are you all right? What are you doing here?"

"I need your help," I blurt. "They're…" I stare at him blankly, wishing I had thought this through. I want to confide in Law. I know he would listen, and I'm pretty sure he wouldn't tell anyone. But what if he did? I wait too long, the silence awkward and unbearable, and then finally change the subject and say, "Why are you answering the door? Where is everyone?"

He raises his eyebrows. "They're all on the lower level preparing for the ball. Now your turn. What do you need my help with? Is it…?" He tilts his head, and I get the feeling he knows something, maybe the same something I know. I can't be sure.

I draw a long breath, stalling again. What can I say that doesn't sound completely insane? I don't even know how much I'm allowed to tell him, separate from the Jackson bit. Dad doesn't divulge his theories and experiments to President Cartier until they're fully developed. That much I know.

"Ari?" Lawrence says, pulling me from my thoughts.

I decide to start with the truth. "I had a rough training session today. I just needed to see someone. Sorry to come unannounced."

He closes the door behind him and leads me to his front steps. "Not at all. But come on, you're not telling me everything. You seem rattled. There's no training that could shake you like this, so what's the real story?"

I stare up at him and all my resolve crashes. He's not ready for this. To Law, life is still in perfect order. I don't want to be the one to wreck that for him, at least not yet.

I smile at him, hoping to lighten the mood. "It's my new trainer, Cybil. She's intense. I think I just got a little overwhelmed. I'm fine now."

He studies my face, and I can tell he doesn't believe me. "Well, let me walk you home." The sun has just started to dip behind the trees, mixing orange and yellow hues into the gray sky. Law takes my hand as we pass through his gate and onto the main walk that leads to my house. He's quiet the entire way, as though he's enjoying the peacefulness and doesn't want to complicate things by talking. We reach my house and I'm about to turn to thank him when I feel his hand stiffen in mine.

"Are you okay?" I ask, then, hearing a voice call my name from behind, turn around. Gretchen stands a few yards away. She seems dazed for a second, her eyes darting between Law and me, and then she breaks into a grin and points to my front door.

"Hey, I messaged you earlier," she says. "Your dress came!" She tugs me away from Law toward my door.

"See you tomorrow," Law says to me. "See ya, Gretch." He doesn't look at her when he says it, and he's halfway down the auto-walk before I can ask him why he's acting so weird.

"Okay, look," Gretchen says, "I know we have Ops testing tomorrow, but promise me you'll go try it on right now and message me what you think." She claps her hands together like the whole thing's too much for her to take.

"Fine." I pick up the box and dart inside, hoping she doesn't

ask to come in with me. I need to think without anyone around.
I enter my room, turn around, and almost shriek.

"Well, go ahead, try it on," Jackson says as he leans against
the wall beside my window, his arms crossed. "I won't watch.
Much." He breaks into a grin that quickly fades when he notices
the look on my face. Seeing Jackson has brought everything back
from training. I feel sick. I feel sad. Every emotion swirls through
me, and somehow this boy seems to be the only one who can
understand.

I allow my eyes to find his. "Shouldn't you be a bit more
stealth? Especially after last night? And you can cut the arrogant-
boy act. I know that's not really you."

He stares at me for a second. "I took care of that. Or should
I say *her*. And I'm not… What happened?" he asks.

"Her? Who…Mackenzie?" I should have guessed that she
was the one outside my room listening.

"Forget Kenzie. What happened?"

"I found out what happens in lab three," I say as I sit my
dress box down on the floor. I give him an abbreviated version of
my afternoon, including the old woman who will likely cause me
nightmares for weeks. Jackson starts forward, his face conflicted,
then he stops and backs up against the wall again, crossing his
arms. "We'll figure it out, Ari," he says.

I look down. "It was terrible. What we're doing…"

"Hey…" He opens his mouth to say more, but the words
catch as his eyes slip over my face. I must look wrecked.

Jackson clears his throat and looks away. "Did you notice
anything else? Like what they're planning to do in those
chambers?"

I shake my head; my entire body feels numb, empty. "No, nothing." I walk over to my bed and sit down, noticing that it's not quite time for the Taking and wondering what Jackson's planning to do for the next hour or so.

"I know I'm early. I thought we could…talk. Is it okay if I stay?" he asks, his voice more vulnerable than I'm used to.

I study him. "I guess so," I say, fumbling with a loose string on the edge of my shirt.

Jackson hesitates, sensing my unease, but eventually slips down beside me, leaning back against my headboard.

We sit in silence for several seconds before I finally say, "Can you tell me about Loge? I've always wondered what it's like. Is it different? The same?"

He glances at me, smiling at the mention of Loge. "It's beautiful all year round. The sky is a purplish blue; the grass is always green. We have no pollution or trash. And Logians…" He stops for a second, like mentioning them hurts. "They're pure in every way. Logians, by nature, are nothing like Zeus. Well, nothing like Zeus is now."

"And what about your family and friends? Do they miss you when you're away? Do you miss them?"

"I miss my friends every day, some more than others." He grins. "My family…" he continues, though the tone of his voice has changed, "I love them. I try to please them…but they can be difficult."

I nod in understanding. I'm not sure I'll ever truly please Dad. "What about your parents?"

Jackson clears his throat, his eyes finding the wall opposite of us and never leaving. "I don't have parents. My dad died before I was born and my mom… She didn't… I wasn't… She couldn't keep me."

"Couldn't keep you? That's horrible. Why?" My cheeks burn at my forwardness. "I'm sorry, I shouldn't have asked. I'm sure it's personal."

Jackson reaches around me to check the time. His expression turns playful. "Time for me to Take some of your goodness."

I roll my eyes, but can't keep from grinning. "Ha-ha. You really are a jerk, you know that?"

He leans over me. "Is that right?"

I open my mouth to respond with a smart comeback, but close it back. The truth is, I don't think he's a jerk. He's confident, for sure, smart, and ridiculously good in all our trainings. But there's also something deeper. He cares. I see it in him from time to time, only a brief flicker. And the look on his face when I told him about the old lady—he seemed as upset about it as I did. It's like he's putting on a front, something I know all too much about.

The truth is…Ancient or not, I'm starting to think Jackson and I may be more alike than I ever could have guessed.

CHAPTER 10

The next day I stand at my locker, anxious. It's the first day of Op testing. There are four sections, just as with true Op training—combat, limits, resources, and weaponry. No one knows the order of the testing or how many tests we'll face each day. The Engineer coordinators may separate them into different days, or we may face all today.

Gretchen walks up quiet and reserved, her face green. "Are you all right?" I ask.

"Yeah, just nervous."

I rub her shoulder. "You've been prepping for this for years. We all have. You'll be fine."

"Easy for you to say," she mutters as we slip into the gym.

The class takes a moment to calm down, all of us either jumping with excitement or nerves. Coach Sanders lowers the T-screen. He runs us through the terms of the testing, which basically says that we can't hold the school, Parliament, or the

Engineers accountable for any injuries. Our parents had to sign waivers, though they didn't even send one to Dad. My role has always been known.

Once he's finished the terms, he clicks a blue box on the T-screen. Instantly, testing stations rise from the floor at the far left of the gym. The transformation completes, leaving ten different stations, each with large walls surrounding them, blocking what's inside. There are twenty-five of us in the class but only ten stations. That's odd. Coach clicks another box and the numbers one through ten appear on each station, and below each number is a name. My eyes dart from station to station until I find mine. Station nine. Gretchen has station two, and Jackson, station five.

"You will see your names located below your station number," Coach says. "If your name is not listed, then I'm sorry to say your scores have not qualified you to continue with Op testing. You may leave."

A round of gasps echoes through the room. Not allowed to test? Wow. I try not to stare as they exit, a few angry and one girl sobbing. It seems cruel to not give them a chance, but Operatives aren't known for their kindness, as evidenced by my dad.

We're instructed to go to our stations. I stand outside nine, my hands shaking, but I know I'll get it under control once inside. Mom offered a relaxation supplement this morning, but I couldn't bring myself to take it. Lots of Ops take them, even some trainees, but the result is that you never really master self-control. A real fight isn't likely to occur when we expect it. *Inability to master fear will result in death.* I can hear Dad's voice saying the phrase to me during our earliest trainings. Dad taught me to know my weaknesses and face them head-on.

The door to nine opens and a woman beckons me forward. She bears the Lead Op badge, but I don't recognize her. I'm sure that was intentional. Her black hair is pulled back in a tight bun, causing her eyes to slant to the side. She doesn't smile or wave or hint at any form of civility.

"Today's test is limits. Your headset is there," she says, pointing to a chair against the opposite wall from her. "You may sit or stand while you conduct the test, though I'll warn you, eventually you'll find yourself standing. I suggest you stand or sit in the center of the room. Less injuries that way."

I walk over to the chair, grab the headset, and step back over to the center of the room.

She nods for me to begin, and just as I slide the headset on, blocking her from view, I hear her say, "Your test is unique, Ari. Keep that in mind."

I try to think of what she might mean, and then it hits me— Cybil. And if she had any say in my test that can only mean one thing. Ancients. I draw a steadying breath, forcing back any doubts, and open my eyes.

I am alone in an abandoned warehouse. It reminds me of a food-processing warehouse but older, decaying. Bits of orange light shine in through a half dozen windows, streaking out across the top of the warehouse, never dropping to where I stand a story below. Dust floats in the air above me. Birds crow in the distance. The hinges of the warehouse door creak as it swings back and forth, back and forth. I push through the doors to outside, peering around. There's nothing, no one, only the single warehouse in a field surrounded by thick, overgrown woods.

Something urges me forward, something like curiosity or need. I walk out into the open and turn around in a circle, watching the trees, but for what I'm not sure.

Then I see her.

A tiny woman walks out from the woods' edge. She's lean with an agile look that instantly flicks on my defensive side. I wait where I am, somehow sure that she'll come to me. What I don't expect is for a thick arm to wrap around my neck from behind, cutting off my air supply. I rise onto my toes and then slam down into a squat, jerking the offender over my head and onto the ground in front of me, where I slam my fist into his face. I glance up to where the woman stood before and now there are three, five, ten of them, one after another, stepping out from the forest depths. I do the only thing I can do—I turn and run, crashing through the woods opposite from them into the overgrowth and thorns, desperate for distance so I can think up a plan.

I'm well into the woods now, darkness closing in overhead. The wind picks up, carrying whispers through the leaves. I stop at an open clearing, hoping I can take on one at a time, but that's not really how an attack works. They're all going to jump me. I wait several seconds, widening my stance and preparing myself mentally for the fact that I might fail this test, when I hear a strange sound coming from a great oak to my right. First scratching, then what I can only describe as something growing inside a space that's too small. I back away from it, staring with wide eyes, as first a hand, then a leg, then an entire body emerges from the tree, like the bark spit out a person—an Ancient.

I scream just as someone yanks me back, causing my headset

to scatter to the ground. For a moment, I'm disoriented, caught between the simulation and reality, then my focus returns and I realize I'm being dragged from the simulation room. I claw and kick against the offender, fighting to regain control, then I wheel around, prepared to punch, when I see Jackson, his face filled with urgency. "What…?"

"We have to get out of here. Now." He grabs my hand and drags me through the door of station nine and into a cloud of smoke. At first I think it's part of the simulation, but then smoke spills into my lungs, and I cough, clamping a hand to my mouth. "There's been an explosion," Jackson says. "I don't know where. We have to get out."

We reach the exit to the gym before I'm able to wiggle from his grasp. "I can't leave Gretchen."

"She was in two. Come on." We rush through the smoke, barely missing people as we go. How Jackson finds station two, I'll never know, but he has the door open and pulls Gretchen from the center of the room, headset still over her head. She screams and fights against him until I yank the headset off and force her to look at me.

"We have to go!" I say and tug her toward the door. She pulls back, but then her gaze shoots past me, her eyes widening. She nods without a word. As soon as we're out of her station, I realize we can't leave everyone else. Jackson must sense my thoughts and rushes from station to station, opening the doors and commanding everyone to run. Most seem as confused as Gretchen, but eventually the smoke causes primal instinct to kick in.

A voice comes over the intercom instructing students, by code, to the secret exits and protective shelters planted around the school. They've been ingrained in us as prep for war. Chaos ensues in the gym as the announcement sparks fear and worry. People begin to shove others out of the way, desperate to get out. This feels like a war.

I motion to the emergency exit doors of the gym, where bright red lights flash, directing us to safety. Gretchen looks hesitant—the doors are all the way across the gym and the main doors that exit into the school are closer. "No, let's go this way," she screams over the high-pitched alarms echoing through the school.

I shake my head and point to the emergency doors. "Those go directly outside of the grounds. Come on, we don't have time to argue." Just when I'm about to drag her with me, the ceiling starts to cave in, debris crashing to the gym floor. I duck down, covering my head with my arms, and when I stand back up, she's gone. "Gretchen!" I spin around and around. "Where are you? Gretchen!" Nothing. Panic crawls up my spine. "Jackson?"

"I'm here. She ran; I'm not sure where. We have to get out of here." He grabs my hand and directs me toward the emergency exit, but it's a dead end. Debris is scattered all in front of it, blocking access to the door.

"This way." I tug Jackson to the left toward Coach Sanders's office, which I know has its own exit to inside the school grounds. We rush through the hallway, pass his office door, and turn left down another long hallway with a door at the end. But once we barrel through the door, the world stops, as if in slow motion.

Smoke floats through the air, heavy, suffocating, so much

worse than the smoke in the gym. My eyes dart left and right. Coughs chorus from every direction. Everyone's running. A boy falls to the ground. I reach out for him, but Jackson gets to him first, standing him up and pointing him to the exit closest to us. The boy stumbles forward and I fear he's going to fall again and we'll be gone and no one will help him. "We can't just—" Then I look around. There are too many to count. Girls and boys coughing and sputtering on the ground, some crying, all paralyzed with fear. I rush to a tiny girl hunched in the corner to my left and motion for Jackson to help another one a yard or two away. I'm not leaving this building while all these people are inside. We lead the two girls out the main double doors and turn back to go get more, but this time thirty or more students who were safe outside now rush in after us, everyone joining together to save as many as possible. Finally, emergency medics arrive and usher us outside. I start through the crowd, eager to find Gretchen, when an overwhelming pain slices through my head and I collapse to the ground, screaming.

"Ari!" Jackson reaches for me. "What is it? What's wrong?" My head twitches, and I wrap my hands around my skull as if I can press the pain away. Jackson cradles me in his arms and starts to run away from the crowd. I want to ask where he's taking me, but each second brings on a fresh wave of pain, like a heartbeat. *Relief-pounding-relief-pounding.* I bite down on my lip, tasting blood almost immediately, sure I'll pass out any second from the pain.

"What happened to her?" a voice calls. Then fast footsteps followed by, "Where are you taking her?"

Lawrence? But I don't dare open my eyes because I can still hear the piercing screams of my classmates and professors, inside the school and out. Screaming, so much screaming.

Before I know it, we've reached some alcove that feels spongy and wet. I open my eyes fleetingly. Jackson and Lawrence kneel beside me. They're talking too quickly to keep up. The world spins in a mixture of pain and nausea and dizziness. I try to keep my eyes open but the pain slams them shut.

"Just do it!" Law commands.

I wonder who he's so angry with when Jackson yells back, "It isn't that easy! It'll expose her. I can't—"

I start to drift off, unaware of where I am or who I'm with or what's happening.

"Do it now. Please, look at her," Law says, his voice rattling.

A second later, I feel intense warmth, and then ice pours over my head, moving down my neck and into my body. I breathe in, and with each release the pain begins to diminish. More and more seeps into my body until it's as though I'm floating through a gentle stream. My body is weightless matter, nothing more than a beating heart inside an empty shell. I'm sure I can open my eyes now, but I don't. I want every bit of the icy liquid. I want it to never leave. Maybe I can stay here in the majestic stream, light and airy, without worry…without the screams.

CHAPTER 11

When I wake, I expect to see blood or bodies or, worse, nothing at all. I'm so afraid that I hesitate, my eyes closed while my mind processes my environment. I hear an argument, and then a door closes, blocking out the sound. I sit up as my mom comes toward me with a tray of food.

"I'm so glad to see you awake," she says, placing the tray on my nightstand. "How are you feeling?" She runs a hand over my forehead and through my hair before easily patting my back as though I'm a young girl again.

"I'm...okay. What about everyone else? What happened?"

She sighs that long, drawn-out breath that means she's trying to avoid the question. "There was an electrical fire at your school. What do you remember?"

I remember Jackson and Lawrence and... "Where's Gretchen?" I barely remember being taken from school, but somewhere deep in my fractured mind I remember not knowing where Gretchen went and worrying whether she would make it out.

"She's at the Medical Center, but she'll be okay," Mom says. "I spoke to her mom. She said Gretchen had a breakdown. Something to do with being pulled from the Op simulation too quickly. She's fragile right now, but her mom assured me she would be fine and to let you know."

I slump back against my pillows, relieved. I remember an excruciating pain just before I blacked out. That must have been my breakdown, but then…then came the cold. But not an agonizing cold, it was soothing, almost like drinking something iced on a hot day. I remember basking in it, not wanting it to end.

"Honey," Mom says. "You have a few visitors. I've kept them away while you slept." She shakes her head in obvious annoyance. "They refuse to leave until they see you." She opens my bedroom door, and Jackson and Lawrence fight to get through the doorway. Mom rolls her eyes. "You have ten minutes. She needs rest."

I wait until I can hear her descend the stairs to speak. "Why are you two together?" I ask.

"We— I— Jackson?" Law shoots him a look.

"A bomb was planted at the school," Jackson says.

"Bomb? Mom said it was an electrical fire."

Jackson stares at me, almost in disappointment, like he expects better than for me to just accept what someone tells me. "No. And we're running out of time." He paces the room, raking a hand through his hair and scratching his chin. "Zeus is growing impatient, and he's not the sort of leader to care who he kills. I think… I fear…"

"Genocide," Law says. The word hangs in the air, a dark cloud over us. "Which is why I had to help. I'm the next leader. Besides, Jackson thinks they'll kill our mom soon if she doesn't cooperate. That's all he told me. He approached me as soon as he found out. I'll admit," he says, glancing at Jackson, "it took me a while to believe him, but there's too much evidence. Plus—"

"Wait," I say, waving my hands in the air, confused. "What do you mean o*ur* mom? Who is *our*?"

Lawrence's eyes shift from me to Jackson. "Seriously? You couldn't even be honest with her about that?"

"You're…brothers?" I ask, putting it all together. I cover my face with my hands, wishing I wasn't so tired so I could think. "Get out," I say. "Both of you. I want to be alone."

Jackson starts to explain, but I point at the door before he can continue. "I said, get out!" I'm so sick of all the secrets.

Mom rushes in, hearing my shouts. "What's wrong?" she says to me.

"I'm tired."

She looks from me to the two of them and nods. "Okay, guys, she's had enough."

Once they're gone, I'm able to think through what they've said and what it means. I feel gross inside. Law kissing me in public all the time, like he was marking his territory. Jackson stiffening every time he saw Law with me. I can't believe they didn't tell me. No, I can't believe *he* didn't tell me, because I know this was all Jackson. He could have told me at any point that Law was his brother. Why not tell me? Why not be honest? I slump down in bed, wrapping the covers tightly around me. Exhaustion overcomes me, and before I know it I'm asleep.

When I wake it's dark outside and my alarm clock reads one a.m. I slide up in bed, rubbing the sleep from my eyes, and freeze as my foot connects with something hard.

"Glad to see you awake." I lower my hands to find Jackson sitting at the foot of my bed. "Sorry, did I startle you?"

I hesitate, torn between telling him to leave and wanting to know more. "Why didn't you tell me?" I ask, my voice hard.

He walks around the bed and sits next to me. "I'm sorry. It was selfish and mean. I just… I wanted you to trust me because of me, not because of him."   His face turns bitter, and I realize he's jealous of Law.

"You know, honesty builds trust, not withholding stuff. And I was beginning to trust you, but now…I don't know." I lean back, taking him in.

"I'm sorry," he says again.

I stare out into my room, wanting to stay angry, but I can't keep my curiosity from bubbling up. "So tell me how this works. How are you and Lawrence brothers?"

He straightens. "We're not brothers. We may share the same blood but he isn't my brother. I don't know him, not really. My family is on Loge. To the Cartiers, I was just a mistake." He pulls back, his face reddening, but not out of embarrassment, out of anger. "Did you know the patch used to not exist?"

"No, I didn't."

"Yeah, years ago there was nothing blocking humans from seeing Ancients. You can guess what happened—hormones kicked in, attraction overcame logic, and a few mixed breeds were born. Sandra Cartier, my birth mom, was twenty-two when she had me. I think she cared for my dad, and he for her, but none of that mattered. My grandparents came for me. See, half human or not, once xylem enters our bodies, it multiplies. With half of me already Ancient, it took very little time for the xylem to spread. I became a full Ancient within three months of my birth. I never saw my mother, or even knew who she was, until I came here. My grandfather was afraid I would sense a connection to her and seek her out, so he told me everything. I agreed to not speak to her, and I haven't. But once I learned she was in danger, I had to tell Lawrence… Regardless of what's happened, I don't want a war."

"That's horrible," I say.

He glances up. "I know. I guess my grandparents assumed I would hate her for ditching me. I should feel that way, but I don't."

He seems so sad and broken that my body moves before I remember that I'm supposed to be angry. I lean in, wrapping my arms around him in a hug that sends a flood of warmth through my body. I ease away slowly, so slowly I can feel his breath against my neck, my cheek, my mouth.

Jackson separates, and it's as though all the warmth in my body went with him. He smiles awkwardly and scratches his chin. "I thought you were mad at me."

I look down. "I am, or I was. I guess I understand why you didn't say anything, but that doesn't make it all right. If you want me to trust you, you have to be honest with me. From now on, got it? And you need to trust me, too. This isn't going to work unless we can be open with each other."

He tilts his head as though contemplating something, and then finally says, "I do trust you, and I'll prove it. Come someplace with me."

"Where are we going?"

"You'll see."

Jackson opens my window, letting in an easy breeze. I reach behind me for a sweater and slide on some shoes. "Okay, ready," I say, then stop. "Wait, what about the Taking?" Most of his Takings lately have been short, but still he hasn't missed a night.

"Nah, not tonight. You're just recovering. I don't want to risk weakening you."

Jackson slips out my window onto a wooden ledge and waits for me to follow. The platform stretches from my window to a giant oak behind my house—the Ancient tree assigned to my family. I glance to my right and left, seeing tree after tree, all similar to this one, all allowing Ancients into homes along my street. It's a surreal sight, viewing it from here. I've always known how the Taking process works, how an Ancient is assigned to each of us at age ten, but I've never witnessed a visual like this row of trees that shows just how connected the Ancients are to our lives. I can't believe I've never walked out on this platform until now.

"We're pretty high up, so watch your step," Jackson says as he maneuvers his body under one of the branches. I freeze. We are seriously high up. My heart begins to race, and then Jackson swings through the limbs, his body curving and folding around branches as though he is one of those gymnasts in our athletic tablets. I watch him in awe. Then a thought leaks into my brain. Can I do that? Surely not, but something inside me screams that

I can.

Jackson reaches the ground and looks up. "You can jump. I'll catch you."

"Jump?!" I whisper-scream. "I'm not jumping." I eye the branches in front of me, tangled and chaotic, and a moment later I'm within them, swinging from branch to branch just like Jackson before finally landing on the ground, a triumphant smile on my face. "Did you see that? I just…um…well, whatever you did, I did it, too! Isn't that amazing?"

But his expression seems worried, even afraid. "Uh, yeah, amazing. Let's go."

I hesitate, wondering what's with his changed mood, but then my focus is on the forest trail. Goose bumps rise across my skin. The forest isn't just dark, it's blacker than black and thorny and overgrown. I stop short. "Won't they sense us?"

"They?" He smirks.

"Never mind. Let's go."

"No, no, no. Who's 'they'?"

I sigh, shaking my head. "You know the stories. The wild Ancients who stalk the forest like animals wanting to feed off our souls."

I glance over to see him fighting back laughter. "Trust me, there's no one in the forest but you and me. And besides, am I detecting fear? Is the future commander actually *afraid*?"

"No, of course not." I stare through the thick branches and leaves, trying to find wandering eyes or razor-sharp teeth. "Fine, okay. Let's go."

Jackson leads the way, tearing down spiderwebs and

overgrowth. We're several yards into the forest and away from earshot of anyone when something dawns on me.

"Hey," I say, turning on him. "My patch. I lost it the night you asked for my help, and then the next day it just reappeared. Did you—"

"Yes. I took it and then returned it when I told you to close your eyes. I was afraid you wouldn't believe me if I just told you what I was. You're too skeptical for that. I had to show you."

"So have you always been assigned to me, or was there someone before?"

"No, all the leaders are assigned RESs, and with you being a future leader, you were assigned an—um—trained RES." He looks away like he's hiding something.

I stop. "What aren't you telling me?"

"Nothing. Look, we're here." He motions beside us, and I crane my neck to peer up at the largest tree I've ever seen in my life. It's like someone took a normal tree and then stacked a couple more on top of it. The knobby branches fork off in strange directions, like it's reaching out for something, but that's not the weirdest part. In the center of the trunk, as though it's been cut out of the wood, is a dark triangular opening that must be six feet high. The opening slants to the right in a painful sort of way, and I wonder if this tree can feel, because if so it seems miserable. "What is this thing?" I ask.

"This is our original entrance, called the Unity Tree. It's the only port not monitored by Mainland."

"What do you mean, *monitored*?"

"We created and continue to control all the ports on Earth so leaders of your world can travel to ours as needed," Jackson says. "But humans still monitor them. Not this tree." He points to the Unity Tree. "It can only be seen if you know where to find it. I thought maybe this could be, you know, our place. For coordinating and stuff." He glances up, looking nervous.

I inch forward, reaching out to touch the tree, when Jackson takes my hand gently in his, surprising me.

"It's a portal, remember," he says.

"Oh, right." I step back from it, pulling my hand from his. The chill of the forest seeps through my clothes and I wrap my arms around myself.

"Jackson?" I ask.

"Yeah?"

"I need to know what happened at school."

"I thought you might," Jackson says, walking over to lean against a nearby tree. "Though I don't know much. Zeus gave a last-minute order. I found out moments before the bomb exploded."

"But why the school of all places? Didn't he know you and Mackenzie were in there? Didn't he—"

Jackson pushes from the tree, tossing a twig to the ground he'd been fiddling with. "Oh, he knew; he just didn't care. Zeus has changed, hardened. He doesn't care who he hurts, least of all me. The clock ticks away, and everyone *thinks* it ticks toward Zeus's decision, but really it's his mind. He's closer and closer to losing it, and trust me, when he does there won't be anything or anyone left to fight for. That's why we need the strategy now. He's convinced that if he knows the strategy, he can stop it from happening and negotiate coexistence. That bit of information could have prevented the attack at school today, but I can't find it." He kicks at a rock, causing it to crash into a patch of leaves. "I've tried everything I can think of. I've involved anyone that could be useful, but still I couldn't prevent this. I couldn't help those people today. I—"

"Stop," I say. "This isn't your fault. You're doing everything you can. You aren't the one who can prevent this, anyway—I am."

That night I dream I'm running through the forest screaming Jackson's name, but he doesn't respond. Laughter floats through the leaves, as sharp as the wind before a storm. It taunts me forward, yet I can't make out the words. I stop in front of the Unity Tree. But where darkness lay in its center before, I'm now greeted with a light as small as a candle. I walk toward the light, reaching out to touch its warmth, and then I'm inside the tree, a sparkling waterfall gushing down from above me and disappearing into a sea of roots below my feet. It sparkles green and yellow with hints of shimmering pink mixed into the water like flecks of glitter. I think I'm there alone, absorbing this magical place, until the scene changes and I'm standing on a stone cliff overlooking a lake, Jackson by my side.

He leads me out onto a path beside a smaller pond, where several Ancients stand on flat bamboo-looking boats, an older one watching me. Lightning fills the sky, and then the man is in front of me. He releases a musical laugh, and then leans in until his face rests against mine. "Danger lies with those who ignore the signs." I pull away to look at him, my words failing me, but he doesn't say more. Instead, his eyes dart to Jackson, and only one word can describe the expression on his face—*fear*.

CHAPTER 12

Bang! Bang! Bang!

I jerk up in bed and stare at my door. What the—?

Bang! Bang! Bang!

The last of sleep evaporates from my brain, and I go to my closet, pulling out the gun Dad gave me for my birthday last year and edge to the door before the next round of banging can start up. I slip beside the door, hit the open button, and whip around to blow the head off my intruder, only to scream in unison with Gretchen, who is on the other side, her fist still midair, her face painted with shock.

"Seriously?" she says as she pushes the gun out of her face and walks into my room. "You need to invest in some quality nerve pills. Like the kind retired Ops take so they can sleep at night. The hard stuff. That's what sick people like you need."

I sigh heavily as I return the weapon to the small gun cabinet in my closet. Maybe my reaction was a little rash, but after yesterday's attack, I'm not sure what to expect. "What are you doing here?" I ask.

"Have you seen the news?"

"No, what's going on?"

"It's insane." She taps my T-screen to awaken it, clicks the convert button, and then surfs through the channels until she reaches the news. And she's right; it's horrible. Protestors have popped up all across the country, maybe the world. Some are burning their patches, others chopping down their Taking trees. It's the largest show of rebellion I've ever seen, and I can only imagine what horrors lay in store for these people. Their passion is admirable, but it's also futile. They still think we have the control, when I'm starting to wonder if we ever had control. Something doesn't feel right to me. Jackson claims Zeus wants the strategy so negotiations can be made before a war erupts, but it feels like the war has already begun—if nothing else, droplets of it, spreading through our world. I'm not sure delivering the strategy to Zeus will stop the attacks, but knowing what we have planned is vital to figuring out how to stop the rising tension. I can't say what Zeus will do—I can't even guess—all I can do is trust Jackson.

"Hello, anyone in there?" Gretchen asks, snapping in front of my face. "I asked you if it's all right if I click that message." She points to the screen where an emergency message from Parliament flashes in red.

I reach over her, tap the message, and then crack each of my knuckles one by one as the letter fills the screen. A voice-over sounds through my speakers, reading the letter to us in a thunderous voice.

"Today, October 15, 2140, Parliament announces a mandatory education day. All applicable students are expected to arrive promptly to their respective schools. No excuses will be accepted. Any student not accounted for will be summoned into questioning. We appreciate your cooperation."

Then the letter folds away, disappearing as quickly as it emerged. Gretchen and I stare at the screen. A mandatory school day. That's never happened before—ever. I can't imagine Dad agreed to this, but maybe he did. Maybe it was his idea. The only reason they would do this is to show the Ancients that we can't be bullied into coexistence. Everything is moving much faster than I thought.

Gretchen reaches over to click off my T-screen when another letter appears from Coach Sanders—Op testing continues today.

Gretchen and I walk into school wary. Everyone looks as uneasy as we do, even the professors. The Chemists must have sent their construction team to work through the night because everything looks exactly as it was before, as though nothing happened. As though the Ancients didn't try to wipe out our school just twenty-four hours ago. Sure, no one died, but plenty of students and professors were injured. Forcing us to come back so soon is torture. They want to show face to the Ancients, but they're doing it by punishing us. It isn't right. And what's even more shocking is that we have another round of Op testing today, which means Parliament wants a stocked military as soon as possible.

The halls are silent, the students are ghosts, dazed and empty.

Law is waiting at our lockers when Gretchen and I arrive. "You okay?" he asks, his eyes darting from me to Gretchen, where they linger. I glance from him to her. Gretchen's cheeks redden, her eyes looking anywhere but at me. Hmm, that's odd.

I start to ask what's going on when I spy Jackson in the middle of the hall. Mackenzie walks up to him and whispers something. He straightens, smiling, and then pulls her to him, wrapping his arms around her. I look away.

"Hey, are you okay?" Law asks, and I can hear the question in his voice. He's worried I'm mad at him for not telling me about the brother thing. And maybe I should be, but I know it wasn't Law's fault. Besides, from what they told me, it sounds like he hasn't known for very long himself.

"Yeah, I'm fine." I crack my neck and drop my notes tablet into my locker. I won't need it for testing today anyway. "We should get to testing. See you later, Law," I say.

Gretchen steps in line with me and loops her arm into mine. "What's going on, Ari? You can tell me. Is it…Jackson? I know you said you're just friends with him, but it sort of seems like—"

"I told you, we're nothing." I shake my head, but I can't meet her eyes. I don't understand how I've gotten myself into this. I can't have feelings for Jackson. Can't.

Gretchen's face fills with hurt. "I'm your best friend, Ari. You can trust me, you know?"

I stop outside the F.T. door, fighting the overwhelming emotions swirling through me. "I don't know. Okay? That's the truth. It's like gravity disappears when he's around and I'm lost, no longer sure of anything. I think… I don't know… He's just different than what I thought." I tug at my ponytail, twirling it around my finger again and again. I can't bring myself to admit I have feelings for him, even to Gretchen.

She tilts her head, her expression full of concern. "Does he feel the same way?"

I shake my head. "I'm not sure."

"Not sure of what?" a familiar voice says from behind us.

I cringe as I turn.

CHAPTER 13

Jackson opens the F.T. door, holding it so we can go in front of him. Gretchen shoots me an excited look and then nods toward him. "I'm going…um…on in," she says. "See you after, Ari."

I start to follow, but Jackson grabs my arm. "Wait."

"Yes?"

"What's wrong?"

"Nothing," I say.

"It doesn't seem like nothing."

Then before we can say anything else, Coach Sanders flashes the lights then yells from the back door, "Testing is out here. We're all set up."

Once we're outside, Coach lines us up in front of a giant metal obstacle course. I've heard these are used in actual Operative training to force Operatives to think quickly on their feet. I have no idea what we'll face inside, but I do know whatever it is will use every form of simulation and advancement the Chemists can throw at us.

"As you know," Coach says, "you have all passed your limits test and have advanced forward to this very crucial element of testing. Today, you will be judged on your resourcefulness and your ability to handle unusual weapons. I can't tell you what you'll find in the obstacle, but I can tell you to expect anything and to trust no one. Your job is to get through in ten minutes. Anyone not on the other side in ten will be disqualified."

"Do we all go in at once?" Marcus Wilde, a tall, slim boy—another Engineer legacy—asks. His father is a Lead Op and has a reputation for being as tough as Dad, so I can imagine he's asking to prevent any mess-ups that would then get back to his father. Little does he know asking this sort of question suggests weakness.

Sure enough, Coach gives him a hard stare. "You'll figure it out."

"But," Lexis says, "how are we supposed to—"

"Begin!" Coach shouts.

Everyone jumps into the entrance at once—everyone except me. I wait for the others to disappear and then enter, not wanting anyone else to see which way I go. As soon as I'm inside, a loud *bang* followed by *click-clack-click* sounds from behind me, and I turn to see a metal door where the opening to outside stood just moments before.

There are only two directions from here—right or left. I have no idea which way to go, so I choose right and hope my instincts serve me well. I draw a deep breath to steady myself.

I press my hands against the metal walls that line my sides and push, just to see what might happen. Nothing does. That's both good and bad. The good is that it didn't open up new paths, which would have potentially led me farther into the obstacle course. The bad is that I'm coming up to a corner, and every instinct in my body tells me something dangerous lies beyond the turn.

I can't go back. And there's nothing but metal on my sides. So, I have no choice but to push forward and face whatever waits.

I peek around the corner to an open area and spot an Op sitting between two paths. I recognize him at once. Lane something. He's a trainee under Dad and always has a smug expression plastered across his face. He calls me—

"Fancy seeing you here, Princess," Lane says. I step out, my eyes on the two paths behind him. If I knock him out I won't know which way to go, which means he needs to be disabled but coherent. My eyes dart around the open area. There's nothing but composite bushes. What am I supposed to do with— Ah-ha! I spy a tiny silver mass on the far left, no larger than a trick knife. I have no idea what it is, but it has to be there for a reason. I dash for it at the same time as Lane, barely nabbing it before he shoves me to the ground. I jump up and widen my stance. He grins, his expression sardonic. He knows what it does, and he knows that I have no clue.

Lane straightens. "You're tougher than you look, I'll give you that." He gets into position. I have less than five seconds to figure out what the thing does before he attacks. My eyes flicker to it. There's an indentation in the bottom. Maybe… I slide my thumb into the indentation and press. A spark followed by buzzing. It's a Senso-Taser. No way! I thought these things were a myth. Most

Tasers stop muscular control. These things shut down all senses so the victim can't see or hear or feel.

I smile up at him. "You have no idea." I run forward, flip through the air, and land in front of him. He punches me in the gut, causing the Taser to fly from my grasp. I scramble for it, but Lane is fast and jerks me up by my hair, dragging me back. I kick and thrash against him, managing to wiggle free and driving my fist into his face. Blood pours from his nose, the smile on his face vanishing for the first time.

I know this is the only chance I have, so I kick Lane in the chest, causing him to stumble back, and dive for the Taser. I'm close, so close, but then I feel a jerk and realize he's dragging me by my feet back, back, back. I dig deeper into the ground, what little fingernails I have breaking under the pressure in painful snaps. The tips of my fingers graze the metal and then wrap around the Taser. I turn just as Lane is about to jump me and shove the Taser into his chest. His body spasms and shakes as the electrical current courses through him. "Which path?" I command. The Taser will strengthen with each zap until he passes out. The first hit should only last a few seconds, with each sense coming back one by one. He can speak now, but he can't move. "Which path?" I scream and jerk his arm to me, nearing the Taser to his skin. He flinches. "One, two—"

"Okay, okay! Go to the left. You'll find three more paths. You'll need to get through the center one. Once through it, go left, then right, then left again. You'll hit another set of paths. The right one leads out."

I release his arm. "Thanks."

His expression turns serious. "Good luck. You're the kind of fighter we need if we're going to beat them."

My eyes widen. *Them.*

"Hurry, you only have seven minutes left."

"Thanks again." I race down the left path, realizing that while the sun was shining bright when I entered the obstacle, now the paths are all dark and shadowed. I repeat Lane's directions again and again in my mind so my body will act on a subconscious level. I can't trust my eyes to lead me right now, and thoughts just slow down our body's natural ability to survive. Dad taught me that. But he didn't teach me how to handle this.

I stop short in front of a group of children, by their faces they look to be about ten, but they're tiny, the size of toddlers. They sit on the ground in front of the middle path. The other two paths aren't blocked, but Lane said to take the center one. I back up, planning to run and jump over them, when I hear something. Whispers. They're whispering to me, beckoning me.

"Follow the light…follow the light…" they repeat over and over.

What light? My eyes dart from path to path and around the large opening. There is nothing else, only the strange children and me.

Thunder roars in the sky. The children stand and point, their heads tilting back. Black clouds hover over us, lightning strikes, and the children cry. Their eyes mirror the sky—black, emotionless. Their faces break into devilish grins while tears pour from their eyes, washing away the blackness. They shake their heads, as though disoriented, and edge toward me, calling my name, beckoning me to the light.

I draw a shaky breath. *This is just part of the test.* I search the composite greenery lining the walls. Nothing but leaves and sticks. If the first test involved weapons then maybe this one is resources. Thunder rumbles again. The children's heads tilt upward. I watch them with curiosity, pressing myself against the wall to my right. Lightning strikes and their blue and green and brown eyes all turn black as though a painter colored in the irises. The children weep, and the black washes away. They chant my name, but this time it's as if they can't see me. A second passes and then they all turn, facing me, begging me to come to them. I study their faces, their eyes for half a second, putting the pieces together in my mind. Lightning—disoriented. Crying—clarity. So if I'm right, the lightning somehow blinds them.

I wait for the next rumble and prepare to test my theory. The children huddle together on the west side of the opening. If I time it exact—and if I'm lucky—when the lightning strikes they won't see me slip around them. The thunder dies down. Lightning hits with a deafening *crack*! I race around them, dash into the center path, and fall onto my hands and knees. I spin around, prepared to fight, but the children stare away from me, calling my name, oblivious to anything but the storm.

A shiver crawls up my back that I quickly push away. I don't have time to get spooked.

I follow Lane's directions, turning left, then right, then left again before slamming to a halt. There are two paths. But blocking the way out isn't an Operative like Lane or a simulation like the children. Blocking my escape is an Ancient. He stands over two bodies. From this distance, I can't tell if they're alive. He smiles widely at me, crossing his arms. "Good to see you, Ari.

Your name has grown rather popular back home."

I peer down the right path behind him. The exit is close, ten yards at most. If I can get past him, I'm sure I'll make it out before he grabs me. He notices me looking and laughs. "Such a pity." And he lunges for me. I dodge him, racing for the path, and just as I reach the threshold, Jackson steps up to the exit. His eyes round out in terror as the Ancient hits me from behind. I fall forward, but then something comes alive inside me. My veins pulse, my muscles spasm, my senses heighten. The Ancient grabs my arm, and I swing around with the other, connecting with his temple. Typically that's a knockout move, but he just seems unbalanced.

I pull back to hit again when Jackson lands between us. "Go," he says to me.

"I—"

"Go!"

For once I don't argue. I reach the clearing and spin around, expecting to see other Ancients or hear alarms, something that tells me we're in response mode. But no one else is out of the obstacle course. For a moment I consider going back in. What if there are other Ancients in there? What if they've hurt Gretchen or one of the others? My eyes flash to Jackson, my chest tightening as he circles the Ancient, who says something I can't make out.

"Who gave the order?" Jackson commands. The Ancient laughs, races for the exit, and leaps past me into a patch of trees behind the clearing. He disappears.

Coach Sanders claps loudly when he sees us. "Great job!"

"He doesn't know," Jackson whispers. "No one knows."

"Knows what? That the Ancient breached the testing?"

"Yes. I think they've been ordered to interrupt Op testing." He checks behind him to make sure no one is around. "I think they want to weaken the military. I'm afraid—"

My phone buzzes, a new message from Mom flashing across the screen. *Come home now. It's urgent.*

CHAPTER 14

Mom stands a foot from the T-screen with her hand over her mouth, her eyes glued to a live newscast of an attack downtown, then one two cities over, and before I can process the totals, the screen separates into ten mini screens.

Ten attacks, all today, all happening simultaneously.

Mom reaches out to me, and we lock hands. We watch the attacks in silence. More than fifty people died within a ten-minute stretch. Operatives exit from Engineer trucks at the site of each attack. They look so young from here, but then, they are young, no older than twenty-five. I've never understood why we send our future into the fight, but that's how it has always been and how it always will be…if we survive this.

Gunfire and explosions and screaming jar me from my thoughts. My heart skips a beat as we wait for the dust to settle, wait to see how many bodies lay lifeless on the street—wait to see whether they are our bodies or theirs. But we never get the chance. The T-screen goes black and then a message appears that communication is down.

The front door announces Dad and we both lurch forward to see what he has to say about the attacks. His phone buzzes the moment he nears, but instead of stepping out of the room like normal, he jerks it to his ear. He nods a few times, pacing, and then slides the phone back into its holster.

"They bombed our off-site lab. All our research… How did they know?" he says to no one in particular.

"What research?" Mom asks.

His head snaps up. "Composite plant life. It produces oxygen and absorbs CO_2. We were ready to launch final testing. How did they find out?"

Composite plant life. So the rumors are true. The Ancients not only rise from trees; they produce them. That explains the fields of crops even in the dead of winter. One thing's for sure, they control way more than I ever guessed.

The door alarm sounds again, and Law rushes into the room, his face pale and empty.

"Is everything okay?" I ask.

"Yeah, but can we…" He gestures to the back patio.

"Only a second, Ari," Mom says, noticing us leave. "And stay close to the house."

I nod and close the patio door behind us. When we turn around, Jackson and Mackenzie are there. Law lunges for them before I can stop him. "What are you doing here?"

Jackson backs up. "We're trying to help, Law. You know that."

"I don't know anything anymore." Law drops into a chair. "A pair of Ancients came by my house, waiting, stalking our front steps. Mom never showed, but what if she had?"

Jackson shakes his head. "Don't worry, that was just a visual. They want everyone to see their capabilities. They can get to anyone, even the president. It's a fear tactic."

"Well, it worked," I say. "How are we supposed to stop this?"

"*We* can't do anything, but he can." Law glowers at Jackson. "Place the order. You know they'll listen to you."

"To me? I'm not Zeus. This order came from the top. There's no countering it. The only thing we can do is respond. We need info, stat. I need— "

"Did you see the news?" Law says. "Why would Ari and I try to *stop* an attack against Ancients? It seems to me like we should support the rebellion, not stand in its way."

Jackson's eyes flash to me, but I can't respond. I agree with Law; we can't let them kill our people. Law and I have a responsibility. We're the next leaders. Humans may be the weaker species, but we can't go down without a fight. I cross my arms, preparing to speak up, when Jackson interrupts.

"You don't get it, either of you. This is minor. And time is running out. We need the strategy. Now."

I walk out to the forest edge, needing distance so I can think. Something doesn't make sense here. Either Jackson doesn't know the whole situation or he isn't telling us. I want to trust him—I do trust him. But I don't trust Zeus, who is the one giving Jackson his orders. I release a long breath as I hear footsteps approach. Law comes up and drapes his arm around me, glancing over his shoulder before walking me farther into the woods and out of earshot of potential listeners. "If we refuse to help, then we're accepting war. I can't do that, Law."

"I'm not sure it's that simple. And I'm not convinced giving them our strategy will do anything but weaken us further."

"I know. I'm starting to wonder…"

More footsteps. Jackson. "Wonder what?" he spits out.

I wheel around, all my frustration bubbling to the surface. "None of this makes sense! Why should we give the strategy to you? What good will that do? Do you honestly think we'll stop fighting now that you've killed our people? We won't. We won't just lie down and let you take over."

I see the hurt flash across Jackson's face, but I don't take back my words. I can't.

"You are deciding between surviving or the total elimination of your kind. How can you not see that? This isn't a fair fight. You. Can't. Win."

I start walking deeper into the forest, so nothing but trees and the wind surround us. "Maybe not," I say. "But we have never in history agreed to work with our enemies."

"Are you insane?" Jackson shouts. "Your kind has *always* worked with your enemies. They have done what they needed to do to survive. That is what this is, Ari. Survival. Not who appears strongest or in control. I'm trying to help you stay alive."

"And how do you know Zeus will do as he says? How do you know he'll stop the attacks once he knows the strategy?"

"Because he always does what he says, both good and bad. He's reliable, if nothing more."

Law steps in front of me, squatting so we're eye to eye. "I hate to admit it, but I think he's right, Ari. I think we will have our time to fight. I'm just not sure that it's right now. I think we need to appease Zeus, get him what he wants, so he'll stop. Then we can rethink how to move forward. Besides, what choice do we have? It's take a chance and he keeps his word, or do nothing and we're all blown to bits."

I wish I could scream. I hate this. I hate this plan. It goes against the grain of my existence, makes me feel like I'm giving up when I should be rallying troops to fight. We're trained to give our lives, but how do you enter a war that is already lost? How do you send people to fight when they are already dead?

I sigh, long and heavy.

I turn to face the group, resigned with my decision because if nothing else I'm not the sort of person to go back on what I say. There are too many things to consider, too many people at risk, to do anything but keep moving forward and hope for the best.

"What do you need me to do?" I say.

Jackson glances up, all his anger and frustration disappearing as he takes in my face. "Do what we've needed done from the beginning. Find out the strategy."

I nod, feeling a sudden determination I haven't felt through any of this. Because inside I wasn't sure I'd made the right decision in helping Jackson. Now I know it isn't about the rightness of the decision so much as the necessity of it, and realizing that difference has somehow freed me. I've regained control. And I'm ready to do what I need to do to protect my kind.

I fix my gaze on Jackson. "Consider it done."

Law walks over and hugs me tightly. "You can do this," he says before leaving to go check on his mom. I watch him go, glad that he knows, that I have someone human on my side.

"You coming?" Mackenzie says to Jackson.

He shakes his head, never looking up, and I feel the hard walls around me beginning to crumble slightly. I don't know why he has this effect on me. My eyes find the ground, and I kick the dirt, both of us looking like children who refuse to give in first.

Mackenzie starts for me, her expression full of resentment. "This isn't a game, human. We have roles to fill here. Our people—your people—are all counting on us to make this happen. There's no time for this—this—"

"What are you talking about?" I almost scream.

"Look at him!" Mackenzie points at Jackson. "Can't you see what you're doing? Don't you care?"

My head twitches, words failing me. Then Jackson steps between us, easing Mackenzie back. "I'm fine, Kenzie. Go back to the others. Report our findings."

"But—"

"Just go. Please."

Hurt replaces her anger, and then with one giant leap, she's in a nearby tree, disappearing before our eyes.

And then we're alone, Jackson and me, watching each other, both unsure of what to say next. I walk back toward my house, knowing I don't have long before Mom calls me inside, and sit down on the porch swing that hangs below our deck.

Jackson stops in front of me, close enough so when I rock forward our knees touch. "What happened today? Everything was fine last night. What happened? Was it the attacks? Do you feel like I'm…" He runs a hand through his hair.

I look up at him, fully absorbing him. "No. It isn't that. It's… I don't know. I just feel so unsure."

"We'll get the strategy, Ari. Don't worry. We'll get it."

I clear my throat and glance away. "That's not what I'm unsure of."

He seems to consider this for a moment, then kneels on the ground in front of me so we're eye to eye. "I remember when this happened," he says, brushing a finger over a large scar on my left knee. "You were ten and carelessly walking on the edge of your bed with socks on. You slipped and sliced your knee open on the bed corner."

"How do you…?"

"Five stitches if I remember." He raises his eyebrows.

"But they were useless because it was all better the next morning. I told my mom I had superpowers. She let me pretend to heal her for the rest of the week." I smile at the memory, and then realization hits. "It was you, wasn't it?"

"And this one," he says, pointing to a tiny scar on my elbow, "happened a year ago. That one worried me. What were you doing on the roof, anyway? You slipped and fell into that big oak over there. You could have broken something, but instead just got a large gash on your arm."

"Why did you do it? Heal me, I mean."

"I've always looked out for you."

We stare at each other for several long seconds, unsure of what else to say. A war is brewing all around us, linking us together, the only two people who can stop it.

CHAPTER 15

That night I wait by my window for Jackson. Dad scheduled a meeting with Zeus two days from now. Zeus agreed to stop the attacks in favor of communication, which apparently Parliament has refused up until this point. Voices sounded from Dad's office well into the night, only stopping moments before midnight. I'm surprised we're still agreeing to host—after all, we're just strengthening the group that's trying to kill us. But I suppose stopping would guarantee another round of attacks. I can only imagine how afraid people are tonight. They've watched the attacks all day, watched as humans died at the hands of the Ancients, and now they have to slide on their patches and lay immobilized as the creatures climb into their windows and hover above them, sucking out their nutrients. There are no guarantees that the Ancients will abide by the legalized percentages. I wonder how many people will die tonight, if from nothing else, then from fear.

But after well past midnight, I realize that my Ancient isn't coming, and like the rest of the world, I'm gripped by fear, but not of death. I'm afraid that he's gone. That the war has already begun.

I stare out my window, searching for movement, craving something, anything, but when no one comes, I slip out my window, still in my pajamas, not noticing the cold. I sleek down our Taking tree, making sure to go unnoticed, and slip into the woods, hoping if nothing else I find him where he promised he would always be.

Sure enough, when I reach the Unity Tree, he's already there, kneeling in front of it as though in some prayer pose. "I knew you would come," he says. I tread around him so I'm standing in front of him. His eyes raise to mine, broken, worried…afraid.

"Did something else happen?" I whisper, kneeling down so I can see his face.

"No, it's just that a lot of innocent people died today. I'm trying so hard to stop this, but it's no use. First the school, now this." He shakes his head and I can see the pain moving through him.

"Jackson…" But I'm lost for words.

He glances down at me and lifts his hands to my face, tracing a line down my jaw. His fingertips hesitate at my lips, and his gaze drops. I draw a breath, and then his lips find mine. It's an explosion of emotions—first warmth, then contentment, then fear, so much fear. Of what this will mean, of whether we can succeed, of the guilt that threatens to overcome us both. Because of all the things we should be doing right now, after so many people died, this isn't it.

This isn't it.

Jackson pulls away, resting his forehead against mine as though he can't stand to move any farther away. "I'm sorry."

"I know."

I wrap my arms around him and we stay this way for a long time, listening to the eerie silence of the forest. I'm sure I hear whispering dancing with the wind, but for once I don't succumb to my curiosity. No matter what happens in this war, I realize in that moment that I care about Jackson. I can't ignore it any longer. I will do whatever I can to stop this for my family, my friends, for the innocent people who don't deserve to die. But also I will do it for him, because if I'm certain of nothing else, it's that Ancient or not, I trust Jackson. And if he says the strategy will prevent a war, I believe him.

I have to.

I climb back into my room, exhaustion taking over, and slip into my bed. I hear my own breath release, slow and sure. Then the dream begins. I'm walking through the forest, and they're there—Ancients. Hundreds, maybe thousands, all with their eyes on me. They cling to the trees, taunting me forward.

I reach the Unity Tree and a man steps out from its dark center. He watches me, and I return the same questioning look. I've seen him before, but I can't place his face. Withered and important and absolutely Ancient. His long white hair flows back as he steps forward and bows low. Then one by one the others in the forest join him. There's a smirk on his face that says his move is more for their benefit than mine.

"What are you doing?" I ask.

"Bowing," he says. And then his face constricts and he adds, "To bend downward or forward."

Chills spread across my skin. "To who?"

"Our queen."

CHAPTER 16

I wake in a cold sweat. Zeus. The old man was Zeus; I'm sure of it. I tear off my covers, stumble to my bathroom, and splash several rounds of water on my face. I glance into the mirror and wrinkle my brow. I just woke up, from a nightmare no less, yet I look…healthy, alive. My dark brown hair is shiny, almost black. My skin—luminous. I study my reflection, hoping to figure out what caused the change, but when I come up empty, I allow my mind to drift to the nightmare. Fear clutches me as I remember Zeus's expression, how he seemed to know me. Goose bumps rise across my skin even though my shirt is soaked with sweat. Zeus Castello was in my dream.

When I get back to my room, I notice a new message flashing on my T-screen. I click the letter, and a gold and silver scroll appears on the screen with the words 2140 TRINITY MASQUERADE BALL AGENDA at the top. My mouth hangs open as I stare at the words. After everything that's happened, I can't believe they didn't cancel the ball. The lead Chemists, Engineers, and members of Parliament from each world sector will all be present. This is insane, dangerous.

I reach for my phone to dial Lawrence but set it back down. The phones are monitored. I'll have to wait to ask him at school. I'm about to click off my T-screen when another message appears from Coach Sanders. Op testing continues today.

I leave my room and pound down the stairs, rounding the corner to the kitchen, the tang of cinnamon and ginger in the air. Mom smiles widely when she sees me, her dark brown hair sprinkled with flour, her ivory arms splattered with specks of pancake mix.

"This mixer has a mind of its own," she says at my raised eyebrows.

I laugh and sit in a stool beside the counter. "You said that about the last one. What is this, your sixth mixer?"

She drops her head. "Seventh. Don't tell your father."

I wait for her to explain why she's home, cooking pancakes (my favorite), after what happened yesterday. Something tells me this is a bribe. But after several long seconds, she doesn't say anything. "Mom…"

"Yes," she says, refusing to look up.

"What's this about? You don't cook pancakes during the week. And shouldn't you be at the lab, especially after yesterday? I heard Dad leave hours ago."

She slowly sets down her spatula and peers up at me. "I'm staying home today, and I want you to as well."

I start to object, but she cuts me off.

"I know about Op testing, and I know how much that

means to you, but things are getting bad out there. I can't risk…"
She raises a shaking hand to her mouth. "Your father doesn't
understand. He feels that you can protect yourself, he trained
you after all, but this isn't some training session. This is real,
with real people dying. I know you well enough to know that
I can't force you, especially when your father doesn't agree, but
I'm giving you the choice. Please, stay home from school today.
I'll send a note. Here." She passes me a stack of pancakes with
tiny smiley faces made out of chocolate chips. I look down at the
plate and then to her.

"Mom, I…"

"I thought you might disagree, so take this." She hands me a
small silver piece, maybe two inches long. "I had your father give
you clearance to bring a weapon to school today. The scanners
won't flag you. Keep it on you at all times."

"What is it?" I pick up the piece and rotate it around in my
hand.

"A newly invented trick knife." She presses the bottom,
causing a blade to pop out of the top. "But this knife contains
a poisonous tip. It's still in development, but contact with blood
causes the poison to incapacitate your assailant. I hope you don't
need it, but since you're as stubborn as your father, I need you
to be able to protect yourself." She passes it back to me, her face
grave. "And I expect you home immediately after school. No
training this afternoon, understand?"

An hour later, I slide onto the tron seat, my heel tapping against the steel floor, causing the trick knife to hit against my ankle. It seems a little cliché to place it in my boot, but we don't have pockets in our training clothes. For some reason having the knife on me makes me nervous, not because I'm unsure of how to use it, but because it suggests Mom knows more than she's telling me and whatever she knows gives her reason to question my safety. Regardless, I can't miss an Op test. No way would Dad allow it. Safety or not, my future job is to protect others. I can't hide from danger; that's just part of the Operative life. Though it's true that each Op test so far has been interrupted by an attack.

The last two tests covered limits, weaponry, and resources. That leaves combat. I crack my knuckles and stare out the window. I don't think any of the other testers faced an Ancient in their maze, and Jackson kept asking who gave the order, which means that attack was directed at me and me alone. If the Ancients are targeting me now, maybe it's time I talk to Dad. Jackson seems to think he can protect me, but he's not always—

"I see more than you think," Jackson whispers, slipping in beside me, sunshades over his eyes. It's a warm day for fall, so he's wearing only the brown pants and a white tank, a common outfit for the poor when it's nice out. I lean back in my seat, studying his profile.

He's not put-together, not at all. From his messy hair to his untied boots, everything about him screams carefree and effortless. But at the same time…he's gorgeous. His golden skin contrasts against the white tank, making him look healthy and full of life. His muscles protrude from the fabric, showing his strength. It's as though chaos and perfection slammed into each other and he's the result. The corners of his mouth twitch, and then the tron stops and he files into the crowd.

I jolt up, almost shouting for him to wait for me, but then, thinking better of it, file into line a few people behind, forcing myself to keep my eyes away from him.

There's a sign waiting when we enter the school for all Pre-Ops to report to the F.T. gym. Gretchen walks up to me, and we exchange worried expressions. This is the final test. By the end of this session, we'll either be Op trainees or cut from the program.

Gretchen opens the gym doors to a pitch-black room. "Is it supposed to be dark?" she asks.

"I don't know..." I ease forward, but someone jerks me back.

"Let me," Jackson says, stepping in front of us. He disappears into the darkness, a second passes, and then rushing footsteps, a loud *crack*, followed by a *thunk*.

Gretchen backs up, accidentally shutting the door so I'm left in the dark. I raise my fists, preparing to jab if necessary, but nothing happens so I move forward a few feet at a time. Still nothing. I can't even see my hands in front of my face. My foot hits something hard and I reach down to pull the trick knife from my pocket, but then think better of it. If this is part of the test, I don't want to permanently hurt someone.

"Jackson?" I whisper into the darkness. Then hands wrap around my shoulders and toss me to the ground. I try to jump up, but more and more hands secure me to the floor. I draw a breath, hoping to steady myself before I panic, when a spark ignites inside me. Adrenaline pumps in my veins, like a switch turned on, and suddenly I can see. My muscles contract, pulsing, pulsing, pulsing, and then...the hands are off me. I'm on my feet, listening to each heartbeat drum around me. There are five of them. Five humans, I'm sure of it, yet I don't know how. I wait for the first to attack, a guy I can tell by his smell. He lunges forward just as I swing around, kicking him in the face. He drops on contact. A brief flutter of guilt moves over me, but then two attack at once and my mind moves into a blur, kicking and punching, no longer needing thought or vision to guarantee a solid hit. I hear grunts and thuds, as one by one my assailants fall.

Finally, I stop and listen. I hear their heartbeats, hear their breathing, but that isn't possible. I lower my fists to my sides. Luminous skin, healthy and alive. My mind flashes from Jackson on the tron to me this morning in the mirror. But that isn't — No, not possible.

A loud whistle sounds over the room, jarring me back to the moment. The lights flicker on. I stare around me and raise a hand to my mouth. There are five Ops lying around me, all unconscious. Gretchen is not far from me, looking as dazed as I feel. My eyes register a petite black-haired woman. Cybil. I almost laugh. I knocked out Cybil.

Applause starts from the north end of the gym. "Congratulations, the four of you have advanced to Operative training."

What? That was it? I smile wide, searching for the other three who will train with me. Gretchen wraps me in a big hug. "We made it!" she screams. Marcus Wilde sags onto the ground, exhausted but grinning. So that leaves... My eyes land on Jackson, but he doesn't look happy. He looks worried. He shakes his head, his mouth open.

We're directed down the hall to the main library where a large banner greets us, already with our names inscribed on it. There's a crowd and they break into cheers as we enter. Gretchen's dad, Oliver O'Neil, races to her, embracing her in a hug. Marcus's dad finds him and does the same. I glance around, wondering if Dad will show, but after scanning the crowd twice, I realize it was stupid to even hope. Instead, Cybil, now conscious, walks up behind me and hugs me. "Your father said to tell you he's proud," she says. "And to come see me after school today."

I nod. "Hey, sorry about…" I motion to her swelling eye.

"You don't need to be sorry. What you did was amazing. Your father isn't the only one who's proud." She hugs me again. "Now, remember, my office as soon as you can. There's a lot to discuss." And with that, she leaves the library, letting in a sea of students. A few congratulate me, but most rush over to the food tables stationed on the back wall. They reach in with their bare hands, stuffing their faces with the only real food beyond fruit they'll get this month.

I turn around, hating the sight of it. When I'm commander, I'm going to force them to change the food laws. That is, if I become commander. A war could change everything.

I'm about to search for Jackson—for some reason I want him with me more than ever right now—but Lawrence walks in, stopping me before I can go.

"Congrats," he says, pulling me into a hug. I glance up at him, but his eyes aren't on me, they're across the room on another person, on Gretchen. My eyes dart from him to her. She smiles a little when she sees him, then looks at me and redirects her attention elsewhere. Wow, I hadn't even considered… Wow. I press my lips together to keep from grinning.

"So did you get your invite for tonight?" I ask Lawrence.

"Yeah, I think we're supposed to go together. Meet at my house?"

I nod, trying to keep my composure. Gretchen and Lawrence. I can't believe I didn't notice it sooner. There were hints for sure. I consider pointing it out to him, but he would never admit it, especially to me. Lawrence is all about expectation and as long as he's tied to me, he would never publicly act on something with Gretchen. The thought makes me want to tell him about Jackson and me, give him the freedom he needs to be happy. Though, maybe he already knows.

He looks down at me, his face serious, and then to Gretchen, and then back to me. "I… I've got to go. I'm supposed to report to Mom's office." He kisses my cheek and leaves before I can even respond. I want to tell him not to feel guilty, that I'm okay with them being together, but I can't. I turn around and find Gretchen watching me. She walks over once he leaves and we both just sort of stare at each other, unsure what the other knows and what we're each allowed to say.

"You know it's okay with me," I say finally.

She sighs with a sarcastic laugh. "I wish it were that easy. He"—she lowers her voice—"he hasn't… Let's just say he isn't as sure as I am."

I don't know what to say to make her feel better, so I reach out to take her hand, but she pulls away.

"It's fine." And she leaves as quickly as Lawrence.

I feel a lump form in my throat as I make my way to class,

tired of the party and what it suggests, tired of being me for the day. I slip into world lit, anxious to see Jackson, but when I get there his chair is empty. Gretchen leans over to me. "Sorry about that. I shouldn't… It isn't your fault."

"Regardless, the last thing I want is for you to be unhappy. I'll do whatever I can to fix it. I'm so sorry."

She shrugs and the final bell sounds before we can say more. Where is Jackson? I peer around the room to be sure he didn't sit somewhere else today but come up empty. Worry begins to soak into my mind. Maybe the war is starting so he was summoned back to Loge.

The rest of the class settles down. Professor Kington writes notes on the overhead, which then transfer to our note tablets. I chew on my lip, thinking of possible reasons that Jackson is missing class, when the door slides open and he enters, handing Professor Kington something. She directs him to take his seat behind me.

I cross my arms to keep from fidgeting.

"Ari," he whispers. "We need to talk."

"I—"

"Enough talking!" Professor Kington snaps.

I lean back in my seat, dread pouring over me. The dreams. The unnatural speed and strength. I can't deny it any longer. Something is definitely happening to me. All I can hope is that it isn't what I'm thinking. I can take anything else but that. Because that—*that*—would change everything.

CHAPTER 17

I step into Cybil's office unsure of what to expect. Mom replied to my message with a cold *I know*, which tells me both Dad and I will hear it when we get home. She has to understand that this is my job, but even though she's married to the commander, she's never been one to support the rigors of an Engineer schedule.

Cybil motions me inside and closes the door behind me. "We're going to the lab again today, but first we need to talk. Did you receive your invitation to the ball?"

"Yeah, I was a little surprised it's still on."

"That's not a coincidence. The masquerade ball is just a rouse, giving the four world leaders an opportunity to meet to discuss how we will proceed. The attacks are not going unanswered. We have had tests in place with both the Chemists and Engineers for weeks now. This meeting will decide our final strategy."

"Negotiation strategy?"

Cybil laughs. "Our attack strategy. We are preparing to

siege war on the Ancients, just not by the traditional means. By midnight tonight, the decision will be made. There are…risks involved when planning an attack. Key leaders often become key targets. I don't want to frighten you, but your father, we believe, is being monitored."

My mind flashes to the list Jackson showed me, to Dad's name at the very top. "But isn't that why we should try to negotiate before attacking? They have all sorts of advancements. We can't possibly—"

"Ari, you really don't understand what we're capable of. We won't lose. There's no chance, nothing to worry about. I only tell you this to explain where I'm about to take you."

I'm speechless. She really believes what she's saying; they all do. They all think this is going to be easy. No wonder Jackson sought me out to help find the strategy and insisted I keep quiet. He knew then what I know now—they would never have questioned our superiority to the Ancients, and that arrogance would have guaranteed the wipeout of humankind. Any doubt from before fades away. I won't let ignorance murder the people I love. I will fight for peaceful coexistence.

I look up at Cybil, everything in me focused on the strategy. "Well, what are we waiting for? Let's go."

Moments later, we're back at lab three, but this time the lab is hopping with people—and not just Chemists, but Engineers, too. I want to eavesdrop on what they're doing, but Cybil ushers me to the tight hallway that makes me feel like the walls are caving in, and then to the room full of Ancients and their body parts. The room has changed since the last time I was here. Now the back wall is a T-screen and the front wall is lined with Ancients in water chambers.

Cybil goes to the T-screen, types in a series of codes, and waits as a photo appears on the screen with data beside it. She points behind her to the first Ancient in line—a male, young, but older than Jackson, maybe twenty. He doesn't move in the chamber, so I assume he's technically dead but his body kept alert, like the old woman from before (who is no longer in her previous chamber). I try not to think about where she may be now or what they may have done to or with her body.

"Check out his bodily fluid percentages," Cybil says, zooming in on the data with a couple of taps on the screen. "Notice anything?"

I scan down the list and stop at xylem. "Can that be right?"

"The human body," Cybil says, "is roughly sixty percent water. Our blood is roughly ninety-two percent water. Ancients? Water comprises only twenty-five percent of their body, yet like our blood, xylem is roughly ninety percent water. But the composition of water in xylem can hardly be called water. Take water from a human and eventually what will happen?"

"Death."

"Right, but that wouldn't happen with Ancients because xylem carries water continuously through their body, almost recycling it. They claim that they want to come here because Loge's water supply is deteriorating. So what? They don't technically need water. Which is why we know they would never maintain a peaceful coexistence. Their reasons are built on a lie, so why would we believe anything they say? We can't and won't."

I fight the urge to question her. Jackson told me they need

water, but if what Cybil says is true, I can't see why. Maybe they need it to flush out their bodies; I don't know. But something isn't adding up.

Cybil closes the screen and opens another one titled INJURY ANALYSIS. "Watch this." She turns around, crossing her arms. I watch the first chamber, but nothing happens. I assume it's too technical for me to see, but then the male's eyes flitter open and round out in horror, while a dark liquid surrounds his left arm.

"I thought they were dead?" I half shriek, and then force myself to maintain my composure.

"These? No, they're Latents sent to spy on us. And they are... asleep," Cybil says with indifference. "I just gave the command for him to be stabbed in the arm. That's the blood you see there. It's a simulation of sorts, but the physical reaction is real." She points to the dark liquid now floating through the chamber. "Now, watch, watch. It's fascinating." She pulls me closer to the chamber and jabs at the place where his arm is slit. We stare at it for several seconds, and then just as quickly as it appeared, the wound vanishes.

"How did it...? Xylem." I knew it healed, but I had no idea it was so fast.

"Exactly. So whatever we do has to slow down xylem's ability to heal. That's the only way to kill them."

"So the strategy is to stop xylem? How can we do that?"

She looks at me as though I'm such an amateur. "We have several options already in development. As I mentioned, the meeting tonight decides which course we proceed with. There isn't a second chance here. Whatever we do has to work and it has to work quickly. Otherwise—"

"We're all dead."

"Well, that's a little dramatic. We have this under control, but I needed you to see this so you would know how to read the data. Should something happen…well, there are only four people who have access to this room and this information. President Cartier, your father, me"—she passes me a gold keycard—"and now you. Though I believe Lawrence Cartier will also receive access. This is a restricted area. I cannot convey enough how important it is for you to keep this room and that keycard safe. Keep it where only you know to find it, because that key accesses more than just this room. It's a universal key. In the wrong hands, it could be very dangerous."

I nod, wishing the knot in my stomach would go away, but with each day, I feel closer and closer to losing it. Dad isn't giving me this card so I can learn. This isn't part of my training. He's passing along the torch, just in case he isn't around to see this thing through. Little does he know, I would never go along with killing off the Ancients. It isn't right.

I slide the keycard into my boot beside the trick knife and leave the Engineer building. I hop the first tron I see and wait for my stop, but three stops later I stand in the center of Landings Park in front of a row of apartments, all steel and stretching to the sky. I have no idea where to go from here. I consider phoning Gretchen to look up Jackson's address, but she'll ask too many questions. Just when I'm about to turn back, I notice that each building has a large letter etched into it like a name. This section is *H* through *J*. Three identical buildings are across the street—*K*, *L*, and *M*. Leave it to Parliament to stay organized.

I wait outside the main door, wondering if a guard will come or if it requires a special keycard, but after a minute or two, I edge closer and almost jump back in surprise as it opens. Weird. I've never been to a building that opened without a keycard. Inside, the building is all business, no composite carpet or tile here. The floor seems to be made of cement, the walls all steel, and the elevator is no different. I slip inside and glance stupidly at the floor numbers, unsure how I'll find him, and decide I have no choice but to ask Gretchen. I send the message and wait, the elevator doors sliding open and closed every few seconds as though asking me to make up my mind. Finally, my phone beeps— *This is all kinds of crazy. 5C. Don't get caught.*

I shove the phone in my jacket pocket, press the fifth floor, and wait for the doors to reopen. Once on the floor, I ease down the hall, my nerves wound tight, and then tap 5C's door.

The door opens and my heart stops. Jackson is sliding on a shirt, his abs still exposed, then his head peeks through the hole in the shirt and his eyes find mine. "Okay, not who I expected." He steps out of the way and directs me inside. All thought drips from my mind and all I can do is watch as he smoothes out his shirt.

"Everything okay?" he asks.

"Yeah, I— Well, no, but…" I turn away from him so I can think and take my time examining the tiny apartment. They at least used composite flooring, though I can't place what it's supposed to look like. Not carpet; it looks harder than carpet, but it has a texture to it that isn't common with composite hardwood or tile. A deep brown sofa sits against the back wall with a small T-screen to its right. There is only one window in the main room, cut into the wall across from me, and Jackson has the blinds closed, blocking the outside view. In front of the window is a small table and to the left an open kitchen that would fit inside my food pantry. A door breaks up the right side wall, which I suppose leads to his bedroom.

Bedroom.

Heat rises up my neck, and I wonder if I've made a stupid decision coming here. I can't seem to think. I clear my throat and turn back to Jackson.

"The ball tonight is just so the leaders can get together. They're planning to decide tonight what to do. Oh, and they're researching xylem. Whatever they decide, they want to make sure xylem can't heal it." Jackson nods while I continue on with everything Cybil told me, even the part about how sure she is that we will win. When I'm done, he raises his arms, locking his hands behind his head. I've noticed he does this when he's deep in thought, and I can't help wondering what he's thinking and how much of it, if any, he plans to share with me.

He doesn't say anything for a long time, just finally stands, pointing to the clock beside his T-screen. "You need to get home. I'm sure everyone's waiting for you."

"Wait, aren't you going to say something?"

"I'm not sure what to say. I need to think about it. I knew the ball was just to hide their meeting, but I haven't thought out how we'll listen in on it yet. By tonight I'll have a plan. But you can't help if you're stuck at home. So"—he points to his door—"see you tonight." He stands, and I can't help feeling a little hurt. I'm not sure what I expected, but I hate his shadowed emotions, so obvious yet not detailed enough to reveal anything.

I edge to the door, trying not to look as pathetic as I feel. Jackson grabs my hand before I go. "Don't worry. I know it's a lot to take, but we'll figure it out."

I nod before heading out the door. I hope he's right.

CHAPTER 18

When I arrive home, Mom waits on our front porch for me, her expression lethal. I'm torn between apologizing and acting like I've done nothing wrong. She stands as I step up the stairs, and without a word, she points for me to go inside. This is bad.

Dad is already home and looks as tense as I feel.

As soon as the door closes behind her, she whips around, jabbing her finger between the two of us. "I know you both seem to think you are immortals, somehow able to survive when others can't, but I'm here to tell you that when I ask for Ari to come home after school, she is to come home right then, not a second later. Forget training. She is still underage, and I will not have you two pretending that she has the experience that those who have been doing this for years have! Now, we will all be leaving this house as a family in forty-five minutes." She walks around us without another glance.

I release a long breath and turn to look at Dad, who just

shrugs and follows Mom to their room to get ready.

What feels like hours of hair pulling and nail clipping and sucking in my breath so I fit into my dress later, I stand in the Cartier home, sipping a bubbling drink that tastes both sweet and sour. The sparkling bubbles rise to the top of the lavender liquid, burst once they reach the surface, and send alcohol pouring into the drink. It's a clever way to ration alcohol based upon the age of the drinker. Around the room older guests' drinks bubble continuously, while mine bubbles only on the rare occasion, like an afterthought.

I walk into the foyer, which could be a mini ballroom. Its massive size, crystal chandelier, and real marble flooring—not composite like the rest of ours—reveals the grandeur that is the Cartier name. As I'm staring into the twinkling chandelier, I hear someone enter and smile as Lawrence, dressed in a white tux and simple gold mask, bows in front of me. I wish I knew if Gretchen was watching. I don't want her to see how he's expected to act around me and think it's real. Law's feelings for me are only a result of expectation, but I know firsthand that actions can hurt, intentional or not.

"You are…" He takes my hand and brushes his lips against it. "Sinful."

I glance down at my dress and give a half smile. It is spectacular. Golden bronze, strapless, with an empire waist. Draping that cascades in folds down to my knees. My hair is swept up into a messy array of loose curls, my makeup simple and enchanting, while a black feather and gemstone mask conceals my eyes. "The perfect blend of innocence and seduction," Gretchen had said when she created the outfit.

He leans over to kiss my cheek just as the lights dim, saving me from figuring out a way to avoid the kiss. It's time to attend the formal portion of the ball. We file into line by the elevators, again a Cartier perk, which lead to the belowground ballroom. There, we will enjoy more drinks and expected mingling.

Law guides me to the far left elevator. It closes before anyone else can enter. Mirrors surround us, so I'm able to see, really see, Law for the first time tonight. His dark brown hair, full and wavy, hangs over his forehead and ears in that perfect sort of way. He notices me staring and smiles, his teeth startlingly white against his olive skin.

"What?"

"Nothing." I look down. I want to ask him about Gretchen but wonder if she would rather I not. Maybe they haven't worked out their feelings and I don't want to be the one to make it awkward between them. So, unsure of what to say, I just stare at him, remembering how it used to be—simple, easy. Even now, I feel so normal with him. Just me. I wonder if he, like Jackson, senses the changes in me. I avoided the topic at Jackson's. I'm not ready to talk about what's happening to me or what the changes suggest. For now, I have enough to worry about.

The elevator doors pop open, and we're escorted into the atrium. It's the shape of an octagon, with alternating silver and gold walls covered with ornate framings of past American presidents. The atrium leads to a grand marble staircase, sloping down into the main ballroom where hundreds of round tables, topped with the most expensive linens and silver available, circle the dance floor. From this view, we can see all the guests, all the splendor. I've been to these sorts of things before, but they were nothing like this. With the orchestra music playing below and so many eyes on us, for a moment I feel like royalty, like nothing is wrong with me.

Law smiles at the onlookers as we descend the stairs. I take the final step off the staircase and wish I could turn back. In front of me stand my parents, along with Alaster Krane, the European president, and to his right, his creepy son, Brighton. He's the worst kind of guy. At last year's ball, he got drunk, blurted out that I was too pretty to be a commander, and then smacked my backside. He didn't expect what came next—a blow to the face.

I walk over to President Krane, intentionally avoiding Brighton, who seems fixed on staring at me until I look his way. My parents have yet to notice I'm here, but then they all turn and grin at Lawrence and me.

"Oh, there you are," Dad says. "I'm sure you remember President Krane and Brighton."

I nod to both of them. Brighton is handsome for sure, with his dark skin and equally dark hair. Too bad he's a total lemur. I wish he'd bother the African heiress, who seems to appreciate his forwardness, and leave me alone. I scan the room for her, curious if she's in attendance, and find her chatting it up with Qwen, the Asian heir. They'd make a nice couple…if international marriages were allowed.

Law and I stand post for another few minutes before the president and Brighton move to the next group of attendees. I release a long breath when they leave. The last thing I want to do tonight is hang around Brighton. I wait until they're out of earshot and lean in to Law. "Where are the others?"

"No clue; time to eat."

The lights dim, and we take our places. Law ends up sitting at the presidential table, while I meet my parents at one of ten Engineer tables. Murmuring starts around the room. The Ancients. The attacks. What we plan to do. Finally, President Cartier rises from her seat and moves to the front of the ballroom, preparing to address the crowd.

"Thank you," she says as everyone quiets down to listen, "for joining us yet again for a celebration of food and dancing on this very important day. It is necessary that we remember why we celebrate. Remember, dear friends, peace is not a guarantee and humanity must always prosper. No matter the costs." All eyes focus on President Cartier, all movement and noise cease. She stares with fierceness into the crowd, and then suddenly her face breaks into a wide smile. "Now, let's eat!"

Dad clears his throat beside me, ignoring the gaze of the people at our table. Everyone in the crowd doesn't miss whatever President Cartier meant by her speech — Dad knows. I switch my attention to Mom, whose hands are shaking in her lap. This isn't good.

I search the crowd, curious if Jackson was invited as an Op trainee, and find him at an Engineer table three back from my own. His eyes burn holes into President Cartier, never leaving her. It must be hard for him to be in the same room as his mother, knowing she won't speak to him, knowing she likely doesn't even recognize him.

My gaze drops to my plate, and I glance up only when spoken to. Luckily, I'm not the only one mesmerized by the food. It's as exquisite as the ballroom. Essence of butternut squash soup with a seared sea scallop. Fire-roasted corn cilantro and buttered leeks atop a lump crab cake. Roasted beet carpaccio with creamy goat cheese and aged balsamic. Grilled fillet of beef with caramelized red shallot, potato rösti, and white asparagus. Everything tastes amazing, and if I weren't focusing on not throwing up, I might actually enjoy it. Finally, when I can handle no more, they bring the dessert.

I scoop the last bite into my mouth just as the lights flicker. The help enters to disassemble the tables and escort the older attendees to a lower level. This is it. The leaders will have the perfect opportunity to sneak off to meet without anyone noticing.

My eyes dart around for Law, and then Jackson, but both have disappeared. The meeting will start any minute, and it does me no good to get there after they've made the decision. I move through the crowd, keeping my eyes peeled. The lights dim and the band sets up at center stage. They look more rugged than usual. All leather—well, composite leather—clothes, purple-black hair, and a mix of silver and gold tattoos.

Drumbeats fill the air and the lights dim until we're almost in the dark. Colorful lights flash across the room and most everyone rushes to the dance floor, their bodies causing shadows to dance across the walls. I strain to see around me, fearing Jackson and Law went to the meeting without me, when I feel someone touch my shoulder and I whip around to see Jackson, a finger to his lips. He points to the steps and motions for me to go left while he goes right.

I make my way around the crowd to the stairs, glancing behind me briefly before ascending to the top. When I get there

Law and Jackson are standing close, their tones both hard, like they're arguing. They shut up when they see me. "Try to be less obvious next time," I say. "Care to share what you're talking about?"

Law presses the elevator button. "We'll explain later, right, Jack?"

Jackson shoots him daggers and says through clenched teeth, "Of course."

There's no time for me to push the issue, because we're already exiting the elevator into Law's house. He waves to the guard outside the elevator and then directs us upstairs, as though we're going to his room, but as soon as we're out of sight, he dips left, leading us to a door at the end of the hall. He slides his keycard, and the door opens to another set of stairs. We slip into the open room just inside the door and wait as the door clicks closed. The stairwell is tight, barely enough room for two people to stand side-by-side. It drops one flight, then there's another open room like the one we're in with two doors, one to the right and the other to the left. I assume they lead to the main level, but there's another flight of stairs that shoots down from that landing, and where it goes I'm not sure.

"Okay," Law whispers. "Someone should stay here as watchman—or watchwoman in your case, Ari." He grins as though he made the wisest crack on the planet.

I roll my eyes. "Funny. So, who's staying here?"

"Well, shouldn't it be you, Law?" Jackson asks. "Considering you're the one with access to this stairwell?"

"I thought of that, but if we're caught down there it would be better for Ari or me to be caught than for you."

I can see the logic working through Jackson, and finally he sighs. "Fine, but what's our warning call?"

Law smirks. "How about honesty. Scream honesty and we'll know someone's coming."

Jackson looks like he might deck Law but instead grinds his teeth together. "Then go already. Hurry back."

We get past the second landing and down the next flight of stairs before I tug on Law's arm, stopping him. "What was that about?" I whisper.

"Ask him." Then he places his finger to his mouth. "We're almost there."

Law tiptoes down the final flight of stairs, which ends at another landing. There are three doors at the bottom, one on the right and left, then a set of double doors straight ahead. He slides his keycard in a scanner beside the double doors and then ushers me into President Cartier's private office. The room is dark except for a few recess lights, and even though there is no one there except us, I can't keep chills from racing up my spine. This is so risky.

Her office reminds me of Dad's—bookshelves line three walls, windows the fourth. A giant mahogany desk sits against the windows with a matching mahogany chair in front of it. Beyond the desk, there is no other furniture in the office.

We edge past the desk toward another set of double doors, opposite from the ones we just entered, when I hear a voice that stops me cold—Dad, thunderous and angry, booming from the other side. "The situation no longer lends itself to negotiations," he says. "I vote for an immediate attack as soon as final analysis can be made."

"But how accurate is your data?" a voice I don't recognize says, but his accent suggests that he works for President Krane. "Do you understand the ramifications on human life if you are wrong? Humans could die right alongside them! We need more research. Send your findings to our lab. Let us test your theory." His tone hints that he thinks the European labs are more qualified than ours, something I'm sure doesn't go unnoticed by Dad.

Law's eyes meet mine. He knows Dad isn't going to let the conversation die there, but before Dad can argue, the African president chimes in, her voice meek compared to the others. "I would prefer to compromise with Mr. Castello. Are you sure negotiations aren't possible?"

Everyone starts talking at once, until finally President Cartier silences them. "I'm afraid not, Ninkini. Our attempts have not been successful. And of course, all research will be shared among the four major Chemists labs. Now please remember, we must stay a united front if we hope to succeed. The attacks continue daily; we have no choice but to respond. Can we all agree an airborne tactic is best?"

A muffling of agreement comes from the room, and then a clicking sound against the double door sends Law and me racing back to the secret stairwell and up the two flights of stairs until we reach Jackson. Law pushes us out the main door and then slows to a walk, his breathing as heavy as mine. "So, it looks like they've made a decision," Law says to Jackson. "Airborne attack."

"Hmm," Jackson says. "Do you think satellite missiles?"

Law shakes his head. "I can't say for sure, though I know they've talked about that before."

"I don't think so," I say. "Cybil said the strategy would involve xylem, something that prevents its healing ability. Did you get a gold keycard to the lab?" I ask Law and he nods.

"Yeah, the research there tells me this isn't a traditional attack. It's something more inventive than that. I don't think they plan to use missiles. I think their plan is biological."

We stand in silence for several minutes, trying to find the answer, when finally Law says, "This is crazy. We aren't going to figure it out tonight. Let's get back to the party before someone notices and then start fresh tomorrow. Work for everyone?"

Jackson wavers but eventually agrees. We time our entrance back into the party so it doesn't look obvious. When it's my turn, I weave my way through the crowd in front of the band, everyone jumping and singing along. I decide I should keep away from Law and Jackson for a bit and, unsure of what else to do, head to the bar for some water.

It's overcrowded, so I stand to the side, waiting to be helped, when an arm yanks me backward. I stumble as I'm dragged back, back, back. Finally, I wheel around and see Brighton, who looks like he's stolen two or ten of the adult drinks. He jerks me toward him, kissing me hard before I'm able to wiggle free and punch him in the face.

He rubs his jaw and grins. "Love it; hit me again." I back away, but he matches my steps. The music is too loud behind us for anyone to hear. My eyes scan the abandoned hall, searching for a door, exit, something, and come up empty. He outweighs me by a hundred pounds. Still, there's no way his reflexes are as good as mine.

"Look," I say, hoping to reason with him. "I don't know what you're doing. But I'm going back to the party. Okay?" He doesn't say anything. I inch backward, spinning around to run, when he grabs my hair, dragging me deeper into the hall. I cry out, and then heat strikes my chest, burning through me, like a flame turned on in my soul.

I flip over him and thrust my hand into the back of his head. He hurls forward, but it's not enough. I kick him again and again and again.

Someone screams from the entranceway. Then I feel arms wrap around me. "Ari, what are you doing?" Jackson lifts me off Brighton and carries me through a doorway I didn't notice before. It's a plush room with a large bed in the center and not much else.

"Answer me," Jackson snaps.

"What?" I ask.

"What were you doing out there?"

"What are you talking about? I was trying to get away from Brighton, and then you found me. What's your deal?"

He studies me, and then his shoulders relax. "Nothing. I must have…I don't know. I thought…" He sits on the edge of the bed and peers up at me as though I'm someone else.

"What's happening to me, Jackson?" I say, breathless and tired. "And for once, can you just be straight with me?"

He ignores the question and walks toward the door. "We should get back out there. Dance or something."

"I'm not going anywhere until you tell me what's happening."

He spins around, his eyes wild. "I don't know what's happening, okay? None of this should be happening. None of it." His head shakes as though he's fighting to keep from saying more.

"None of it?" I feel the weight of his words smashing into my chest. "You mean us, don't you? You're such a hypocrite! You want me to trust you, yet say I can't. You act like you care, then push me away. I'm not built that way! I can't just turn off my feelings."

"Well, you should! Trust your instincts, Ari. What do they tell you? To trust me? I'm betting not. I can't be trusted."

My face burns with anger and frustration. "What's this really about? You say I can't trust you. I think the problem is that you don't trust yourself. Why? Why do you hate yourself so much?"

"Because they own me. Why can't you see that? What I want doesn't matter, and the sooner you separate yourself from me, the safer you'll be."

"I don't care," I say, my voice barely a whisper. "I know you're worried. I'm worried, too. But I can't help it. I care about you. There, I said it. I care."

Jackson lifts his head, his expression so cold it sends a chill down my spine.

"Don't."

CHAPTER 19

Now that I passed Op testing, Dad canceled our morning training permanently, which would normally be a relief, but this morning I wanted to work off some of my frustration…and anger.

I cried myself to sleep waiting for Jackson to arrive. He never came. I considered going back to the Unity Tree, but I couldn't let my dignity drop that far. I told him how I felt. There's nothing else I can do. And now that the sadness has buried itself deep in my heart, anger has taken its place.

I enter the main hall at school, my eyes straight ahead, unfocused. I don't want to see him. We'll go back to the way things were before. All business. All animosity and sarcasm. And I'll pretend that I don't feel like he shot me in the heart.

Gretchen finds me and loops her arm into mine. "Guess what?" she asks, practically beaming.

"What?" I say, the word almost a whisper.

"Wait, what's wrong?" She eyes me with concern.

"Nothing."

Gretchen starts to press me for more when Jackson rounds the corner. He stops. I cut over to my locker as though I'm computerized, void of any emotion.

"Ari…" Gretchen whispers. "Jackson is staring at you. No, wait, he's coming over. He's coming over!" she squeals, shaking my arm.

Within seconds, I feel his presence behind me. I close my locker, swallow hard, and turn around, faking disinterest. "Yes?"

"Can we talk?" he asks.

"I think you said enough." I turn back to my locker, afraid if I continue to face him I'll either cry or hit him.

He edges closer, so close I feel his body against my back, his breath on my neck. "Please. Let's talk."

"There's nothing to say."

"Ari, please…" He tries to turn me back around, but anger lashes through me and I jerk away, my emotions taking over.

"What do you want from me, huh? I told you how I felt. You don't feel the same. It's fine. Let's move on."

Jackson glances around and then back at me, lowering his voice. "You didn't give me a chance to finish. You stormed off. And then I wasn't sure you— It's— Look, I'm sorry. I overreacted. I was stupid, a coward…but that doesn't mean I don't feel the same way."

I open my mouth to argue and then snap it shut. "What did you say?"

He brushes my hair from my face, and then before I can say another word, he kisses me, ignoring the crowd of people in the hall. I want to lose myself in the moment, but the presence of everyone around us comes into focus—the jocks who worship Jackson, the stupid girls who chase him, Gretchen…Law. Oh no, Lawrence. I pull away and look over at him. His face is hard, unreadable.

Jackson stiffens and steps between us in a flash. "Don't even," he says, shaking his head at Law.

"I think Ari and I should have a conversation this morning. You know, the truth. Ever try it?" Law smiles. I hate that smile. He's being cryptic and mean, two things so rare in Law it's impossible to miss them now.

Jackson sputters, his face growing tense. Everyone in the hall freezes, anxious, waiting to see what the two most popular boys from opposite sides of town will do.

"Think about who you will hurt. Is that really what you want?" Jackson asks.

Law looks at me, his face full of pain. "Ari, please just think about what you're doing. For me."

I start to ask what they're talking about, but Gretchen interrupts, her fists clenched tight. "Are you serious?" she screams at Lawrence, pushing him in the chest. "What about— Am I just—" Her head twitches, and I wonder if she's going to punch him or break into sobs. "She doesn't want you. Can't you see that? And you don't want her, either. I know it, and deep down you know I'm right. Why can't you just let her go?"

Law looks like she punched him in the gut even though she never moved. His eyes shift from her to me and back. "I…I don't know." And he walks away, his hands in his pockets.

Gretchen leans against our lockers.

"Gretch…" I say. "I'm so sorry. What can I do?"

Her face falls. "Nothing. It's his decision. You've already made your choice."

Jackson studies Gretchen with strange curiosity and then says, "He feels the same way."

She looks up with skepticism, but there's hope in her eyes. "What? No, he isn't sure."

Jackson laughs. "Oh, he's sure all right."

Gretchen shrugs, but I can tell she feels better. We go to class, hoping to quiet the gossip before it starts, but it doesn't help. Talk spreads through the entire school, some claiming the four of us are in some crazy affair, though most seem to focus on Jackson and me and my decision to be with him over Lawrence. The professors ogle as much as the students, watching us with a new curiosity. The privileged, like me, don't normally mix with the lower class. So even though Jackson is gorgeous, it's a shock that I would choose someone considered by most to be beneath me.

I'm about to leave school when a stab of reality hits me. *Dad.* I hadn't thought that far and now my throat feels tight, my stomach jelly. My future is planned out, not by law or anything, but it may as well be. Dad will lose it. And Mom. She loves Lawrence. Suddenly the kiss in the hall feels reckless, selfish, even. On top of all that, Jackson is an Ancient. If Dad knew I'd fallen for one of them…well, I may not have a future at all.

I make my way to the orchards out back, stalling for time, hoping I can think up what to say to Dad. Mom is a bit more romantic. She *might* understand. Dad cares about nothing but obligation. He'll view my decision as a mark against me, as though I'm one of his staff instead of his daughter.

It's a nice day, full sky with a slight overcast, which makes everything look peaceful. I'm jealous. I wish the clouds would cover my worries, shadow them with white fluff so I no longer care, or at the very least no longer think about it. Everything with Jackson gave me a moment's pause to think of something other than the attacks and the risk of war, but soon, I'll be back at the lab with Cybil, face-to-face with the horror.

I try not to think about it. One thing at a time. Besides, if Dad kills me then there's nothing I can do about the rest anyway.

Gretchen spots me from the hill and breaks into a huge grin, which I hope means she and Lawrence talked. "Hey, hey, hey!" She pounds the space beside her, telling me to get up there, to no doubt discuss what we couldn't earlier. I release a long, relieved breath, feeling giddy.

"Soooo?" she probes before I've even reached her. I look around. Good, we're alone.

I wonder if I can get away with, *It just happened*. Likely not, so I start with the truth. "It was nothing at first. He started working with my dad a few weeks ago. At first he annoyed me, but slowly things…changed." I smile, remembering how angry I was when I saw him in Dad's office for the first time. Now for the lying. I sigh, wishing I could just tell Gretchen the truth. "Dad started having him over for more detailed trainings at home. He would stay for dinner, come over on the weekend. Before I knew what happened, I'd fallen for him. I never imagined he felt the same way until we danced at the ball." I glance nervously at her, but she just grins back, not picking up on the lie at all.

Gretchen won't let me stop there. She wants *details*, each

question causing my cheeks to grow hotter. What he smells like. What he kisses like. What he looks like naked.

"What?! I don't know!" I shriek, but my eyes scan the orchards for Jackson and find him staring up at me, a giant smile on his face. I can't help but smile, too.

Mackenzie sprints across the field, her blond hair and golden skin dancing in the sun. Jackson notices her a second too late. He turns just as she jumps into his arms, wraps her legs around his waist, and kisses him. My chest tightens. He pulls her away, stepping back, his hands moving fast as he explains something to her I can't make out. She argues back and then speeds to the main gate, racing up the hill, Jackson on her heels. She reaches me, her face a combination of anger and hurt.

"You," she says.

I stand, preparing to defend myself if I have to, but Jackson steps between us. "Leave it, Mackenzie," he says.

"Leave it? Leave it! You are all I have and you're ditching me for this?" She motions to me. I open my mouth to say something equally mean, but then I shut it back. She begins to cry and then sob. "I… You… Please." Her round blue eyes, drowning in tears, plead with him to change his mind.

"I'm sorry," Jackson says, and the finality in his voice makes the whole thing even more painful to watch. I thought their relationship was all for show, but maybe it was real to her, maybe even real to him at some point.

Mackenzie's eyes flicker to mine and back to Jackson, a slow smile forming on her blotchy face. "Hmm. Well, then. I think it's time your family knew about this."

"You wouldn't," he whispers.

She laughs and returns her attention to me. "Time to meet the parents. Or should I say *grand*parents. Good luck. You'll need it." And she's gone.

I turn on Jackson. "What was that about? Why is she so upset?" Then I remember where we are and grit my teeth together in frustration. I want answers, but I can't ask more with all these people around.

"Later?" I ask him.

He releases a long breath and rubs his hands over his face. "Yeah…later."

An hour later, Jackson and I sit in Dad's lobby. Cybil messaged me that today's training would be intense, resurrecting the sickness in the pit of my stomach. I tell myself over and over that no matter what I see, I can handle it. I have to. We need the information to stop this and I plan to get it today. Of course, that's assuming I get to train once Dad finds out about Jackson and me. I know I have to tell him. I can't risk the news reaching him from one of my professors, but still, I wish I could just hide it. At least for a little while.

Jackson places his hand on my knee. "Everything okay?"

"Yeah, just thinking." I place my chin in my hand and lean against the armrest. The lobby feels cold and emotionless. The flooring is a brown composite tile that brings the only warmth to the room. Hidden doorways and passages line the composite wood walls. I can only imagine what's behind them. There are three elevators on the floor—the main elevator, the Chemist elevator, and then one for Parliament.

It dawns on me that I'll be working here in another year. Op training begins the moment I graduate high school, and then I'll be assigned fieldwork. Traditionally, for someone like me, that's research and development, sort of like what Cybil does, but there's still a chance that I could be sent to fight, especially now. Those calls used to be rare—uproars in rural areas, maintaining our borders, or policing. But everything's changed and regardless of what happens, life on Earth will never be the same.

I don't want to think about it anymore. Now is technically later, so I decide to push the Mackenzie thing. "Why did Mackenzie get so upset earlier? I thought the thing between you two was all for show."

He tilts his neck back as though he needs a second to think through what to say. "She's an old friend who hasn't really gotten over that we're *only* friends. She sees you, a human, as beneath her. I'll talk to her."

"So what did she mean earlier with the comment about your grandparents?"

"Remember how I told you that she was sent to assist me?" he says. "Well, she was sent by my family. She's threatening to tell them about you, but I don't care. I'm tired of doing exactly what they want, when they want, all the time. It's my life."

I start to ask him more when the Chemist elevator springs open.

Dad closes in on us faster than expected. His eyes dart from Jackson to me, and then like some super lens, zoom in on our interlocked hands. "*Ex*plain."

I drop Jackson's hand and stand, swallowing hard. "Dad… um, see…we're—"

"You're what?" Dad says, his eyes landing on Jackson.

Jackson stands beside me.

"Jackson and I are...together, Dad," I manage to finally say.

His face bucks and sours and grimaces. "Impossible. You can't—" His jaw sets and I can tell he swallowed what he wanted to say. "You're to marry Lawrence. You know this. There are no changes in plan. Forget whatever this is," he says, motioning between us. "You're not allowed to be *together* with anyone other than Lawrence Cartier." And he turns to leave.

"No," I scream after him.

He stops cold and spins around. "No?"

I walk forward. I want Dad to see my face. "You've trained me to think for myself. Act for myself. For the good of the country. I've always behaved as you want me to behave. I never deviate. But not with this."

His chest rises and falls, his eyes burning a hole into me. He glances over my shoulder to Jackson. "You have exactly three seconds to get out of my building. Do not step back in until I've decided what to do with you."

Jackson edges forward. "Sir—"

Dad shoots him a lethal look and walks around me toward Jackson. I try to block his path, but he has a clear head over me and his eyes never leave Jackson.

"My daughter apparently cares for you. Do you her?"

"Yes, sir," Jackson says. "I do."

Dad's gaze turns deadly. "Prove it. Her future is set. Surely you realize you can't give her what Lawrence can. If you care about her, really care about her, then walk away."

All feeling leaves my body as I look up at Jackson and see

the logic enveloping him.

Then Dad turns on me. "Cybil will arrive soon to take you to your training for today. You are to go with her. You are to listen. You are to act as I have raised you to act. Understand? Now, this has occupied as much of my time as I am willing to give it." He shoots Jackson another menacing look before turning back to his office. "I expect you out of my building, Mr. Locke. Effective immediately, you are no longer part of my program." And his office door closes behind him before either of us can utter another word.

We both stand, staring at each other. I knew this would be bad, but I had no idea it would be this bad. Cybil rushes from her office, her expression changing from worry to shock as she takes in Jackson and me.

"Ari..." Cybil turns her head just enough to let me know something is wrong—very wrong. Then she stands tall and addresses the Ops who have arrived to guard Jackson. "Remove him from the premises. At once."

My mouth falls open and I feel like there's something I'm missing. They can't know he's an Ancient. They would arrest him, they would...I don't know. But the way they're acting, it's as though they do know, or maybe they suspect. No, they wouldn't just let him leave.

Jackson nods toward me, shooting me a weak smile, before leaving without another word.

CHAPTER 20

Cybil motions for me to follow her, but I hesitate, staring at the spot where Jackson stood just moments before. If it weren't for the strategy, I would have left with him, but I can't risk the only chance we have of stopping this.

I try to clear my mind and prepare for whatever horror lies in store for me today. Cybil notices my distance and turns around. "Are you good? I need you focused today, so if not let me know and we can catch up tomorrow."

"No, I'm fine, really," I say, hoping I sound more sure than I feel.

She smiles widely. "Great, because the first stop today is the training room."

My head snaps up. "The Operative training room?"

"Uh-huh. I'm guessing you've never been?"

I follow Cybil down the hall to the main elevator. I wait for her to press a button, but she turns to face the back wall.

She flattens her hand against it, causing a silver scanner to pop out, and swipes her keycard. The back wall slides open like the double elevator doors at the medical center. Cybil motions me forward, her demeanor switching from carefree to rigid.

The elevator dumps us onto a landing with two sets of stairs, darting down on the right and left. The landing overlooks a giant room broken into four sections, where a dozen or so men and women stand in line at each end, none of them a day over twenty-five—the cutoff age for Operatives—but most look younger, maybe eighteen.

Cybil starts down the right set of stairs. "As you'll see, the training room is broken into four stations. Combat, weaponry, resources, and limits. Traditionally, the stations are designed to test agility and strength, but today, we're experimenting." She stops in front of the first station to the left, where a group of ten men and women circle around a guy in the center wearing a headset. I assume he's in limits and experiencing a simulation, but then his body begins to shake and he falls to the ground. A Lead Op rushes over to him, jerks off his headset, and starts yelling at him that resistance is key to survival.

Cybil *tsk*s. "I designed that one myself. I had hoped they would be responding better by now."

"It's a simulation, right? What are they seeing?" I ask.

She smiles with pride. "The program simulates the Taking. The trainees feel as though they're being Taken to death, but I did extensive research before I approved the program for use. Their vitals aren't changing. It's all psychological, which is the point of limits. We have to act in spite of fear, never succumbing to it."

I can't help hearing my dad's voice in her words. It's something he would say, likely something he did say. I peek at the boy as he steps back into line. His face hangs in disappointment, and from this distance, I can tell he's shaking. I wish I could tell him how pointless it is to be afraid. If the Ancients want him dead, he's dead. There's nothing this training can do to prevent it, which I suppose is why Dad always said we had less than a minute to figure out how to kill the enemy. I always thought he said that to scare me into working harder. Now I know he was just trying to prepare me.

Cybil and I move on to the next station, which I can only assume is combat, but instead of two people in the center of the mat, there is only one, and she seems to be fighting herself. "What's she doing?" I ask after several seconds of watching.

"We believe the Ancients have force-field technology that they could use during a war," Cybil says. "Here, we have a minor one in place—static, really—that gives a brief shock when a trainee passes it. To leave the mat, she'll have to use her other senses to weave out of the force field, like a maze. We depend too heavily on sight, which I believe is our greatest weakness."

Now that one I'm sure I've heard Dad say. She's like a younger, female version of him. The thought sends chills down my back. One of Dad is enough.

Cybil moves on to the weapons station, where trainees are testing guns and knives I've never seen before. I study each of them with interest. I'm about to ask about a flashing trick knife that some tiny girl studies when it whips out of her hand and flies through the air toward us. I snatch the knife moments before it would have jabbed into Cybil's face, flip it into my other hand, and throw it at a knife target ten yards away.

"Bull's-eye," I say, unfazed.

Cybil's eyes burn into me. "What was that?" she asks, a strange excitement in her voice. But before I can answer, her phone buzzes and she smiles widely. "We're done here. Time for the main part of our training."

A few minutes later, Cybil and I stand outside lab three. My heart races in anticipation. I have no idea what I'll see inside the lab, but I can tell by Cybil's demeanor, it's going to be big.

"Before we go inside," Cybil says, "it's important that I reiterate that this information is classified. No one can know what you're about to see."

"Of course."

She slides her keycard at the door and then presses her right thumb into a jelly-like square beside the scanner. Her photo fills the scanner screen followed by the words: ADVANCED OP CLEARANCE.

"Ready or not, what you're about to see may change the way you think."

"The way I think about what?" I ask.

"Everything."

An alarm sounds through the labs, signaling the close of regular business. It must be about five. I fight off the chill in my back and the nervousness in my stomach. I steel myself, readying my mind for whatever they throw at me.

We step inside to a room full of white-coat Chemists. The room is different than it was before. There are ten large T-screens against the left-hand wall, each with a Chemist in front of it, studying data I can't make out. The screens flash continuously and then one of the screens flashes to a face, then the next screen to a different face, and before long all ten screens show the face of an Ancient, all different, all ages. Cybil nods for me to follow her over.

"Marique," she says to the Chemist on the end, a female with bright red hair and fair skin. "This is Ari. We're observing today. Can you show her what you're studying?"

Marique eyes me with a kind smile. "I know who you are. Pleasure to meet you." She taps her screen, switching it to the data screen I saw before, then clicks on XYLEM LEVELS. A reading fills the screen that reminds me of the heart monitors at the Medical Center. It flows up and down, up and down.

"It fluctuates," I say in amazement. "How is that possible?"

Marique turns to me. "We believe xylem operates very much like an organ would. It moves, and it has a pulse to it that is unlike anything we have ever seen. Before, we compared it to water in the human body, but it's nothing like water. It's almost..." She glances at Cybil as though embarrassed of what she's about to say and finally whispers, "Magical."

Cybil gives a curt laugh. "You Chemists will romanticize anything. It's not magical. It's deadly. That liquid evolution is what prevents us from killing them. Remember our goal, Marique." Then she pulls me away, her head shaking. "I can't blame them for being fascinated—that's what they do—but as Engineers, we don't admire its strengths; we look for its weaknesses. Which brings us here." She motions to the split back wall and the exposed glass testing chamber she revealed to me the first time we came here. But as I edge to the glass, I realize it looks less like a testing chamber and more like a torture chamber.

The Chemists stare into it with intensity, and then one—a short guy with black hair and olive skin—presses a button on the outside of the glass and speaks into an intercom. "Admit subject one."

I watch as two Operatives bring in a male Ancient. He wears nothing beyond a small cloth that covers his private region, and the rest of his body looks frail and broken. The five Chemists around me begin jotting down notes on their notes tablets. The same Chemist who pressed the intercom walks over to a keypad on the right side of the glass. The door inside the chamber closes behind the Operatives, and the Ancient is left alone in the huge two-story room, visibly shaking. His head twitches in nervousness, and then he darts from one side to the other, hitting each wall, before latching onto the glass we're looking through like a frog to a tree. He tilts his head to the side and screams out, but no sound releases.

Cybil steps up beside me. "Meet Ryden. He is a longtime friend of the Chemists' cause. Ignorance is our greatest weakness, which we must rectify if we hope to succeed."

"Succeed in…?" I ask, probing Cybil to tell me what I need to know but keeping my eyes on Ryden. He doesn't look like a spy, but Cybil said all their test subjects were Latents. This guy looks like he should be in the croplands working fields, not risking his life to learn information about humans. Something doesn't add up.

"Destroying them, of course," Cybil says.

"Of course, but what's the plan, the strategy?" I hope I don't sound as desperate as I feel.

She grins. "I like where your head is, but we haven't decided our final strategy just yet. I will tell you that it hinges on this research."

"Speaking of, where did you get him?"

She looks away, uncomfortable, avoiding the question for far too long to respond with the truth. She forgets who trained me. "I told you, they're Latents," she says.

Well, that's a lie. Either she doesn't know or she doesn't want to tell me.

My eyes drift to the Chemist beside the keypad. He punches in a series of codes and then walks back over, biting his nails as he comes.

"What are they doing?" I ask Cybil.

"Electrical therapy," she replies.

At that moment a bell sounds from within the testing chamber. The Ancient spasms and jerks, his body jumping from within itself like his organs want to escape. A bell sounds again, and his body relaxes. He falls to the ground. The Chemists around me jot down more notes, and from the looks on their faces they seem pleased with the results.

Cybil leads me away from the glass. "This lab focuses on airborne tactics that affect the Ancients without harming humans. The goal is to create a weapon that will hit without them knowing. So they breach our surface and *bam*!" She slams her fist into her hand. "They're dead. The problem is that xylem heals them within moments. So our strategy is to come up with something that interacts with xylem, changing it."

I nod, wondering if I should ask the question that hasn't left my mind since we started all of this. "Cybil," I say with hesitation. "I thought they want to join us once they're strong enough. I thought they wanted a peaceful coexistence. So, I guess what I'm wondering is why are we trying to kill them?"

"Two such different species can't coexist on one planet. It's survival of the fittest and we must survive."

She walks back, and I follow as a giant hole spreads in my chest. Everything we've been taught about the Ancients, all of it, has led up to this moment. They want to push fear into us so we don't pity the species we plan to annihilate. I glance through the glass. Ryden cowers in a corner, his eyes jerking from person to person before landing on me. He studies me, and then mouths a single word—*help*.

CHAPTER 21

I cut through the woods behind my house, jumping over thorny overgrowth and swiping away spiderwebs. I messaged Jackson the moment I left training, hoping I have enough information to appease Zeus. But even if I do, won't Dad just come up with a new strategy? I don't know. I don't know. I don't know.

When I reach the Unity Tree, the sun has set and the forest is dark. Wind blows through the trees, causing the fallen leaves to scatter. I kneel down in front of the tree and stare into its hollow center, aching to inch closer, feeling like I belong there, not here.

I reach out a shaky hand. My fingers disappear into the triangular opening and warmth crawls through my fingertips, down my hand, up my forearm. I jerk back, but the ghost of the sensation lingers on my arm. My heart races in my chest. Then I hear something from within the tree. I stand slowly as whispers echo in the trees. They call to me as though they know me, as though I'm one of them. I close my eyes, allowing the whispers to grow closer, swirling with the wind. I can't understand what they're saying, but I can feel the passion of their words in my chest and I want more than anything to join them.

The whispers blend with the beats of tree limbs around me, each sound pushing me further from reality. My arms latch on to an oak tree behind me, clinging to the bark, and within moments, I'm to the top of the tree, peering down before a single breath escapes me. The whispers and beats continue below, harmonious pounding, and then the forest goes still, the sky peaceful. I feel a sense of belonging and comfort unlike anything I've felt before. I stare down at the forest floor and back up to the sky. With one final breath, I lift my arms out to my sides and swan-dive into the open clearing. Air rushes past my ears, cold and inviting. I should be terrified, but I'm exhilarated, electricity in my veins instead of blood. I flip in the air and land easily on my feet. Laughter bursts from my mouth.

"Ari..." a voice says from behind me. I freeze, cringing as I turn to see Gretchen, her mouth wide open, her eyes round with fear. "I saw you come here... I came to check. I—I..."

"Gretch, stop," I say as she backs away. "This isn't... I'm not..." I stare at her and she stares back, but not like my best friend; she stares as though she's seeing me for the first time. Tears well in my eyes, and before I know it I'm sobbing uncontrollably. The weight of what I just did, Gretchen seeing, Ryden, the war strategy, Jackson, everything culminates in my mind and I can't take any more. I feel like years, decades, have passed since my life had any sense of normalcy. I want a normal life. I want to *be* normal.

But I know I'm not. I feel it in my gut, yet I have no clue

what's happening to me. Am I becoming one of them or am I already one of them? I don't know. I know nothing. I am nothing. Everything in my life feels foolish now. If I'm half of each species, I can't choose which part of me is real, which part gets to live. It's too much. I break into a fresh round of sobs and feel a hand press against my back.

"Ari, talk to me," Gretchen says. "I won't judge. I promise. Talk to me."

I glance up at her, my eyes burning from the tears, and lean back against the large oak tree I just dove from. Gretchen sits in front of me, no judgment, no pitying expression. I can trust her; I'm sure of it. I draw a shaky breath and release it, the words spilling out. "I guess it all started with Jackson." And I tell her everything. About him being an Ancient. The war strategy. What I've done, what I plan to do, what I think I'm becoming. She listens with interest, never interrupting. When I finally stop talking, I look over at her. "So…what do you think?"

"I think I'm sickly jealous that you get to kiss someone as tasty as Jackson and can jump off a blasted tree without dying." We both break into laughter. It's dark now, the moon beaming down over us. Gretchen stops laughing, and I'm worried she's about to run off screaming, but she hugs me tightly. "You're my best friend, no matter what. Everything will be all right. I'll help if I can, okay?"

I nod. "Enough about me. You came looking for me. Is everything okay?" She leans back, aiming for the tree behind her, but slips on the scattered leaves. I catch her moments before her head would have hit the tree. We both freeze.

"How did you…?" Gretchen starts.

"I don't know."

"Can you do other things, too?"

I shrug, but Gretchen's face morphs into a sly smile.

"Let's see." She bounces with excitement, but I'm not in the mood to test whatever weirdness exists within me.

She picks up a rock from beside her and tosses it in the air again and again, then eyes me, preparing to toss the rock behind me. I don't know why I move, but something inside me wants to prove that I can stop the rock from sailing into the air. The rock leaves her hand one second, and in the next, it's in my hand. I moved, I felt my arm move, yet my reflex responded faster than I could process what I wanted to do, like an inane muscle response. I stare down at the rock, feeling more confused than ever. I'm faster than before, have quicker reflexes, but I wonder if I can do the one thing that separates humans from Ancients.

I flip the rock around in my hand until I find a sharp edge, and then I slice it over my forearm. Blood trickles down the sides of my arm.

"Ari, what in the world?"

"Just wait," I say, staring at the wound, but nothing happens. It continues to bleed more and more, never healing as the Ancient in the water chamber healed. A sense of disappointment washes over me. I don't know why I hoped it would work, but I guess I would rather be all of one species than part of two. I must have very little xylem in me or the cut would have healed.

Gretchen pulls my arm from me and wraps her jacket around it. "Come on, you need to get home and get some healing gel on it."

I sigh. "Thanks. And thanks for not thinking I'm a freak."

"Who said I didn't?" she says with a smile as she loops her arm into my other arm. "Let's get you home. I don't want to risk being your first sacrifice or something."

A few minutes later, I slip into my house, listening for either of my parents, but all I hear is the eerie hum of silence. I contemplate calling them, but instead head up to my room, thankful for the peace. My body is exhausted in every way, and my face is still puffy from crying. It's been a long time since I've allowed myself to let it all out, and now all I want to do is crawl into bed and forget about everything for one night.

My room is dark when I step inside, yet I'm somehow able to see or at least sense everything around me. I tell myself it's because it's my room, but inside I can't help wondering if it's yet another change. I reach my bathroom, clean the cut, and then coat it in healing gel, catching sight of my reflection in the mirror. I ease closer until my eyes shine back at me, their color previously the same emerald green of my mom's but now a deep blue-green. Amazing. I step back into my room, feeling both uneasy and elated.

"Ari?" Jackson calls from my window, startling me.

"Hi," I say.

He walks over, taking my arm, his face crinkled in concern. "What happened?"

"Oh, it's nothing. I was just being stupid. I thought I could... It's stupid." I hesitate and then add, "I waited for you."

"I know; I'm sorry," he says, sitting beside me on the bed. "I was called back to Loge. Is everything okay?"

I look down. "No, not really. They're planning to use an airborne tactic, something that prevents xylem from healing you. There was this Ancient; they called him Ryden. He asked for my help. That's why I called you." My eyes train on his. "I want to go back to release him."

"Ryden is dead."

My chest constricts. They killed him. No, I *let* him die. I swallow my sadness, anger overcoming all other emotions. "We have to do something. Enough talking. We have to act." I detail every moment that I spent in the lab and wait as Jackson processes everything I've told him. He leans against my headboard and wraps his hand around his neck.

"Is that all?" he asks.

I draw a long breath. I can't tell him about Gretchen, though maybe he already knows. "No, that's not all. I climbed to the top of an oak tree and dove off." I expect him to jump up or act surprised or something, but instead he just nods. "Tell me what's happening to me," I say.

"What's happening to you is me. I did this to you. I understand if you hate me, if you never want to see me again. I'm not proud of what I did. I couldn't... You were... I'm so sorry." His eyes plead with me to forgive him.

"What did you do?"

"The day of the explosion at school. You were screaming. You were in so much pain. I... Lawrence said... No, it was my decision—"

"Just tell me."

"I healed you, and not like the tiny healings I did when you were little that have no consequences. A full healing. And do you remember what I told you about xylem?"

"It multiplies," I say, my words almost a whisper. I stare out into my room, seeing nothing, lost in my thoughts. We sit silently for several minutes, him wrecked with remorse, me with fear.

"I should go." He starts to rise, but I grab his arm, our eyes connecting. He must sense what I'm thinking. I don't want to worry any longer. He lies beside me, our faces inches apart. "Or maybe I'll stay." He kisses my lips and cheeks and neck, filling my body with warmth.

I maneuver on top of him. My body takes over, all restraint gone, all thoughts of anything but us vanishing from my mind. His hands move into my hair, down my back, farther and farther. I wiggle a hand under his shirt, tracing lines on his stomach, and ease off his shirt. He does the same for mine so we're bare chest to bare chest, our breath heavy. Then, suddenly, he sits up, pushing me back until I'm straddling his waist. "You've had a hard day. We shouldn't…" He shifts in the bed, reaches for his shirt, and hands me mine. I slip it on but keep my eyes on him.

"What's wrong?" I ask.

He rakes a hand through his hair and looks up at me, seeming conflicted, then he says, "Come take a walk with me."

"Now?"

He slips out of bed and holds out his hand for me. "I have a surprise for you."

A minute later we're in the forest, crunching down the trail, the moonlight as our guide. It's a full yellow moon—unrealistic-looking and so big I want to reach out to it. Jackson takes my hand and I slow my pace. It's electrifying being here with him with no one else to see.

He pulls me to him. We walk the rest of the way to the Unity Tree wrapped in each other's arms. I feel sliced in half, cut by guilt. My loyalties are to my dad, to my family, my people. It's who I am, the kind of person I want to be. Dad's disappointed face swirls through my mind. I divulged information to the enemy, information that may prevent a war.

We reach the Unity Tree in silence. Jackson likely heard my thoughts, but he doesn't say anything. He walks around the tree and brings back a large basket. I study it. "What's that?"

He grins. "It's a picnic basket. I thought you could use a distraction."

"A what basket?"

"Picnic. Haven't you ever heard of picnics?" He opens the basket, pulling out a small blanket, and lays it on the ground in front of the tree. I eye it and then him and then lie down on the blanket. He breaks into hysterics, laughter echoing through the woods. "You don't *lay* on it. You sit on it and eat."

"You want me to eat in the middle of the night on this"—I glance at the blanket—"crisscross blanket."

He laughs again, this time fighting for breath. "It's called plaid. And this is all human stuff you should know."

"Whatever. Do you know my parents?" I say sarcastically. "I can just see Dad now, sitting on the ground, eating a— Where is this food you speak of?"

"In here." He motions to the basket and takes out all kinds of food. "Do you like it? I mean, we don't have to eat. I just thought…"

"No, it's perfect. I love picnics, do them all the time. Let's eat."

He smiles again and sets everything out.

A bright red strawberry catches my eye and I pick it up to take a bite.

"How do you know about this stuff?" I ask.

"We're required to learn your history. I am more than others. It's drilled into my mind on a constant, daily basis. What happened and when and why. You can't imagine how frustrating it is to be expected to know so much in so little time."

I raise an eyebrow. "Have you met my father?"

"I retract previous statement. Let's talk about something else," he says, tilting his glass back to take a drink.

"Yes, tell me about your family."

Jackson chokes, coughing and hacking.

"Are you okay?" I ask.

"Yeah, sorry I…" He moves a strand of hair from my face and kisses me. I wrap my legs around his waist and look at him.

"Can I…touch you?" I ask.

"Touch me? Where?" He grins.

I pretend-punch his chest. "Not like that. I just want to…" I trace my fingers down the sides of his face, forming lines on his cheeks, down his neck, smoothing my hands over his shoulders and arms. He leans back on his elbows, and I loosen his shirt, exposing the contours of his toned chest. He's so perfect; it's unbelievable that anyone could be this perfect.

I lean forward and kiss him, letting his body warm mine. Heat rises between us and I wonder when he'll pull away, but he doesn't stop.

He lays me on the blanket, his body pressed against mine, his lips enveloping mine in a fit of passion that causes my skin to tingle from my head to my toes. "Will you stay with me tonight? Out here?" he says, pulling away to look at me.

I nod and Jackson slides down so that we're side by side on the blanket. He kisses me again and then closes his eyes. His breath is heavy but soon it slows to a peaceful rhythm. I close my eyes, drifting off.

Then the dream finds me.

I'm alone in lab three, watching as Ryden's body jerks and spasms. No one will know if I release him. I can do it. I can save him. But I don't. Instead, I watch as he slowly begins to die. Then I catch sight of my reflection against the steel wall across from me. My skin is golden, like the sun rises through my skin, bronze and beautiful…then fear eats into my mind. I'm an Ancient. As soon as I think the words, the door behind me opens, and Dad walks in with a gun in his hand. He shakes his head, his lips pursed, and then he shoots me in the head.

CHAPTER 22

I sneak into my house at four a.m., beyond exhausted. Mom is an early riser, so I knew if I waited too long I risked running into her...and being locked in my room for the rest of my life. She used to sneak into my room when I was little just to watch me sleep. I would wake up to find her sitting beside me on my bed, but when I would ask her why she came she would always say just to make sure. I never knew what she meant, but now I wonder if she was making sure I survived the night.

I have no clue what time Jackson and I fell asleep, but I know nightmares stole my dreams. He must think I'm a terrible sleeper. Though he'd sleep terribly, too, if his dad shot him in the head. I shake the image from my mind and climb into my bed, allowing myself another few minutes of sleep before I get ready.

Big mistake.

I wake twenty minutes late, missing the first tron. Mom bursts into my room just as I'm setting my alarm clock back on my nightstand. "Are you feeling okay? You have training today. You need to get going."

"Training. You mean this afternoon?"

"No," she says. "Didn't you read your messages last night? Your father authorized early Operative training. You're supposed to be there at eight this morning."

I jump out of bed and race to my bathroom. "Can you pull out my training clothes?"

"Sure, but I can message your father."

"No, no, no! I'll be ready in ten."

Fifteen minutes later, I'm out the door and running to the tron. I slide onto it seconds before the doors close and drop into a seat, my chest pounding. I can't be late for my first training. This is unbelievable. I crack my knuckles, each joint one by one, my mind distant. I wonder if Jackson knows to show—or if he'll even be asked to after what happened with Dad. I wonder if Gretchen will act weird. I wonder, if I do well, whether she'll think it's because I'm part Ancient. And maybe she'd be right.

The tron stops at Business Park and I'm off, running down the auto-path without another thought. I fidget for my keycard at the door but slam to a halt when I get inside. I have no clue where to go. The training room is a keycard-only access zone. My keycard isn't coded for training yet…or is it? I step into the elevator and press the third floor. When the elevator stops, I turn and slide my keycard through the scanner on the back wall. Instantly, the doors open and once again I'm overlooking the training room.

"Alexander," the head Operative calls out. "You're late! Get down here before I drop you from training."

I fall into line beside Gretchen, Jackson to her left, and Marcus beside him. The rest of the thirty or so people in the room are strangers. I had forgotten we wouldn't train alone. Trainees are chosen from around the country. All schools offer F.T. training, though most don't have the resources to test properly. I'm not the smallest girl, but I'm definitely not the largest. Depending upon our training today, I might leave bruised and bleeding.

The training room isn't what I remembered. There are no longer four stations. Instead, one large station occupies the majority of the room, blocked off by four steel beams with rope draping from beam to beam. At the opposite side of the station from us is a large T-screen.

The Operative motions to the screen and then to the tables that line the station. There are four large black boxes on each of six tables. "You can call me Terrence. Today, you will learn how to shoot every legal weapon known to mankind...and a few that aren't yet legal. The T-screen allows you to advance from a still target to a moving target. I expect you all to master this skill to prevent dead bodies. Understand?"

Dead bodies. I wonder if he means us or other people. Either way it doesn't sound good. Terrence walks to each of the tables, clicking open all the boxes. From this distance, I can only see the first two tables. Both are stocked with handguns. All training guns have a switch that transfers the weapon from practice to lethal. Hence the T-screen. Practice mode utilizes lasers. Lethal mode uses lasers only for sighting and otherwise uses traditional ammunition—whatever is appropriate for the weapon.

"There are thirty-five of you," Terrence says. "The T-screen behind us will separate into seven sections. I have you in five rows of seven. The first person in each line will take a gun from the first table, fire until you hit the moving target, and then circle to the back of the line when the screen flashes. Remember, if your aim's bad you're going to rile the ones behind you. So I suggest you figure it out fast. You must successfully use a weapon from each box before you can leave today. Get started!" He struts over to a chair against the left wall, smirking as he walks. I'm guessing he's seen everything in this training and is anxious to see which of us makes an idiot of ourselves.

Thankfully, I'm well trained with most weapons. I shot my first gun when I was ten. I remember how heavy it felt in my small hands, how Dad pushed me to shoot again and again until my arms ached from holding it up. It took me weeks of hour-long practices every day to hit the target. I still have that gun, tucked away in my gun cabinet right now. Something about mastering your first weapon is like a rite of passage, so Dad let me keep it. I was so proud that day, until he brought in the next weapon and the next, each more complicated than the last. That training went on for years, but it left me with impeccable aim. Ancient or not, I should do well today.

The four of us from my school stand first in line along with a tall guy with long black hair beside me. He glances over and smiles. "Alexander, huh? The commander's daughter. We'll see if that heritage proves anything today." He steps up to the table and grabs a handgun. I do the same, ignoring his jab. I widen my stance, feel the weight of the gun in my hand, and wait for the T-screen to click on. A grid appears on the screen with a black target in the center. I count to five, click the release, and shoot.

A mark appears in the center of the target. The screen switches to a person walking across the street with a target over his head. I shoot again, and the screen switches to a bird flying through the air at absurd speeds for a bird. It flies across the screen and back. I study it, timing its flight, and then shoot a second before the bird comes back into the screen. My section of the T-screen flashes, and I circle to the back of my line.

Jackson is already done and smiles over at me. "Great job," he says.

"You, too," I say, smiling back.

Gretchen steps into line behind me, bouncing with excitement. She's a good shot so I knew she'd do well. Seconds later, Marcus and the black-haired guy finish. I thought their times were slow until the second group starts. None of them can hit the still target.

"Locke," Terrence calls. "Go demonstrate before we all fall asleep."

"Yes, sir," Jackson says, making his way to the front of the line. He shows them first how to stand, then how to hold the gun, how to sight in the target (with and without a laser sight). Within a few minutes, he has all of them through the sequence. I expect him to step back in line, but instead he stays, helping the next group and the next until it's our turn again.

Gretchen edges toward me. "Are you all right?"

"Much better, thanks to you." I smile up at her, hoping she knows how much it meant to me that she didn't trip out last night. I expected her to be a little uneasy around Jackson, but so far she's acted normal. I would say it speaks to our friendship, but really it speaks to her ability as an Operative. She's able to hide emotion better than anyone I know. I just hope she isn't hiding her true feelings from me. I'm sure I'd notice. Besides, even if she were worried or afraid, she'd never put me at risk by telling anyone.

The next hour goes faster than the first. We switch from handguns to assault rifles to sniper rifles and every type of gun in between. Terrence walks over when we get to the final table. "The last set of tables contains a new, experimental weapon. This is classified information. If anyone leaks this…well, you can imagine what will happen. The first group," he orders.

We go to the tables and pull out silver guns that resemble rifles, though smaller and definitely lighter. I balance the gun in my hand, getting a feel for its weight, and step over to my spot. The gun is light, but it must be powerful. I remember Dad's Newton lesson from years ago—every action has an equal and opposite reaction. Whatever force comes out of this gun will recoil back at me, and I'd hate to embarrass myself by screaming or, worse, falling backward.

I wait for one of the others to fire first. Jackson shoots; there's a red blur and then a flash on the T-screen. A hush goes over the room. All guns propel the ammo fast, but this is something else. A laser gun—no ammunition at all. This thing fires at invisible speeds, no doubt created for use against the Ancients.

I place my feet shoulder-width apart and bend my knees a touch. My finger curls around the trigger and *bam*! The recoil causes me to stumble back, but that isn't what causes me to stare at the gun in awe. My hands tingle as though I've just been shocked. The others sense it, too, and, like me, stare at their guns.

Jackson keeps firing. He seems determined, angry. He hits target after target, and then drops his arm, the gun dangling by his side. He tosses the weapon back in its box and marches to the back of the line. Terrence walks over and says something to him, and then Jackson leaves the room.

I turn back to my station and fire the gun again and again until I've hit all my targets. My fingertips feel electrocuted by the time I'm done. Terrence walks over to me after I've returned the gun. "Great job, Alexander. Your father would be proud. You can report back to school."

I guess that's what he told Jackson, too. I exit the training room and find him leaning against a wall. "You know what they're doing, don't you?" he asks.

"Yeah," I say. Parliament knows the Ancients will attack. Early training can only mean they plan to be ready. Everyone in that room was seventeen, just like me, and we're about to be sent into a war. Soldiers. That's what we are.

"I'm tired," I say, leaning against him.

"We have a few hours before your training with Cybil," Jackson says. "Want to skip class? There are only two left now anyway."

Ten minutes later, we're on the tron to Market District, the only section of Sydia where items can be purchased in person instead of ordered. It's quaint, but some of my best childhood memories happened there. Law, Gretchen, and I used to roam the District begging the shopkeepers for candy or toys or whatever.

Jackson takes my hand as we step off the tron, and instantly my mind relaxes. He makes me feel strong, like I'm more than just Commander Alexander's daughter. Living in Dad's shadow isn't easy. I'll never be good enough at anything I do. I'll never be viewed as an individual, capable of greatness of my own doing. Everything I do for the rest of my life will be judged, logged away, and then compared to how my dad would have done it.

We reach the corner of the District, and Jackson's face pales. He pulls me to the side of Decadent Desserts—my favorite bakery—just as President Cartier and her entourage march past us. Jackson sags against the composite brick, inching down until he sits on the ground.

"Are you okay?"

"Yeah, why wouldn't I be?"

"Oh, I don't know. Your mom just walked by. She didn't say hi or ask how your day is or even glance your way. It's okay to be upset about that, to care."

"Why should I care?" He jumps up. "She sent me away, ditched me. What am I supposed to make of that? Not love, definitely no love coming from the Cartiers." He kicks the wall, dislodging a brick, then picks up the brick and chucks it down the alleyway.

"Hey." I tug his sleeve so he's forced to look at me. "Maybe she wishes she knew you. Maybe she's forced to not see you or talk to you. Maybe it wasn't her decision. You don't know that she ditched you. You don't know that she doesn't love you."

"Whatever, it doesn't matter. I'm not allowed to see her anyway."

"Says who?"

"The people who run my life, that's who," he says, tugging his hair. "Let's talk about something else."

"I have a better idea," I say. "Let's walk around the shops and get desserts and candy. Want to?"

A few minutes later, we stroll down the street toward the park, ice-cream cones in hand. Of course nothing about them is real. It's synthetic sweets, but it tastes so similar that I can't really tell the real from the fake. I've had them a zillion times. Mom's a dessert addict. But Jackson inhales the thing so quickly I can only assume he's never had one. I want to ask but feel rude pointing out something that might make him sad again. Law has definitely had ice cream, synthetic *and* the real stuff. He's experienced all of this and gets his mom. It must be hard for Jackson, whether he admits it or not.

The park is covered in trees, real trees, their leaves orange and red and yellow. I love fall. I love how the world around me changes into color, like a fantasy world or something.

"This is nothing. You should see Loge."

"It's like this?"

"It's full of color and life all year round. You would like it, I think."

"Tell me about it."

Jackson stretches back on the bench, his face disappearing into thought. "There are less of us than there are of you on Earth. We have a school system like you, though, and a work system, but Logians can choose their future jobs. We don't force it the way you do here."

My instinct wants to argue his point. It isn't that we force jobs, it's that we place according to skill set and need at the time, but I know those are Dad's words ingrained in me instead of my own, so I stay quiet, wondering if we are really as bad as Jackson sees us or if his kind has instilled his mindset, very much like ours has mine.

"Most," he continues, "go into knowledge or agriculture. Government is trickier and as we're a peaceful species by nature, no one wants to join the military. Zeus complains about it all the time."

I tilt my head. "And what about your family?"

He stiffens. "What would you like to know?"

"Well, to start, what do they do for work? Are they military like you? I'm guessing RESs are considered military."

He weighs the question for a long time. "I guess you could say a mix of all four." Then he taps his watch. "It's almost time for training. We better head over."

"So does that mean my dad asked you to come back? I was worried you wouldn't show to Op training, that he would take you out of the program altogether."

"No, I received the same message you did about early training, so I showed. As for today, I don't know. You could say he summoned me. Not sure what he wants."

I sigh. That could be good or really, really bad. We make our way back through the park and are almost to the tron when I turn on Jackson, stopping him before he can take another step.

"You know," I say, my voice filled with sugary goodness. "You're not getting out of this. I'm going to learn about your family whether you like it or not."

"I know," he says. "That's what I'm afraid of."

CHAPTER 23

Jackson doesn't talk, not really, the entire way from the tron to Dad's office. He comments on the weather, the tron, whatever to avoid the conversation about his family. Something tells me whatever secret lies with his family is bad. Maybe I don't want to know.

The elevator doors open to Cybil already waiting for me in the atrium.

"You're late," she says and taps her watch. But I'm ten minutes early. "I expect punctuality for all training. And you." She glances at Jackson. "He's waiting in his office."

Her tone, especially for Cybil, seems formal. I follow her to the Chemist elevator, giving Jackson my best supportive smile as I go. I try not to worry over what Dad wants or what he might say, but still my chest feels tight and I know it won't relax until I see Jackson again and know everything is okay.

The elevator doors close, and Cybil turns to me, excited.

"Wait until you see our latest development."

Okay…talk about a mood change. "What is it?"

"Oh, you'll see, but keep it to yourself. Your dad doesn't want this one leaking."

My insides sour. This is it. I feel it in my gut. I think of the room of us today, strong but so young, going into war against a species that even our most trained can't stand against. I can't let this happen.

We reach the Chemist door, and Cybil types in her code. It's past five. The halls loom dark, with nothing but recess lights to guide our path. Lab three shines brightly again today, but as we near it, I realize two others are lit as well. Thirty or more Chemists work busily in each lab, all of them watching over glass rooms similar to three's. Cybil calls them *testing chambers*. I guess that sounds more professional, and less barbaric, than calling them what they are—cages.

Cybil slides her card through the first lab's key slot. Marique stands in front of the only T-screen in the room. It's stationed to the right of the chamber, so her head jerks from the screen to the chamber and back continuously. "Doing okay?" she says to me as we near. "I hear you survived your first day of Op training. It can be intense, or so I'm told." There's a longing in her voice that makes me wonder if she was a Pre-Op in school but didn't pass. I hear many become Chemists, since we work so closely together.

I shrug. "It was okay. I've been preparing so it was…okay." I don't mention why I think we've been drafted early. I don't want her to think I'm afraid, because I'm not—not in the traditional sense, anyway. I'm not afraid to fight. Fighting is easy. I'm afraid that I can't prevent the fight, and all of this—the early drafting, the testing today—just proves I'm losing that battle.

"So what's that?" I ask her, pointing to the screen, where a reading is climbing slowly upward.

"Look in there." She motions to the glass. "This is monitoring his xylem level. Notice how it climbs? We're about to see how high it can go." She clicks the sound on the screen, causing a soft *beep, beep, beep* to fill the air.

The door to the chamber opens and an Operative enters. I recognize him at once—it's Lane, the same one I fought in the maze. He's a strong fighter, but he can't survive against an Ancient. Lane gets into position, but the Ancient in the chamber, a male who has at least a foot on Lane, doesn't budge. The Ancient smirks then tilts his head up to the glass. "Is this the best you've got?" Then he lunges for Lane, tossing him to the floor. He drags his body back to the center of the chamber. "Stand, human. Let's see what you can do."

The beeping beside us quickens, growing louder. Marique exclaims, "Cybil, look at this!" She taps the screen hard, the xylem level climbing higher and higher. "That's amazing. And check out his vitals. They're soaring. Xylem must fuel energy in addition to healing him. It's like an energy shot directly into his muscles. I've never seen anything—"

"Get him out of there!" Cybil yells.

Everyone's eyes dart back to the chamber, where the Ancient hits Lane again and again. His speed, his reflexes, all too much for Lane to compete against. The door to the chamber opens and three Operatives race in just as Lane's body falls to the ground.

"No more one-on-one combat. Do you understand me?"

Cybil says to a Chemist beside her. "If he dies, it's on you."

She marches from the lab and I follow, unsure what to say or do. I assume we're done for the day, but then she slides her keycard through the next lab, and we enter to a pungent smell, like singed flesh.

"More electrocuting?" I whisper to Cybil.

"Oh, no. We came up with something better." She waves a few Chemists out of the way so we can see through the glass on the back wall. Inside this chamber, there are five Ancients—two males and three females. They're all naked, their skin covered in dark marks that ooze some thick yellow goo.

"What happened to them?"

"Ever heard of spontaneous combustion?" A smile spreads across her face. I grit my teeth together to keep from screaming at her to stop acting like this is fun. It isn't fun. It's horrifying in every way.

I draw a breath to calm my anger and say, "Of course. What's that got to do with this?"

"Everything," Cybil says. "See, we release a chemical into the air that, once mixed with xylem, causes the Ancients to literally explode from the inside out. Brilliant, right?" Just then a large wall timer to our left hits zero, a second passes, and then *boom*! The Ancients explode within the chamber; limbs and guts splatter against the walls.

I jolt backward, my hands covering my mouth. Five lives just disappeared before my eyes. This isn't happening. I fight to remain calm. I can't get shaken, not now, not when I'm this close to learning the strategy.

"That won't do," Cybil says to a Chemist at the T-screen

to our right, a lady much younger than Marique who seems as rattled as I am by what just happened. "Clean this up and record the issue. Make adjustments. We need more live subjects."

"Live subjects," I say, unable to hold back. "I thought they were Latents."

"Most are."

"And the rest?"

"Were obtained. What does it matter?"

"It matters because maybe that is why we've been attacked again and again. We stole some of their kind. Didn't it ever occur to anyone that they would fight to get them back?" I know my words border on dangerous, but I can't stop myself now. "All of this might have been prevented and yet you stand here, asking for more of them. We should just call Zeus now and schedule another attack."

"That's enough," Cybil says, grabbing me hard by the arm and yanking me from the lab. "They attacked because they are impatient and greedy. The Ancients don't care whether humans live or die; they only care about inhabiting Earth and to them, their time is now. And you will do well to remember that you are a guest here and a reflection of your father. You are to watch. Silently. Do you understand?"

I shake my head, biting hard on my lip to stop myself from arguing.

"Okay, good. Now on to lab three," Cybil says.

Cybil enters the room with her head high. She'll make a great Lead Operative someday, authoritative and void of emotion. I force myself to step to her side and peer down into chamber three. At first I think my sanity is safe, that there is no one in chamber three. Then a buzzer sounds, and a group of ten men and women and children enters the chamber. My mouth drops.

"Wait, those are kids," I say to Cybil, my voice rich with fear.

"Of course they are. We need to guarantee the weapon works on all generations of Ancients. Some believe the youth are stronger, more able to resist. We have to guarantee full disposal."

Full disposal. I have to find Jackson now, before—

The wall timer hits zero. My eyes jerk back to the chamber. Nothing happens. The Ancients huddle together, protecting one another, all noticeably shaking. Time ticks by, seconds become minutes. I glance to my watch. Ten minutes have passed.

"Nothing's happening," I whisper to Cybil, but it's a Chemist who answers me. He's younger than most, with dark skin and dark hair.

"Wait for it," he says. "This one is magic, Cybil."

Cybil beams at him, all of our attention trained on the chamber. "This test," Cybil says to me, "is subtle. We release a neurotoxin into the air that, once mixed with xylem, slowly and systematically poisons them."

They wanted an airborne tactic that mixes with xylem. This is it—the strategy. A neurotoxin, by its simplest definition, poisons us by impacting our nervous system. It's something the Chemists in the eco-sector have preached for years, stating that WWIV killed many due to the aftereffects of the neurotoxins released by the nuclear bombs. How smart we must think we are to impose the same on the Ancients.

But this time, the toxin won't have a chance to kill anyone. I tap my foot on the floor, anxious for this to get over with so

I can report it to Jackson and stop all this craziness. I keep my eyes on the chamber, waiting for something to happen, but still, the Ancients look healthy. Hmm, maybe it doesn't work against them, or maybe their bodies can withstand the poison.

And then it happens.

A tall male with long brown hair begins to cough. The female beside him—petite and beautiful—looks at him, concerned, and then he pukes all over her, soaking her blond locks with an orange liquid.

She gasps; her hands freeze midway to her hair. She screams at another male to help, but before he can move, he falls to the ground, projectile vomiting everywhere.

The Chemists all exclaim around me, taking notes and rocking on their heels, enjoying the scene unfolding before us. I grab Cybil's arm, prepared to ask her to stop this, when my eyes find the children, gathered in a corner, all screaming and crying. My words catch in my throat at the horror of it. I wonder if the adults are their parents, if this is a family we're torturing. But Cybil was right; the children seem immune—

Then my thought is cut short by the youngest child, a perfect round face and giant blue-green eyes. He kneels on the floor, shaking and crying, and then a pearly liquid spews from his mouth. I recognize it at once—xylem. It's as though he's vomiting blood. Each Ancient falls to the ground in domino-like fashion, one, two, finally all ten, convulsing and jerking in a mixture of vomit and xylem. Finally, their bodies find their way to death.

I race from the lab, running with all my might toward the elevator that leads to Dad's office, jamming the button several times to force it to close. When it opens, I get off and collapse against the wall next to the elevator, trying to breathe through my sobs.

The elevator doors pop open and Cybil steps out.

"Are you okay?" she says to me. "I know our training can be…difficult on your stomach. You should have told me before that you were sensitive. I could have given you something to counteract the nausea."

I'm speechless. She thinks I ran off because the scene made me *nauseous*! What's wrong with these people?

Cybil looks concerned. "It's okay if you need to go home early today, Ari. Tomorrow I'll have the necessary supplements." She heads to the elevator, going back to analyze the success of lab three. My head swirls; visions swim through my mind.

I manage to make my way out of the building. In my haze, I nearly run into Jackson when I open the door to go outside. His arms are already open for me to melt into him. I don't understand how he knows, but I rush forward, tears streaming down my face. I'll never forget what I've seen. I'll never have another peaceful night's sleep.

"Th-th-they… All of them… You have to help," I manage to say.

"I know, but it's too late."

"No, help them. Please, help them. I couldn't…" Then my eyes jerk up. "Wait, you know?"

"Ari, I have something to tell you—" But the door behind us opens and an Operative comes out. We are silent until he passes out of earshot.

"Let's go." He holds my hand, guiding me toward the tron

and away from this awful place that just murdered a family of Ancients.

I'm exhausted in every way, yet I know I won't sleep. We ride the tron in silence. Jackson strokes my hair and whispers comforting words from time to time. He directs me down the street of my house but stops cold a few houses from mine.

"What's wrong?" I say, following his eyes down the street, but everything seems normal.

"Nothing. Look, go on inside. I'll see you later, okay?" He doesn't meet my eyes.

"Jackson—"

His head snaps toward me, his face fierce. "Please do as I ask for once."

I recoil, anger and fear creeping into my mind. "But we need to talk. Will this stop everything? It's a neurotoxin. That's their strategy. You said the strategy would stop everything. Please just—"

"I'll handle it. Now, please, go inside." My fists clench tightly, but I resist the urge to press him for more information and rush into my house. I glance through the front windows to see him planted to the spot, staring down my street. A shudder climbs my back as I realize why he forced me to go inside—someone or something is out there, waiting.

It's one a.m. and Jackson isn't here. I check my phone and my T-screen, hoping there's a message. There isn't. I assume by now Zeus knows about the neurotoxin, and everything will be fine, but then where is Jackson? Something has to be wrong, way wrong. I consider going to the Unity Tree. Maybe he's there, but something tells me he wouldn't want me to risk it. Yet I have no idea what I'm risking. I hate this feeling—lost and confused, no direction or hint at what might be wrong.

I lie down in bed, but my nerves cause me to toss and turn all night. Then the nightmares begin.

I'm standing on a balcony overlooking an army, my army. I'm the commander. I can tell by the way they listen to me speak, as though every word is important. Jackson steps up on one side of me, Zeus the other. They talk about our creation, but I have no idea what they mean until one of the soldiers catches my eye. It's Lane, but he seems...different. I try to figure out what changed when it hits me—he's no longer human. None of them are. I'm staring down into a sea of people...a sea of half-breeds.

CHAPTER 24

Shouts startle me awake. I climb out of bed and peek out my bedroom door. Dad's voice drifts up from downstairs.

"No, you're not interrogating her," he says.

"She's a liability," a man responds. My heart drops to the floor as the voice registers. It's one of Dad's Lead Operatives, Oliver O'Neil, who also happens to be Gretchen's father. "You must follow protocol."

"Don't tell me about protocol. I wrote the thing!"

I back into my room, my hands clasped in front of my chest. My room is still dark. It isn't yet daybreak, maybe six a.m. From the corner of my eye, I catch a continuous flash of yellow from my T-screen. When I click the screen, a message appears from Gretchen.

I'm so sorry.

More shouts carry from downstairs, but I'm not registering what they're saying. Gretchen is sorry. Her father is in my house and arguing with my dad. There can only be one thing that she would do to me that would require an apology.

I slump onto my bed, staring at the words. Gretchen apologizes, Jackson disappears, and it sounds like a war is happening in my living room, which all must mean—

"Ari," Dad says as he bursts into my room. "I need to speak with you." He glances at my pajamas and then motions to my closet. "Put on something appropriate. We have guests." He storms out as quickly as he entered.

This isn't good. I take my time showering and dressing. I don't want to face whatever entourage is down there to question me. I have no idea how much Gretchen disclosed and the last thing I want is to make this worse.

I walk into my family room leery of what I'll find. I expected a crew of Engineers, but instead there are only two—Oliver O'Neil and Gretchen. She stares at her feet, twiddling her fingers as though it's too much for her to look at me. I hope it is. I hope she feels horrible for what she's done. I glare at her, cross my arms, and redirect my attention to Dad.

"Everything okay?" I say.

"No," Dad says. "Everything *isn't* okay. We discovered last night that our offices were infiltrated by a group of Ancient spies led by Zeus Castello's grandson. Care to guess whom that might be?"

I stare at him in confusion and then a chilling clarity washes over me. His grandparents raised him, yet he refused to talk about them or even say their names. He said they controlled him in ways I would never understand. He said he couldn't be trusted. And I guess he was right. I am such an idiot.

"Well, let me clarify," Dad says, his voice hard. "Jackson Locke does not exist. His name is Jackson Castello, the only grandchild of Zeus Castello and the future leader of the Ancients. We have been tracking him for months, suspicious that he was a Latent. Why did you think I requested his early transfer? Did you never question why I would spend so much time with a teenager? A child? Or did you completely allow your feelings to overcome your logic?"

I grasp the wall to keep from falling.

"Then we discovered his true identity, coincidentally the same day that you chose to profess your feelings for him. I requested he return to my office so an analysis could be run for confirmation, honestly not expecting him to come." Dad pauses, as though he can't understand even now why Jackson went back to his office. But I understand. Jackson is fearless. He would never have given up on the strategy. He would have died trying to find it if I'd refused to help. Only, none of that was necessary because I handed it to him—along with my heart.

I close my eyes, wishing I could go back to sleep, wake from this nightmare.

"He was assigned to you as a means to get information on me," Dad continues. "Did you know that? Did you know his specialty is rogue work? Did you know he personally trained every one of our attackers?" I hold out my hand to stop him, but he presses on. "Everything about this boy is poison and you let him seep into your life. I trained you to know better. Instead, you gave the enemy control."

Bile climbs in my throat as the room begins to spin. He was

assigned to me. Me, an assignment. Every nerve in my body seems to die all at once, numbing me. This can't be true, he wouldn't… But deep down I know it is.

My eyes drift to Gretchen, and this time she looks at me, pleading with me. I don't know what to say. I'm torn between my anger at her betrayal and my need for her support. A hole spreads in my stomach, tearing into my chest, but I refuse to cry. I've cried enough.

Mr. O'Neil stands. "Sir, she has to be interrogated."

"She is my daughter," Dad says. "I will handle this. You and Gretchen may leave now."

As soon as Dad closes the front door, he wheels around to me, pacing back and forth in the foyer, seeming unable to keep still. "I— You— How could you do this? Did you understand what would happen to anyone else?"

I've never seen my dad so disheveled, and the thought that I brought him to this makes my eyes burn. "Please, let me explain."

"No, it's done. I assume they broke into our offices to steal the neurotoxin, but they found nothing. I approved it last night. The toxin circulates in our air right now."

I gasp, my hands flying to cover my face. "No. You can't. Tell me you didn't do this."

"As I said, it's done. Let them try to attack us now. The toxin will poison them within minutes of breathing it. They've lost. So you see, it doesn't matter what he told you. I have no time for liars. Now go get ready. You will be on time for Op training today. Understand?"

"Wait. You don't understand. Zeus said—"

He stops cold. "You spoke with Zeus?"

"Well, no, but—"

"That's what I thought."

"But Dad—"

"No, enough. You are to go get ready. Right now."

Arguments race through my mind, one after the other, but finally, I lower my arms to my sides and sigh in defeat. Jackson is gone. The neurotoxin has released. It's over. "What about Mr. O'Neil?" I whisper.

"Don't worry about Oliver. President Cartier and I discussed how to handle you and Lawrence this morning. Did you think I didn't know he was in on this charade? It doesn't matter. You are children and are entitled to a mistake. I won't have that ruin your future."

I lower my head, no longer able to look at him. "That's all that matters, isn't it? My future and how this appears to others. Don't you care why I kept this from you? Don't you want to know my motivation?" I have it on the tip of my tongue, anger pushing the words to the surface. I'm prepared to yell at him that I'm part Ancient when Dad's resolve falters.

His eyes soften. "No, Ari. I don't want to know why you chose one of them over me. I don't want to know why I wasn't your first source of refuge. I don't want to know why you trusted a young girl with this instead of your own father. I don't want to hear any more. What I've heard is enough." And he leaves the room without another word.

I lean against the wall, sliding down until I'm on the floor, my head in my hands. I thought I could do this on my own. I thought I could finally step outside Dad's shadow and prove that I'm capable. I never imagined Dad would feel betrayed as a father. He's the commander at the office, at home, in every way. I only thought about his reaction as the commander, never thinking to consider what it would feel like for his daughter to betray him. He has always been so hard on me, but maybe that's because he believed in me. And now I've let him down.

My thoughts move from Dad, to Gretchen, to the neurotoxin, to the threat of war, and then they land on Jackson and I'm sure my heart is gone, leaving a dark hole that will never go away. It's all too much.

Mom finds me curled on the sofa in our sitting room. She doesn't say anything, but she doesn't have to. To her, I am just her daughter. She strokes my hair and pulls me into a tight hug. "He loves you, you know that, right?" she asks. I nod, because I do know that Dad loves me, even if he will never trust me again. "Now, you have to get ready. I'm sure going to training today will be hard, but that's what being an adult is, dear. We have to face things that frighten us head-on. I'll be here when you get home if you need me."

I nod. "Thanks, Mom. I'll go."

She commands the T-screen on. "Want some coffee?"

She moves back into the kitchen to grab me a cup. I chance a look at the T-screen, unsure if I really want to see the news story. A reporter repeats what has likely been said all morning long. The Engineers, in accordance with international Engineering groups, released a neurotoxin into the air that is said to poison any Ancient that breaches Earth. The release occurred yesterday after Commander Alexander discovered the presence of Ancient spies among the populace. Then the camera cuts to a live interview with Dad.

"Once we discovered the presence of Ancients among us," Dad says, "we knew we had to act quickly. Thankfully, the Chemists developed various weapons over the last few decades, enabling us to execute an effective response immediately."

Mom places an arm around my shoulder and hands me the cup of coffee. "Go get ready, sweetie."

Twenty minutes later, I'm on the tron, hoping I can get through the day. For a moment, I worry that the toxin could kill me, too. After all, xylem runs through my body. But I didn't heal, so I must not have enough of it in me. Plus, the neurotoxin would have had an impact on me by now.

Everyone seems elated, like a giant weight was lifted from their shoulders. Most feared the Ancients, hated hosting to them. Many felt we were slaves. So to them, today is an independence day, our freedom from the force that controlled us.

I gaze out the window and sure enough, each tron stop bounces with people outside celebrating. I close my eyes. There's nothing for me to celebrate, no happiness coming from this independence, and the Ancients will respond. I hope our genius Chemists thought out possible counterattacks, or else everyone I love may die in this war.

The tron reaches Business Park, and I step off onto the auto-path, walking instead of allowing the path to guide me. Inside the Engineer building, everyone is as excited as those on the street. I'm the first one to the training room, and all I can think about is Jackson and how the last time I was here, he was with me. I swallow back tears for the second time today. I wish I could have talked to him one last time. Maybe then I could make sense of everything. But instead, I'm left with a scattering of hidden truths and no clue how to decipher the real from the fake.

Gretchen walks through the main doors, stopping when she sees me. "Ari…"

"How could you?" I say.

"Please, I know how it looks," she says. "But it wasn't my fault. Lawrence came by my house, worried over how different you've been acting. He said enough that I was sure he knew so I told him I did as well. Dad must have overheard the part about Jackson because a minute later he stormed into my room, forcing Lawrence and me to tell him everything. I swear I didn't mean to."

"Well, that explains how Dad knew about Law," I say.

She releases a breath, hesitates, and then rushes over to hug me. "I'm so sorry."

I begin to say it's okay when an overwhelming heat hits me and I burst out coughing, unable to gain control for several seconds. The room moves around me, in and out of focus, while sweat collects on my forehead.

Gretchen steadies me by the arm. "Are you okay?"

"Yeah, I'm fine, just exhausted."

She continues to look worried, but the rest of the training class enters the room, Terrence on their heels.

"There has been a change to our training schedule," Terrence says. "I expect you all back here this afternoon to practice with each of the weapons we reviewed yesterday. But this morning, we will split into groups. Half of you will practice combat training, the other half limits, and then we'll switch. After that you can all head to the celebration at the District. It's a momentous day!"

I start for the combat side just as another coughing fit erupts. My chest heaves, the heat overtaking me. I swallow hard, trying to steady the cough, but with each breath it builds until I'm on the ground, gasping for air. Gretchen runs to my side and tries to help me stand. "Coach, can I take her to get water?"

Terrence must agree, because Gretchen helps me limp out into the hall and down the corridor to the women's restroom. As soon as we cross the threshold, I fall to the floor, my body shaking in spasms.

"What can I do? I'll call your dad."

I jerk my head from side to side. Dad can't know what's happening to me. "Wat-er."

She rushes to the sink and soaks several towels with water, bringing them back to me one after another, but it's no use. I can't get myself calmed down. Heat rises in my chest, crawling up my neck, spreading over my body, yet I'm freezing. I draw a breath and vomit all over myself, on the floor, on Gretchen. Then the shaking starts again, and I'm trembling all over, my teeth chattering. Gretchen cleans off my mouth and splashes water on my face. My forehead feels clammy and hot. A soft knock sounds from the door.

"It's me," a voice says. "Can I come in?"

"Yes, hurry up," Gretchen replies, and I notice her face soaked from tears.

Law stops cold when he enters the bathroom, as though he needs a second to compose himself. "We should get her home before someone notices," he says. "Ari, can you walk?"

"I don't know," I say, my voice a whisper. Law scoops me into his arms and motions for Gretchen to get the door. He looks down both directions of the hall and steps out.

"Notices what?" Gretchen asks.

"Think, Gretch. Why would Ari get sick?"

"No," I say. "It's only a little bit…." I trail off, knowing there is no other explanation. Law is right. Never once during all the xylem talk did I think I had enough of it in me to cause an issue. I thought because I didn't heal, that meant it was only a trace amount, nothing to be concerned with. I just assumed… And now…

No one says anything the entire walk to the tron. Law must be getting tired of carrying me, but he doesn't let on. We take the second seat back and wait while other passengers board. The tron is almost full when an older woman starts to get on but backs away. Her face pales, and then she pukes all over the sidewalk.

Law leans over me and winces. "That isn't good. Maybe you're not the only…"

I face him, goose bumps rising across my skin. "Only what?"

He doesn't respond. The silence grows tangible with each passing second. I lean back in my seat, racking my brain for answers. And then a thought crosses my mind so outlandish that it can't be possible. I can't be… Impossible. Thoughts and memories zoom through my mind in chaotic order, one after another—the dreams, the changes. Jackson said xylem multiplies. I assumed I was part Ancient, maybe a third. After all, I didn't heal after slicing my arm and an Ancient would have. But if I'm this sick that must mean…

Law carries me off the tron and down the street toward my house. Gretchen bursts through my front door, calling for my mom. Law helps me to our sitting area, gets me some water, and sits in front of me, looking more nervous and scared than I've ever seen him in my life. "I can handle it," I say.

He nods. "I know."

"Then what's the problem?"

"I can't." He bites his lip and then rubs his chin. "It's all my fault."

"Your fault?"

"The day of the explosion," he says. "Do you remember?"

"A little. Jack—" I cut off. "He told me he healed me. It wasn't your fault."

"But it was. You were screaming. I was afraid you were dying. So I begged him to do it. He didn't want to. I made him do it, and now…" He reaches for my hand. "We'll figure something out; don't worry."

Figure something out? There is nothing to figure out. I'm part Ancient, maybe even half. Xylem circulates through my body, multiplying by the second. The neurotoxin is in the air I'm breathing right now, which all leads to one hard fact—I'm going to die. The question is, how long do I have?

CHAPTER 25

By the time my mom arrives home from work, sickness consumes me. Gretchen and Law set me up in my room, staying to help me to the bathroom and back, and asking every few minutes if they could call my parents. I thought I could do it on my own. I thought maybe it would get better or I would get used to the overwhelming exhaustion, but each second becomes harder than the one before and now all I want is my mom to fix me.

Gretchen brings her into my room and I can tell immediately that she's terrified. The city has grown more and more troubling; Ops sent out to guard the perimeter, all armed, all told to shoot anyone who looks suspicious. I'm not sure who or what they expect to try to get in — an Ancient army, I suppose, which tells me that even with the neurotoxin, they're afraid the Ancients will find a way to attack.

But if Ancients are still in the city, I've seen no sign of them, or at least not of one…I try to ignore the pain in my chest at the thought of him. I didn't get to say good-bye. Good-bye. I hadn't considered it before, but now, I'm infected, he's gone, and I have no reason to believe I'll ever see him again.

I stare off into my room, ignoring my mom's worried look. She moves her hand over my forehead, checking my cheeks. "You're so pale," she says, her voice rich with concern. "When did you start getting sick? Is it something you ate? Have you—"

"I'm part Ancient, Mom, maybe half. We aren't sure."

Her head jerks to attention. "What? That isn't possible. Be serious. What has happened to you?"

"She is being serious, Mrs. Alexander," Lawrence says.

Mom looks around to him and then to Gretchen, who nods her head in agreement. "No, you aren't. I'm telling you that isn't possible."

Everyone is silent for a long second, unsure of how to convince her, then I realize what I need to do and pull her to me. "Mom, it is. Look at my eyes. They should be the same emerald green of yours, but instead…"

Mom lifts a shaking hand to cover her mouth, tears welling in her eyes. "I don't understand. How did this happen to you?"

"I'm sorry. I—" Heat rises up my neck, and then I'm running to my bathroom, hoping I make it. Mom follows, tying my hair behind me and whispering to herself as I get sick again and again and again. Finally, my body collapses onto the bathroom floor, the cool composite tile soothing my overheated face.

Gretchen rushes in with a glass of water, helping me take small sips. I draw a long breath, then another, and close my eyes. After several seconds, Mom helps me stand and tucks me back into my bed. "I'll be right back," she says. "I have something that might help. Can you watch her?" she asks Gretchen, eyeing both her and Law.

As soon as she's gone, Gretchen is at my side. "How much do you want her to know?"

"It doesn't matter now." I reach for my water, stopping midway, my hand shaking too hard for me to be able to hold the glass. "I'm so tired."

"Let me." Gretchen lifts it to my mouth. Any other time, I'd be embarrassed to receive such help, but right now, I don't have the energy or will to do anything for myself. I hate it. I hate how weak I am, how weak I look, and most of all, I hate that I'd agree to be sick the rest of my life if I could just see Jackson again and ask him if it was really all a lie.

I slump against my pillow, allowing my eyes to close. It feels easier to think about him when the others can't see my eyes, the misery that settles in them. I wonder if Dad was right about everything. Maybe Jackson used me to get information. If he did, I guess it worked. But still…flashes of memories course through my mind, one after another, each more painful than the last.

It felt real.

Mom comes back to my room carrying a metal case the size of a notes tablet, her Chemist demeanor taking over. She opens the case, releasing a puff of cold air and exposing twenty or so small vials of liquid. She fumbles through the case, pulls out a vial of blue liquid, and tears open a new needle and syringe. "I'm going to try to counter the vomiting first, then we'll figure out how to counter the poison." She feels around the bend of my arm and slips the needle into my vein. I feel a pinch, a burn, and then the nausea subsides, relief washing over me.

"How long will it last?" I ask her.

"Maybe an hour, depending upon the potency of the poison." She rubs her eyes. "Tell me how this happened."

"Um, we should get going," Law says, tugging on Gretchen's arm.

"Yeah, we'll be back in an hour or so. Feel better, Ari." Then they're gone, and I'm left alone in the eerie silence of my room as Mom waits to hear how I became infected. I'm not sure where to start, so I begin with the truth.

"I fell for the wrong guy," I say, and then I launch into everything—Jackson, the bomb at school, him healing me, the strategy, what I did to help, what I've seen. I talk until I'm too tired to continue. My eyes close and Mom holds my hand, rubbing it gently, and then the dream finds me.

I open my eyes to a hazy yet beautiful world full of bright colors. The sky is an unusual purplish blue, with giant clouds and a golden sun. I step farther into this world and once again, I'm overlooking the lake from a previous dream. I expect to see the people on bamboo-boats but instead hear my name shouted from below.

"Well? Are you coming?" Jackson says, a huge smile on his face. He wades in the water, flipping and swimming, enjoying the warm day.

I hesitate and then dive in after him, but when I break the surface he's no longer there. I call after him and swim around searching. I dive under, scanning below the surface. Where did he go? Finally, I spot him on the bank. He waves to me before walking off. I scream after him, begging him to come back.

And then a force jerks me under. Water pours into my mouth and nose. I fight and claw to stay above the surface, but it's no use. I'm drowning…and Jackson left me.

CHAPTER 26

"Mom?" I call from the downstairs bathroom, throwing up now more times than I can count. The nausea injections that helped yesterday are now lasting only a few minutes, sometimes a few seconds. Mom has tried a few different concoctions, but so far nothing works and we're still no closer to finding something that will stop the neurotoxin's poison from wrecking my body from the inside out.

"More water?" Mom says from the doorway.

"No, can you help me to the sitting room?"

"Sure," she says, just as the front door security system announces Gretchen and Law. They make their way into the sitting area, and Law commands on the T-screen before either speak a word.

"What's going on?" Mom asks, but she's interrupted by the newscast. Ancient infection. That's what they're calling it. A disease released upon humans thanks to their continuous exposure to the Ancients. My eyes widen with each bit of information, all of it speculation or lies. Parliament refuses to admit they're responsible for our sickness, thanks to the release of the neurotoxin. Instead, they act as though the infection and the neurotoxin are two separate issues, never speaking of one in the same newscast as another. It's so ridiculous. They never imagined humans might have been healed by Ancients, and even still, they seem unaware or unwilling to accept that healing is what caused this, that these sick humans are actually part Ancient. The Chemists took blood samples from some of the infected, all in an effort to figure out how it happened. The problem is no human will admit to being healed by an Ancient.

"Volume down," Mom says. "I need to make a call." And she leaves the room looking even more worried.

Law waits until Mom is out of hearing range and then says, "This isn't the half of it. Testing centers went up all around the country an hour ago. Everyone has to be tested. Anyone not checked within twenty-four hours will be issued a warrant for arrest. Plus…" He glances at Gretchen, who bites her thumbnail as though it's the only thing keeping her from crying.

"Tell me," I say.

"I just overheard— It could be nothing. I mean, they can't. It's—"

"Tell me," I repeat, not dropping my eyes from his.

"Execution base. They're talking about bringing everyone who's infected to one location to be"—he swallows hard—"*disposed of.* I heard Mom say it would be too expensive to send Operatives to issue R1 serum and they weren't sure what to do with the bodies if they did it at the centers. So one site, one blast that kills everyone and incinerates the bodies."

"What?" Mom shrieks as her phone crashes to the ground.

"It hasn't been approved yet, Claire," Dad says from behind her as he walks into the room. We all wait anxiously to see what else he might say. "But the testing has already been announced, and they do plan to make arrests. I had to bring in reinforcements." He closes his eyes, and I realize for the first time just how hard this is for him. He took it hard when Mom told him, refusing to believe it until he saw me, and then he questioned me again and again before finally, his face fell and he left my room without another word. I had never seen him look so…broken, and even now, the thought brings tears to my eyes. I never meant to hurt my parents in this way, though I suppose becoming an Ancient wasn't by choice. Still…I feel like it was, like I brought this on myself and now I can't undo it.

"I requested a home inspection, along with most of Process," he says. "Of course they agreed. Our appointment is tomorrow. That's the best I can do." He slumps in a chair across from me. Law sits next to me on the sofa.

"How are you feeling?" Gretchen asks, her first words to me since she arrived, and that alone tells me more than anything she could say. She's not just worried, she's afraid, something I've never before said of her, and that realization, coupled with Dad's morose expression, is enough to make me want to scream. I may die, but I won't have everyone else suffering my death while I'm still here, breathing.

I consider voicing my thoughts, but I can't bring myself to be harsh. Not now. "Fine, I guess," I say with a shrug.

"Fine?" Mom says. "You're not fine. You're infected and dying and I'm your mother and there's nothing I can do. Nothing. I've tried. I can't figure it out. I don't know what to do. Someone tell me what to do. I'm not supposed to outlive you. I…can't… outlive my daughter…" She breaks into sobs. I reach for her, but Dad finds her first, burying her head in his shoulder.

"What if I have a solution? It's not ideal, but if it would save Ari, would you agree?" Lawrence asks.

"What is it?" we all say in unison.

"Well, I don't want to get anyone's hopes up, so how about this—I'll be back tonight, hopefully with our solution." He leans down and kisses my forehead before heading out the door.

The rest of the afternoon creeps along. I'm getting sicker by the second, my body falling apart, but my mind refuses to shut down. If I could sleep then maybe I wouldn't feel so horrible… and so helpless. The news is unbearable. People are dying all across the world, not just here. So many infected. People die walking down the street, on the tron, as they wait in line to be checked for the infection. Parliament calls it the first epidemic in modern history. The Chemists—who created the neurotoxin— can't seem to find a way to reverse its spread. It amazes me that Parliament approved the release of a toxin that we had no way of undoing. Are humans really that stupid? We throw a chemical into our atmosphere without a second thought of how it may impact us, the humans? Unbelievable.

My skin is no longer ivory. It's like the sky just before rain. Gray and miserable. My body wants to die. I can feel it caving in on itself, begging my mind to let go. But I can't. I won't. Mom keeps giving injections, each targeting a different side effect, and all only successful for a few minutes before the poison burns through them. I wonder if this is what the elderly feel like just before death. Our society gives an option—natural death or an injection of R1, a serum that causes instant, painless death. Most choose natural, and now I understand why. Suffering, while horrible, still gives the inkling of hope. Maybe the infection will pass. Maybe one of Mom's concoctions will work. Maybe, maybe, maybe.

I glance back to the T-screen and see another news bulletin. "Volume up." The sound returns just as the anchor declares, "Mandatory containment." Everyone infected will be detained to guarantee the survival of the human species. My mouth drops as what they're saying—or rather what they aren't saying—sinks in. The execution base. They plan to bring us in to kill us. This isn't happening. This isn't happening. My breathing escalates, panic overtaking me.

Mom walks in and asks if I need anything, but the look on my face causes her to rush to my side. "What is it?" she says, placing her hand on my forehead then cheek.

I point to the screen. "They're going to kill us, Mom. They aren't giving us a chance. They won't even wait to see if the Chemists can reverse it."

Mom swallows hard, and I know she's trying to hold herself together for me, to ease my fears with her strength. She takes my hand and holds it close to her. We're both too speechless to say anything more. It's a matter of time, anyway, I guess. Everyone dies. My time just came sooner than most.

I'm about to command the T-screen off when the screen jolts

and someone else appears there, someone unexpected. Zeus.

"Volume up, volume up!" I scream.

"Good afternoon, ladies and gentlemen," Zeus says. "As you just learned, your government has issued mandatory containment for all infected members of the population." His head twitches then he blurts out, "Population: the whole number of inhabitants in an area or region." His face relaxes and he continues as though the interruption didn't occur. "Surely by now you realize what they mean by *containment*. That is how much your government cares about its people. I offer you another alternative. At five p.m. today, we will open all ports to Loge. Anyone infected who chooses to be healed may join us on our planet. We welcome you. I have only one caveat: choosing to come to Loge means you turn your back on mankind. We *will* attack Earth. We *will* win. Choosing to join us means choosing to live. There is no dishonor in living. The ports will close one hour after opening. I bid you farewell for now and hope to see many of you soon."

The T-screen cuts to black, then a scene over in Landings Park appears. People are on the street chanting, "No assisted killing! Just say no! No assisted killing! We won't go!" They repeat the words over and over. Then the screen turns black again. Zeus couldn't have timed his announcement better. People are angry and afraid. He just guaranteed them life. The only thing they have to do is disown a government that plans to kill them. It's so simple it's laughable.

"Power off," Mom says. We sit for a long moment, saying nothing. Then Mom slides in beside me at the foot of the sofa, resting my legs on her lap. "Do you remember the stories Grandma Bea used to tell?"

I smile for the first time all day. Grandma Bea—Mom's mother—used to tell us outlandish stories about her past.

"One time," Mom says, "she told me there were divers that dove way into the ocean, just to see what was down there. She said the ocean was full of colors, more colors than the rainbow. Nothing like the ocean our tablets describe."

"Do you believe her stories?"

"I don't know, but I can promise you this." Her eyes brim with tears. "If we survive this, if you survive this, we will go."

I sit up, despite the weakness. "To the ocean?"

"Everywhere. We will travel everywhere. I will show you the mountains, the ocean, the desert. I will show you everything I was never brave enough to show you before. And I'm sorry for that. I'm sorry I wasn't strong enough to give your life depth." Tears rush down her face. I grasp her hand, but I won't let myself cry. Not now. I don't want her to think for a second that she did anything wrong by me or my life. I had a life, a wonderful life, because of her, not in spite of her.

I'm about to tell her that when Law enters the room. Mom and I both jerk up. His face shows signs of worry…and glistens with sweat. "Hey," he says, sitting down on the table in front of me. "Everything's in place. Now the waiting."

"But what are we waiting for?" Mom asks. "Did you see what your mom just issued?"

He lowers his eyes. "I know. I wasn't there when she made the decision. Not that she would listen to me anyway. I haven't told anyone about Ari," he says. "I wouldn't—"

Mom tosses up a hand. "Enough. Please tell us what you're

doing. What's your plan?"

Law bites his lip, hesitating. Then he sighs. "Well, Zeus's message today made my plan easier. I sent a message to Loge requesting for Ari to go live there. Now all we have to do is get Ari to a direct port before five p.m. I'm sure they'll be crowded and we only have one in Sydia. But they have healers. She'll—"

"What?" Mom screams. "She's not going there. How could you make such a decision without consulting us? We're her parents!"

He starts to respond but stops. I can see by his expression what he's about to say. He didn't act without consulting my parents. Dad knows his plan.

Mom shakes her head in a spasm of anger, and then suddenly she stops, her face as still as stone. "Lawrence, how did you know how to contact Loge?"

His eyes dart from Mom to me, unsure of what she may know and what I may want to keep from her. I nod. It's time we gave my mom the respect she deserves. "Um, well—" he starts, but I cut him off. It should come from me.

"Mom, Jackson is technically only half Ancient."

Her mouth falls. "Half Ancient?"

"Yes," Lawrence says. "His mother is human."

"And how do you…?" Mom asks.

Law focuses on her. "Because he's my brother."

Mom then starts quizzing Lawrence about his past. Why isn't he half Ancient, too? Which is simple. His father is human. Why did his mom send Jackson away? Then more and more questions about Loge, finally ending the questions by asking if he's ever been there. I expect him to say no, but when he pauses before answering, my eyes jerk to his.

"Not until today," he says.

"What was it like?" I say, unable to stop myself.

He pauses again, collecting his thoughts. "Like a dream… only better. I found myself wishing…" He lowers his head. "Well, wishing I were the one sent there instead of Jackson."

I'm about to respond when a simultaneous pounding from Dad's private entrance and a knocking at the door jars us from the conversation. Mom and Law stand as Dad rushes into the room. "They came early. They're here. I tried to get here first."

Worry and dread hang in the air. The Chemists came to check for infection, but they won't even have to test me; it's obvious I'm infected. My heart hits in my chest. I wasn't afraid before, but now that death is literally knocking on my door I want more time. I need more time. My eyes dart to the back patio. Maybe I can run. I try to get up and collapse back down, my legs no longer strong enough to hold me.

Law scoops me into his arms. "I'll carry her outside. Tell them she's not here; they'll have to come back to test her. You're the commander. They won't argue."

Dad buries his head in his hands. "She'll worsen outside. It's more potent air. She might…"

"What choice do we have, Grexic?" Mom says and nods to Lawrence.

Law leans in close and whispers into my ear. "Try not to breathe. You're strong—remember that."

I close my eyes and draw a deep breath. I hear the patio doors slide open and feel the air rush past me. It's like instant food poisoning. My stomach flips and my body shakes. I consider opening my eyes, but with them closed at least Law won't see how bad it is.

He eases down the back steps and into the forest edge, hiding us from view. I think of all the times I've walked through these trees with Jackson, always fearing them, and now they protect me. It's amazing how ironic life can be. I draw another weak breath, trying to pull in as little air as possible, but this second breath cuts through me. I won't survive this.

My head bobs to my chest and I feel myself being pulled under, in and out of consciousness. I see my family, Lawrence, Gretchen—Jackson. I see my life before him and how complicated it became after him. I wish I could ask him why. But it's too late for that. *Why* no longer matters. I feel Law moving and try to open my eyes to see what's happening. I strain to listen, but all I hear is a soft *hmmm*. The air changes around me. We're back inside my house, where it's easier to breathe, if only marginally. He lays me down on a sofa.

"Baby girl," Mom says, cupping her hands around my face, "can you hear me?"

She continues to talk, her words moving in and out as though she's far away. "I hear you," I say, though I'm not sure whether the words are in my mind or voiced out loud. Wetness covers my cheek. She's crying. I want to tell her to stop and that everything will be okay. My eyes blink; my head becomes heavier. I don't want this misery anymore.

"Ari, talk to me," she urges. "Please, talk to me." She shakes me, then she says something to Dad and I feel her leave my side. She returns a few seconds later and whispers, either to herself or to me, I'm not sure, "Please, let this work." And I feel the prick and burn of another injection.

Nothing happens for what feels like forever. I can hear, but I can't speak or open my eyes. No one says anything, but I can tell they're all there, waiting, watching me for a response. Then... then, it feels as though fresh air blows through the room, into my lungs, helping me breathe. I draw in a long, satisfying breath and open my eyes. When I look around, I realize Gretchen is here, which means I must have been out for a while.

Mom comes back into the room just as I'm looking around and rushes over, tears spilling down her face. "Thank goodness." She starts laughing, and I think she's delirious until I glance around and see Dad, pale as snow, and Law with eyes wide. They must have thought I died.

"Can I have something to eat?" I ask, realizing I'm starving.

After Mom gives me something to eat and some water, everyone settles down, relieved. I feel so much better that I'm afraid to trust it, waiting for the sickness to return, but after half an hour, I'm stronger, finally able to stand on my own.

"What did you give me?" I ask Mom.

"I was so afraid," Mom says. "It's never been tested. I had no idea what would happen, and when you didn't wake, I thought...I thought." She clears her throat. "It's a healing serum, like healing gel but more potent. The one I told you about. I've been working on it for months. I'm not sure how long it will last."

I nod, worry creeping into my mind. This may be temporary. I walk over to the window that overlooks our street and peer out, loving the sight of the sun, wishing I could go outside, but

I'm afraid. I'm about to step away when something catches my eye. There are Operatives stationed outside every house, all of them armed. "What are they…?" Then a high-pitched scream comes from the Roman house across from us. A guard carries their ten-year-old daughter from the house, her mom screaming and beating against the Operative the entire way, until another Op on the steps blocks her. Everyone in my house rushes to the windows, opening the blinds to expose the full picture of what's happening, the full horror.

An Engineer truck sits at the end of our street with the back door open. Down the street, more and more Operatives carry or march people from their homes—some young, some old, all terrified. Before long, the infected line both sides of the street, marching by gunpoint to the truck. Family and friends scream from each of the houses, but Operatives block them from doing anything more. I start for the door, but Law pulls me back. "No, you can't go out there. They'll know."

"I don't care. We can't stand here doing nothing."

"He's right, Ari," Dad says. "You can't go out there."

I charge him, anger taking over. "You did this, didn't you? You approved this. How could you?"

"No," he says. "This came from the top." He drops his head and goes to his office, shutting the door tightly behind him.

President Cartier. My body spasms with anger and frustration as I watch the Operatives herd the infected into the truck. The back door closes and a line of Operatives forms, stopping anyone from following. A small boy runs down the street, calling for his daddy over and over. An Operative grabs him, tossing him roughly over his shoulder. The boy cries out in pain, and then he stops crying, stops moving.

"Mom," I say, not taking my eyes from outside.

"I'm here," she says.

"Can you get more healing serum?"

She wrinkles her brow in confusion. "Yes, of course, why?"

"I'll need it when I break into the execution base."

CHAPTER 27

It took me half an hour to convince them I'm not crazy. Even Gretchen, who usually trusts my ideas, wouldn't agree until the news showed a girl from school getting carted off by the Operatives. She was the first to falter, then Law, and finally my mom, the biggest surprise of all. We decided to spend the next hour formulating a plan and preparing, partially because we still didn't know where the execution base was located, but also because the healing serum wore off an hour after it was injected. I needed time to rest, since I didn't want to waste so much of the serum on me. But with Zeus shutting down the portals at five and the time ticking at fifteen past two, whatever plan we came up with had to happen fast.

Law set off to uncover the location, while Gretchen went to retrieve some weapons from her house and Mom left for the Chemist lab to get more healing serum. I have no idea how much we'll need, but I'm guessing enough to dose a few hundred people. My job while they're gone is to develop the plan, which is next to impossible with me getting sick every few minutes. Mom left me three vials of the serum just in case, and I decide to inject one, knowing without it I'll never have a dependable plan before they return.

The serum enters my bloodstream, lighting up my insides, and just like before, I'm better within a few minutes. It's amazing and makes me appreciate for the first time today just what a genius Mom is for creating it.

I don't want to waste time, so I grab a notes tablet and get started jotting down every possible type of location and any barriers we may face at each. A chamber inside the Chemist building, similar to the Ancient testing chambers, with cameras, guards, and nowhere to run would be the worst, I think, but I'm not sure they could build a chamber inside the building to hold hundreds of people. Not with all the labs already in place. I jot all this down, but the more I think about it, the more I feel sure they'll build something outside, where space isn't an issue. This brings me to the croplands. Acre upon acre of land, woods on one side that go on forever. That might be the perfect place, but then that's where all our food is grown, which means lots of fieldworkers as witnesses to their plan. Most would turn a blind eye, but some might put up a fight. No, Parliament won't want an audience.

I'm wasting time guessing. What I need is a map of Sydia. I climb up the stairs, getting only a tad winded, and slip into my room.

My T-screen fires up, flashing that I have messages. I hesitate, wanting to ignore them, but curiosity wins out and I click the first message, only to jerk back in shock.

I'm coming for you.
—J
P.S. Please don't die.

I stare at the words for several minutes, convincing myself again and again that it can't be from him, but then who else would know I'm sick? He knows. Of course he knows. But then how would he be able to send me the message? He couldn't. No. But then…

I shake my head to force myself back into focus. It doesn't matter if he sent the message or not. I won't let myself hope that he's coming, because then I'll never have the strength to do what I'm about to do. And I have to do this. I have to save these people.

The note closes and files away into my message folder, hidden from view. I won't allow myself to even glance at the folder. I can't risk losing time, and I know if I succumb to it, I'll read the note a million times, craving to find answers that aren't there. Instead, I search my homework folders for a map to Sydia, sure I have one from various history lessons, and it's just a matter of finding— A-ha!

The map fills the screen. "Zoom out," I command it, and watch as the map expands so all regions are visible. I never realized how much larger Process is than Landings, though we have half as many people. Parliament has always treated Landings people as though they were disposable, so I'm not sure why it surprises me they agreed to the execution base.

I start at the croplands. Zooming in on each section, I try

to see if there is anything isolated, but the map shows only field after field. Parliament would have to cut out a major section of crops to build the base, and there isn't time for that. Business Park shows nothing of interest, only the Trinity Towers and shops in the District. There's no amount of land, and I can't imagine they would go underground there. Again, that's too much work for so little time.

Process reveals similar issues, and I'm about to close out the map when something just outside the city catches my eye. It isn't detailed, but just outside city limits, beyond Process Park, is a single symbol—a hovercraft. I've never flown before, so I've never been to the airport, and often forget about it. It's primarily used for business purposes, but it's there, surrounded by land and isolated from potential lurkers. The only problem is that I have no idea how much land surrounds it. I reach for my notes tablet and, realizing I forgot it downstairs, open my desk drawer to search for another one, and I spy two things that I can't believe I almost forgot—the poisonous trick knife Mom gave me and the gold universal keycard. I sigh with relief, feeling somehow better knowing I'll have something from both of my parents with me. I slide them into my right boot just as I hear my front door open and close. I bolt from my room, eager to see who's back and with what information.

Gretchen stands in my foyer, balancing two cases in her arms. "If you're feeling up to it, think you could give me some help?"

"Oh, sure, yeah," I say as I jump down the stairs and grab one of the cases from her. "What is all this stuff?"

"You said you wanted weapons, so I brought all I could that

wouldn't look obvious. Where do you want it?"

I nod toward our transfer door and wait as Gretchen gets into the elevator, a surprised look on her face. She's never been to our training room. Dad's orders. But I think today can be an exception.

As soon as the door opens, the lights click on, revealing our tech-savvy, hardcore training room. I haven't been here in several weeks, and seeing Gretchen's jaw drop, I'm reminded of how amazing the room is and how lucky I was to train here. I motion for her to drop her case on the weapons shelf and start back for the door when Gretchen pipes up. "Can I… I mean, do you care if I…try a few?"

I can't help but smile. Regardless of what's going on, Gretchen is still Gretchen. It's a relief right now when I'm unsure of so many things. "Definitely," I say and lean against the wall as she pulls a few different weapons from their shelves—a trick knife that can change size, several different guns, and then a grenade with a switch that changes its function.

All of a sudden, we're both smiling, happy for the first time today, but all happiness drains away when we go back upstairs to find Law in my sitting area, his expression grim. "This isn't going to be easy," he says, tapping his fingertips together. "Maybe even impossible. The base is a detached metal structure that's really more cage than building. They control it from the outside, and the location couldn't be worse. You'll never guess."

"The airport," I say. "I know. But it doesn't matter. We have to get there, and time is running out."

Law nods; he knows me too well to argue. "The tron goes out there, but that would be obvious. The only other option is through the woods."

"Through the woods?" Gretchen says.

"Yeah, the airport is on the other side of these woods. Surely you knew."

"No, I didn't," I say. "But it's too far to walk. We'll have to take the tron."

We all agree and set in to developing our strategy while we wait for Mom to return home with the serum. The best route seems to be to take the tron in and act normal. I've never flown, but Law has plenty of times and feels sure he can get past the guard. I'm not so confident, but I've packed backup in case we run into issues at the gate. Once we're inside, everything should be easy. Well, until we get to the base, and then it becomes dangerous. My plan is to have Law go up to the main crew and claim he's delivering a message from his mom telling them that they need to switch shifts. They won't budge on that alone unless they're idiots. I wouldn't. But we don't need them to move, we just need them distracted while Gretchen and I find a way inside the base to treat and release the infected.

The only questionable element is whether an alarm will sound once we free everyone. If it does, we're dead. We'll be surrounded in no time, outnumbered and out-trained. So I pack a few grenades to use as a distraction just in case. We need to get in, release the infected, and get out, hopefully without anyone getting hurt. But I prepare myself mentally anyway. I may have to hurt or even kill someone I know, someone who works for my dad, in order to save these people.

There is one port in Sydia, just north of the airport. There will be a few guards there, and it may be crowded thanks to Zeus's announcement. I'm not sure how many people can pass through the port at once. I hope lots. But if not, these people may die waiting to be saved. I try not to think about it.

Mom comes in through the back door carrying two large coolant bags. "I have one hundred and five vials. That's the best I could do." She slumps onto the sofa, and I reach out to hug her.

"Thank you. I know what you're risking. Thank you," I say.

She looks up and shrugs. "I can't support what they're doing. I wish I could go with you, but I'm not trained. Just please, please, please be careful. Please make it back home. Okay?"

I don't want to promise her that I will, so I just nod, hoping my smile convinces her, even though I'm not convinced myself.

We spend the next twenty minutes getting into combat clothes, strapping weapons to holsters, and packing our backpacks with additional weapons—mainly guns but also grenades, trick knives, and flashlights, because you never know. Then Gretchen and I slide a coolant bag each into our packs, zip them up, and test them on our backs. It's heavy but not unbearable. I inject two healing serums into my system to give me the strength I'll need, slip a backup serum into my right boot beside the trick knife and master keycard, and then look around at the others. "It's time."

CHAPTER 28

As we climb onto the tron, I can't help wondering if we look suspicious. Giant backpacks on each of our backs, combat clothes. I can't imagine we look normal, but no one says anything; in fact, no one pays us any attention. I glance around the tron at the long faces and empty expressions. Many of these people lost a family member or a friend or a neighbor today.

It's a sad day for America, for the world.

We ride in silence, afraid to speak for fear of revealing something about our plan by mistake. Thankfully, the ride is short, and we're exiting onto the auto-walk that leads to the airport, the three of us its only passengers. We are so visible. I want to conceal myself, but my identity, along with Law's, is what will get us inside.

A guard station comes into view to the left of the walk, and a guard steps out, eyeing us with suspicion until he recognizes Lawrence. "Hello, Mr. Cartier," he says. "Going on another visit today?"

"No, just delivering some supplies and checking available hovercrafts. Mom might visit the Europeans tomorrow."

The guard nods, but inside I'm screaming at Law to come up with a better lie. President Cartier could have her assistant make a call to find out the available planes or she could check the information herself on her T-screen. There's no way the guard will buy it, but then as soon as my doubts surface, the gate opens and he waves us forward. I fight to keep my composure as we continue on down the auto-walk and farther into the airport itself. It's different than I imagined. A huge single-level building sits in front of us. All metal and no frills, with only a few windows and the set of double doors in the center where the auto-walk ends. On the right and left sides of the building are row after row of various hovercrafts, stretching all the way to the gate. I've seen them soaring over my house a zillion times, but it's nothing like seeing one this close. They're gigantic with shiny black exteriors and windows that hide what's inside, creepy like a spider.

"Hey, did you hear me?" Law whispers and I shake myself into focus.

"Sorry, what?"

"We'll have to go inside," he says. "The guard will be watching to make sure we do. Once in there, this gets tricky. I say you and Gretchen slip into the shadows as soon as we enter. Get to the back of the building. There's another set of double doors in the middle, but to the far left is a single door that technicians use to get outside. Go through that one. I'm guessing the base will be out back. I'll go talk to the crew as we planned, hopefully giving you enough time to slip out without notice."

Gretchen starts to protest, but the doors open and Law starts for the right, nodding me to the left. The "airport" is nothing more than a warehouse of supplies. Bins of scrap parts scatter across the open floor, giving me the perfect cover to skirt along the wall to the back door. It's almost in sight when Gretchen trips behind me, barreling into a stack of bins and causing them to cascade to the floor with a loud clatter. Rushing footsteps close in, and the only thing between them and us is a stack of bins that is only six feet wide and maybe seven tall. If they peek around the bin, we're caught. I'm torn between running for the door, staying still, or ducking into what looks like an office across from me, but what if someone's in there? I suck in a breath and wait, listening, hoping I can tell which way they're coming from. After the longest second of my life, the footsteps stop and a man yells, "Get Alex down here to clean this up." Then the footsteps retreat and I release a breath, thankful luck is on my side today.

Once we're through the side door, there's a set of stairs that leads down, but to what I can't make out. My eyes dart around. I don't see anyone. I race for the stairs, jumping down from the first level to the next and onto a flat metal surface as long and wide as two of my houses. Past the metal surface is nothing but woods, and nothing and no one is visible from the right or left. I study the surface, at a loss for what it is, when Gretchen reaches me, her breath heavy. "Care to warn me before you pull out your freakish abilities? We can't all jump down a flight of stairs," she hisses.

I grimace. "Sorry," I say, and then point to the ground. "What do you think this is? Surely not the base. Unless it's underground, then we'd be…"

"Standing on the roof," she says.

And as though the thing heard us, it begins to shake and rattle, sending us stumbling backward. A four-by-eight section to the right and center of us slides open and a guard slips out, biting into an apple, oblivious to us standing there until I punch him in the gut and right hook to hopefully knock him out, but before I can check, the door starts to lower back down. I scream at Gretchen, "Keep watch. I'll be back in ten. If not…If not—"

"No. Don't even think it. Just hurry."

I dip inside the opening moments before it closes, but I'm met by darkness. My eyes strain to find a hint of light, and then, "Is someone there?" a voice calls. The rest of my senses heighten, and though I can't see an inch in front of my face, I know people are there. I hear their heartbeats, their breaths. I smell their sweat, their vomit, their urine. But worst of all, I feel their fear. It's overwhelming to sense so much from so many all at once.

I fumble in my backpack to find the flashlight I slid into the outside pocket and click it on, only to wish I'd done this in the dark. One long walkway darts down the center of the base, starting at the platform I stand on and ending at the opposite wall. On the right and left sit four cages of people, crammed in so blood drips from those against the cage walls, the metal pressing into their skin. But they look content compared to those in the back. Many are hyperventilating, others sobbing. It's the worst possible nightmare come true for these people. I have to get them out.

"Hello," I say, hoping to get their attention. But when no one says anything I strengthen my voice and call out, "I'm here to free you, but I'm going to need your help." This gets them going, and a few people call out to me, begging for me to free them first.

Then an elderly lady, two cages back on my right, says, "What can we do?"

I rush over to her, realizing she may be the only sane person in the group. "I need to know how to open the cages. Do you have any clue? A keycard? A security system?"

She tries to move but is unable to budge. "They keep going under the steps, but I'm not sure what's down there."

"Thank you," I say and dash back to the steps. Sure enough, there's a tiny room under the stairs, no larger than a closet, and filled with equipment and a T-screen that flashes with a reading every few seconds, but of what I can't be sure. *Think, Ari*, I tell myself.

I click on the T-screen and try to override the password, thinking maybe the cages have computerized locks, but I can't even get into the system to find out. I focus my flashlight on every inch of the tiny room, hoping to find anything that clues me in, and just when I'm about to scream, the light passes over a scanner. Of course. Everything in our world operates by a scanner, but they wouldn't… I reach into my boot and pull out the gold keycard, hesitating, and then slide it through the scanner. Instantly, the words ACCESS OVERRIDE: GRANTED fill the screen, and then two things pop up at once. A timer set to twenty-five seconds and a list of names that must be the people caged in front of me. I fight the urge to scan the list, wondering if I'll recognize any of the names. I close both of the screens and search for anything that could do with locks when I think back to the filing system at Parliament when Jackson and I stole the video to lab three. I had to scan the master key once to get into the room and again to unlock the files. Maybe this is similar.

I swipe the keycard, expecting either the cage doors to open or nothing to happen at all, but instead, another window pops up on the T-screen asking for a seven-digit password. I have no clue what it might be and time is running out. I step around the stairs and address the group again. "It wants a seven-digit password. Any clues or suggestions? It might lock me out if I enter something wrong."

A soft voice speaks up from the very back left cage, so small I can hardly hear it.

"What was that?" I ask, nearing. "I can't hear you."

I shine the flashlight into the cage and stumble back, falling hard onto the ground. "No. How in the world…?"

"I said, try *Freedom*," Cybil says, her voice strong, her head high. Even now, she's an Operative, always on the job.

"Cybil. Of all people, I never would have guessed."

She moves in what I guess is a shrug, but her body can't shift enough to complete the response. "What can I say? I got curious." She breaks into a coughing fit before she can continue. "We have loads of xylem around the office. I just wanted to see… And now, well, I guess *irony* about covers it."

I raise an eyebrow. That definitely doesn't sound like the Cybil I know. I start to question her further when the ceiling rattles and my eyes dart to a sliver of sunlight shining in from the top of the stairs.

Someone's coming, which means something must have happened to Gretchen.

I click off the flashlight and edge around the side of the last cage, wedging myself between it and the wall, concentrating on my breathing. In and out, in and out, in short, smooth breaths, hoping to stay as still and quiet as possible.

The door opens farther, and shrieks sound from the cages closest to the door, making me wonder if these people are being tortured. Light shines into the front of the base, while footsteps click down the stairs, slow and steady. Whoever is in here enjoys this; I can tell by the easiness of his heartbeat and the way his steps ooze arrogance. It takes all of me not to attack him, but with the door open, I'm afraid someone would hear him scream.

He *click*, *click*, *click*s down the walkway, dragging something across the cages so it sends a pinging sound into the air. I grit my teeth and press farther against the cage, hoping I'm not hurting anyone, but knowing if I don't steel myself, I'll lash out at the sicko. He reaches the last cage, turns back, and walks with the same carelessness back down the aisle. I hear him round the stairs and click on the T-screen, and then everything gets bad.

"What the…?" he says.

I realize the screen still shows the security window requesting my password, and he must know that only a Lead Op or someone within Parliament could access that screen. I hesitate, unsure of what to do, and then charge forward just as he's about to ascend the stairs. He whips around, but I'm faster, my reflexes sharper, and I flip forward and kick him in the face. He's a big guy so I know that won't be enough. I pull back to hit him again when the spark ignites within me, and I'm on him, warmth spreading through me. I stop, my heart racing, as I realize what I've just done—the Taking, killing him.

A cry releases from me before I can stop it. I've just killed someone using the very weapon the Ancient attackers used against us. I feel sick. I am sick.

"Ari, the code," Cybil screams.

I swallow hard, forcing myself to put what I've done out of my mind, tucked away for a quieter time—if I make it through this.

The T-screen is still lit, showing the security prompt, but another screen catches my eye, and suddenly terror rips through me. The countdown clock flashes, which means whatever Parliament has planned is about to begin. I say a silent prayer and type in F-R-E-E-D-O-M. The doors all open, and everyone tries to exit at once, causing the children and elderly to scream out.

"Stop!" I shout. "Everyone needs a vial. Wait, don't push," I say as a flood of people swarms past me. "Wait! I have something that will stop the infection!" Some turn back, but many are already gone, running with whatever strength they have to get away. I guess I can't blame them, but it's all in vain. The air is just going to poison them as soon as they breathe it, causing whatever symptoms they have to worsen and all of those people will soon be dead.

I sigh, wishing I would have given out the serum first, but it's too late to worry, so I start passing out a vial to everyone left, telling them to head for the port. Before long, the bag is empty and I'm left staring into hopeful faces with nothing left to give them. Then Gretchen races down the stairs, her shirt smeared with blood, and pulls out her bag, passing out the rest of the vials.

Relief washes over me at the sight of her. She reaches into her bag for another vial and passes it to the elderly lady who told me about the stairs.

"The port is just north of the airport," I say to the lady. "Do you know how to get there? Do you think you can make it?"

"I'm not going to the port. I'm going home."

"But, please. The serum will only last an hour. You'll die unless you go."

"Sweetie," she says, taking my hand, "there is a lot of gray between life and death. Life isn't worth living if you aren't with the ones you love. I'm going home to my Henry. I know I won't live long, and that's okay, but at least I can see him one last time."

I watch her in awe as she hobbles up the exit and out into the poisoned air. Gretchen and I are about to follow when I notice a small girl, maybe eight years old, cowering in the corner of one of the cages.

"It's okay. You're safe now," I say. "Gretchen, I need another vial." I hold out my hand, but when nothing drops into it, I peer around at her. "Another vial?"

She shakes her head. "I'm out."

I look from her to the little girl, who shakes uncontrollably. "Can you check again?" I pull out my coolant bag and dump it upside down, hoping a vial will drop from within, but it doesn't. Just then, an alarm sounds, either inside the room or out, I'm not sure.

"We have to go, Ari, now," Gretchen urges.

"We can't just leave her." I bend down to pick her up and feel something cold press against my ankle. I forgot I slipped the extra vial for me into my boot. I pull it out and hand it over to the girl. "Drink this; you'll feel better. I promise."

She reaches out a shaking hand, leery, but tilts it into her mouth. Once she's ingested it, I scoop her into my arms and rush for the exit but slam to a halt. Alarms echo from the airport, while commands shout out from all sides.

We're surrounded.

CHAPTER 29

Chaos everywhere. Guns blast from the right and left, sirens ring from the airport behind, the only sign of refuge is the forest in front of us, and half of the infected run for its shelter. I don't hesitate, running for the woods' edge, hoping Gretchen is with me. When I'm well into the woods, I stop, put down the girl, and scan the area for Gretchen, who reaches the woods a few seconds later.

"You have to stop doing that," she says with annoyance.

"What? I couldn't carry both of you. Where's Lawrence?"

"Here," he calls from behind Gretchen. "I tried to get them to stop. I tried everything."

"It's okay. Let's sort the weapons." I glance around at the thirty or so infected that made it into the woods, not allowing my eyes to drift to the clearing, to the dead bodies of those who didn't make it or died before the healing serum worked. We pass around weapons to those closest to us, giving brief instructions on how to use them.

Fires continue to ring out from the clearing, but those guns can't reach us and they can't fire a missile into the forest, not with the airport so close. That gives me comfort. The Unity Tree is through these woods, but I have no idea how to get to it from this far away, and the healing serum won't last long enough to get us there. The only way to get to the port is to fight, and time has to be running out before Zeus closes it. Then all of this was for nothing because we'll all die anyway.

I creep to the forest edge to get a look at the Operatives, most of them from my training class, which means none of them is older than eighteen and most are weak fighters. They'll have to come in here to get us. Something tells me these woods are more likely to work in our favor than theirs. Even though we're outnumbered, we stand a good chance.

I step backward, one step, two, and—*bam*—I slam into someone, and everything in my body tells me this someone is trouble. I whip around just as he pulls his gun. I was so distracted by eyeing up the enemy that I didn't consider they might come from behind. He tilts his head to the side and smiles before pulling the trigger. Everything slows down, the bullet zooms toward me, and then I'm on the ground in a flash, swiping the trick knife from my boot and jabbing it into his leg. He looks shocked, then his body turns rigid moments before he collapses onto the ground.

Screams ring out in all directions, madness as half the infected run through the woods, never looking back, while the rest of us scramble to find something to hide behind. Shots zoom out from all directions. I can't tell the difference between enemy shots and ours. I dip behind a large oak, resting one hand on it while I pull out a gun from my holster, but what happens next scares me worse than anything else I've experienced today.

My eyes drift to my hand, which has disappeared into the tree, a tingly feeling moving from it to my arm, and then I can no longer feel my hand at all. I jerk it back, shaking it to make sure it's really there. I need to get into the fight, but all I can do is stare at the tree and then at my hand, wanting to test it again but afraid that it won't come back out this time or that I'll disappear into the tree or that something inside it will pull me in. I don't know. I knew Ancients came through the trees, but I always assumed it was more technical than this. And if we can enter any tree and end up on Loge, then everything is okay. I can call out and tell everyone just to touch a tree. But I can't risk it. There's so much I don't know.

I close my eyes, say a tiny prayer, and charge from the tree, both guns raised. And it's horrible, horrible. In the time I took behind the tree, there are Operatives everywhere in the forest, fighting, shooting—killing. I don't know our numbers, but they can't be good. I start for the first group I see, two Operatives barreling in on an old man who I have no clue why he stayed. I'm about to fire when the old man leaps into the air, his Ancient ability, so innate now, overcoming him. In a blur, the two Operatives are on the ground, stumbling to get back up. The man raises a hand, stopping me from helping, and I smile at him, proud, and then he's shot in the head from behind, blood squirting across the Operatives in front of him.

"No!" I shout, racing forward to catch him, but the Operatives are up now, facing me, ready to attack. Anger hits in my chest, and before I can think, I shoot them both in the heads. There's no time for guilt, even though I feel it climbing from my stomach, and I know if there weren't five others running for me right now, I would vomit. Instead I run to meet them, ready to do whatever I must, if only I could keep my vision straight or the ringing in my ears would stop. I allow my other senses to take over, feeling what they feel. They encircle me, half boys, half girls, all of them from my training class.

"You don't have to do this," I say. "I'm human, just like you. You don't have to listen to what they're telling you. Listen to me. You don't have to die today. You can go home right now, and no one will know."

"Enough," a boy with black hair and equally black eyes says. "You disgust me. Calling yourself human. You're a freak of nature. Stand down, everyone. She's mine."

I shake my head. "I warned you." And then I'm on him, his gun flying from his grasp, punching him again and again. I don't want to kill these people, these kids. Maybe I can just— *Bang, bang, bang!*

I suck in a breath as Law comes into view to my right. How he managed that shot, I'll never know, but what I do know is the look on his face will stay ingrained in my memory for the rest of my life. Shock, guilt. He isn't a killer. Gretchen and I were trained for this, but not him.

"Law," I say, racing over to him because he looks like he'll collapse to the ground at any second.

Law's head twitches, and then his moment of weakness is gone, replaced by resolution. "It's fine. They're coming." He motions behind me as the remaining four Operatives close in.

"I've got this. Go find Gretchen," I say, not pulling my eyes from the Operatives, forcing my mind not to see them for what they are but what they will do if I don't stop them. I reach down and pull out the laser gun I took from Dad's private stash in our training room. They see the gun; some maybe even recognize it from our first training. Two stop cold, a boy and a girl who I remember were both horrible shots. "Go!" I scream at them, and they run off, leaving the two remaining members of their team behind. Another time, I would have called them cowards, but I was ignorant then, not understanding that war is about a lot more than courage. It's about what's right, separate from expectation or orders.

The last two are within three yards of me when I say, "Don't do this." But the first one has already pulled his gun, the second reaching for hers, and I fire, zapping both in the chest. Their faces pale, their mouths drop in shock, and then their bodies fall to the ground, crunching into the leaves.

I release a breath I hadn't realized I held and turn around to examine the situation, but what I see through the woods on the metal ceiling of the execution base is enough to send me running through the woods, screaming. Five infected and Gretchen, all kneeling down in front of four Operatives, Law a few feet away, tied up, pleading with the Ops to stop. They won't kill him; they can't—he's the next president. I hear the first gunfire and an infected hits the metal ground, blood pouring over the silver. I push harder, but someone gets to me first, pulling me back.

"Shhh," Cybil whispers. "We need to get around behind

them."

"No," I whisper back. "I have a laser gun. I can get them from the edge."

"You can get one, not all."

I know she's right, but while we sit there talking, another person is about to die. "Fine, what do you suggest?" I peer around her to the forest, my eyes widening as two, four, ten infected step out from behind trees. We did better than I thought, and some of them ran anyway, so maybe this was worth it after all.

They ease closer to hear Cybil. "Stay at the forest edge, but half of us to the right of them, half to the left. Ari, shoot one of the Ops holding Law; that way they'll all look over, and then when we charge, they'll be off their guard."

I start to tell her that we need to match person to person, so shots aren't wasted, when a cough threatens to release and I grab my chest, swallowing it back. Oh no.

"You okay?" she asks, her face wrinkled in concern.

"Yeah, fine." I don't have the heart to tell her my serum is wearing off, and if we don't get going, I may be unable to move, let alone shoot. I point to each person in our group, assigning a target to each, and then nod to Cybil. "I'll go right; you go left."

We separate, our steps light against the forest leaves, never crunching under our weight. I reach the right side, watching the backs of the Operatives, just as one starts yelling at those kneeled in front of him to disclose who infiltrated the base. Over and over he yells. I guess they realize it had to be done by an insider. My eyes lock with Cybil, she nods, and I fire at the Op standing over Law. He falls back, and then we're storming from the forest, shots ringing out. Gretchen stands, pulls a trick knife from her boot, and shoves it into the chest of the Op in front of her. She races for Law, cutting him from his ties, and the two of them join the fight, but there are more Operatives coming from all sides, and only ten of us left. Only ten.

I motion for my group to get the other infected back into the safety of the forest. Shots come from all directions. I shoot back, aiming at one then another, but it's no use, more and more come from the airport, around the sides of it, everywhere.

And that's when it hits me.

My vision blurs, everything slowing down. I spot the little girl I saved, the one I gave my last serum to, hiding by the airport. She cups her hands around her ears, her knees shaking, while slow tears course down her face as though a faucet were left on. I want to scream for her to run. I want to save her myself. But suddenly a coughing fit erupts from my mouth, blood mixed with bile. I draw a breath, no longer hearing what happens around me. An Operative fires, killing an infected. An infected shoots, killing an Operative. So much death. My eyes find the little girl's, and we're locked on each other, unable to look away. I see her tears, and it's as though they're mine—they are mine. But I can't cry. I can't breathe. I can't move. I draw another breath, and it's like I can feel the poison eating my muscles, boiling my blood.

Then I hear my name shouted again and again. A female Operative, one I recognize though I can't remember her name, hears it, too, and she lifts her gun, squaring her shoulders to fire.

"No!" A scream, a voice I recognize. The female Op falls, blood pouring from her, and then he's in front of me, snapping in front of my face for me to see him, begging me to see him.

Jackson holds my face, burying it in his, but I can't say anything.

"Don't die on me. Come on, stay with me. Please…" I suck in a short breath, and my knees buckle as Jackson sweeps me into his arms. "Hold on. Please just hold on," he says, his voice rattling. He calls my name over and over, but it sounds distant, a cacophony against the peaceful chorus I hear, like birds, singing me to sleep. I try to fight off the sound, fight off the heaviness of my eyelids, but the sound is too beautiful, sleep too peaceful. My body surrenders, relishing in the birds' melody. I smile.

And then it's gone.

CHAPTER 30

My mind flashes in nonsensical scenes. A wrinkled woman hovering over me. Jackson beside me, holding my hand. Screams echo in the background. The woman returns, jerks my head back, and shoves something warm into my mouth that tastes and feels like cooked paper or dried leaves. I try to spit it out, but she clamps my mouth shut.

"Chew, human. Now," she commands.

I fight against her arm, so she yanks my mouth open, pouring icy liquid in so fast I have no choice but to choke or swallow.

I swallow.

The clump of cooked goo rushes down my throat, slicing the sides as it goes. I want to puke; I'm going to puke. Then it hits my stomach, and I'm on fire. Every ounce of my body burning, burning, burning. I wonder if this is how the combustion Ancients felt, because I know any moment my insides will burst out of my skin from the pressure. Sweat collects on my forehead, running down the sides of my face, under my arms, under my knees...all over. I'm drenched on the outside, burning on the inside. Hell encapsulated.

Then as quickly as the fire found me, cold replaces the hot, freezing its way through the veins of my body until every part of me feels first relief then fear. My entire body is numb. I try to breathe, but the air sucks in and out in short bursts. Panic ensues, and inside I'm screaming, outside I can't speak. The woman reappears above me, jerking my eyelids up from their half-open stupor.

"You see, human?" she says.

I nod.

"You feel?"

I shake my head—at least, in my mind it's shaking—and she mumbles something before returning with a tiny ceramic cup. "Drink this; be better," she says, forcing the cup to my mouth. I part my lips but not enough, so she pries the cup through the small opening and tilts it down. I cringe at the bitter taste. A mix of black coffee and lemon pours over my taste buds. My body jerks about, either from the concoction or the horrifying taste, I'm not sure. Then suddenly I feel perfect, neutral, and a tad high, like I've had a few too many drinks but not enough to be reckless.

"Yes?" she asks.

I nod, fighting against the stupid smile enveloping my face, but I can't help it. I've felt so sick for so long. "More," I manage to say.

She breaks into laughter, patting my hand. "You good now, child. Sleep."

And I do.

I wake later—hours, minutes, I'm not sure. Someone approaches at my stirring. The woman from my dreams, perhaps, or maybe that was real.

"How are you feeling?"

I open my eyes, and Jackson slides closer to me. "I was so worried. You took longer to wake…I thought you may never come back to me." He traces his hand over my face, and I jerk back, torn between the Jackson I thought I knew and the Jackson he really is—Jackson Castello, Zeus's grandson.

I wet my lips. They're dry and cracked. "How long have I been here?" I ask and realize that isn't the first question. "Where am I?"

A flicker of hurt passes over his face before he answers. "Loge, at our version of a medical center. We call it the Panacea, and you've been here for three days."

"No, that's not— No." My breathing escalates as hot tears collect in my eyes. "What happened to everyone else? Did we leave them? Did they all die? Wait, no." A sob cuts off in my throat. "My parents, Jackson. Where are my parents?"

"Sydia. I'm so sorry," he says, his mouth set in a deep frown, and the finality in his voice causes me to fall apart, everything culminating with this moment. All the planning, all the death, and now… My chest heaves in violent sobs, everything I've been through and everything I'll never see again, showering over me. I second-guess all my decisions. I should have said good-bye to Mom before I left. I should have been more covert, more Op-like when I broke into the base. There are more regrets than I can process.

Jackson tries to pull me to his chest, but I push him away, anger mixing with my tears. He lied to me all along, and now everyone I love is gone. I want to ask him questions, but I'm not ready to hear his answers. I knew what would happen when I came here, but I thought I would have time to say good-bye—not that one word can make this easier. All I can think about is Mom's face when Gretchen and Law tell her I'm gone. It's not fair to her. She'll worry forever, and there's nothing I can do.

A fresh round of sobs escapes, and Jackson dips his head, his face pain-stricken. He reaches for my hand, but stops mid-motion at the look I give him. I don't want him to touch me. Maybe I should be stronger, or at least put forth the illusion of strength, but I can't. The worry is overwhelming. I have no clue what world I left them in or what horrors wait for them because they helped me. I had them risk everything, and then I vanished, leaving them to pick up the pieces.

I know Jackson can sense my thoughts, but he doesn't say anything, instead just lets me cry as long as I need in silence, never leaving. After what feels like an hour of crying, I ease up in the bed, scanning the room for the first time. It's different than what I imagined. The walls and ceiling are wooden but rough, as though someone built the room without the right tools. Two windows on the outside wall allow light to shine through, and though the room could hold ten beds, mine is the only one in the room, made of a tan fabric and held up by nothing more than wooden posts. On the opposite side of the room from the windows is a curtained doorway, the same tan fabric as the bed. What lies beyond the curtain I can only imagine, but so far I've yet to see anyone pass by my doorway or hear any sounds outside it.

A million thoughts flutter through my mind, and I'm not sure where to begin.

"I know it's a lot to take," Jackson says, "but we'll figure it out…together if you'll let me."

"Tell me what happened to them," I say, refusing to meet his gaze.

He adjusts beside me, buying time. "I shouldn't have taken you before you could say good-bye. And I'm sorry for that. I didn't know what else to do. You were…" He looks away, drawing a long breath. "Dying. I scooped you up and raced to the nearest tree, teleporting us here, before I had time to think through the decision."

I nod. "I just wish…" Flashes of memories hit in my mind, each one slicing through my chest. "It doesn't matter now."

Jackson leans in close, lowering his voice. "This isn't forever, Ari. You'll see them again. I promise you that as long as they're alive, I'll make sure you see them again."

"So does that mean they're all fine?"

He shrugs, looking uncomfortable again. "I believe so. I heard from Law yesterday."

"Wait." I jerk up in bed, causing a sharp pain to shoot from my head down my neck. I grimace at the pain but push it away, too eager to hear more. "Did you say you heard from Law? Does that mean we can talk to them?"

Jackson smiles widely. "Of course."

Tears brim my eyes again, this time a mixture of happiness and relief. I'll talk to my parents again. I can tell them I'm okay.

I can make sure they're okay. "But if we can communicate with them, then why did you take so long to message me? I thought… Dad told me who you really are. He told me you were sent to spy on me. He said it was all a job to you," I say, hurt replacing my anger.

Jackson turns around so he faces me, his expression serious. "I was sent to get information, and I am Zeus's grandson, but all of that changes nothing between us. I know I've done a lot to give you doubts, so I understand if—"

The wrinkled woman from earlier returns and *hmph*s at our closeness. "You ought to rest. Let her rest, young one," she says to Jackson.

"And this would be Emmy," Jackson says to me. "She'll take care of you while you're here." He pulls himself away, saying he has a meeting to attend and will return after.

"What sort of meeting?" I ask, causing Emmy to stiffen.

"Not your business, child. He's—"

Jackson silences her with one look. "Nothing. Just business."

I stare at him, hoping he can sense the questions and concerns running through my mind, but he doesn't respond.

He leaves, and I suddenly realize that apart from Jackson, I'm alone here. Alone with a boy that even now refuses to be straight with me. I watch Emmy as she checks my pulse and heart rate. She's systematic about it, no feeling, no care, nothing like the medics at home. Home. I push the thought from my mind as soon as it appears. Crying in front of Jackson is one thing, but I refuse to melt down around Emmy.

She takes a warm sponge from a tin basin beside the bed, easing it over my face and arms and legs.

"I can do that," I say.

"Best not to overdo."

"Thank you."

She stops mid-motion, weighing my words. I'm sure she's about to go off on me, but instead she smiles. "You are one of us now. He chose you long ago."

"Long ago? But we just—"

"No. Nothing by chance."

I try to comprehend what she means, but it's crazy. He couldn't... No. "Jackson didn't plan this; he wouldn't." The room grows hotter by the second. She can't mean... No, no, no.

Fear crosses her face and she leans closer, so close her face is almost touching mine. "Not young one. Old one."

Old one? Who is she...? My mouth falls open, realization clearing my mind.

Zeus.

ACKNOWLEDGMENTS

First, thank you God for guiding me daily and challenging me to be better, always better.

It takes a small army to produce a book, and mine has been nothing short of amazing. Thank you to Heather Howland for discovering me from your endless slush pile. You breathed life into this book and designed the cover of my dreams. I will forever be grateful. Thank you to Liz Pelletier, my fierce editor, for loving the book I wrote, the way I wrote it, and calling it "magic." I feel so blessed to have you. And I feel sure no one would know that *Gravity* exists without the help of my ninja publicist, Heather Riccio. You have been my rock.

Thank you to my husband, Jason, for making sure all the scenes involving weapons were accurate and for being so supportive through all of this. It's easy to write about true love when I experience it daily with you. And many, many thanks to my daughters for keeping me young and laughing. You are my light.

Much love and thanks to my family, most notably my mother, sister, and niece who have been my biggest fans. Also, thank you to my mother-in-law for watching my daughter so I could write even before anyone considered me a writer.

A continuous and unending thanks to Laura Hughes, my critique partner, who has read *Gravity* more times than anyone else. This book would not exist without you. Also thank you to early and beta readers—the Oobies critique group, Shelley, Jenn, and Amanda for helping me add depth to the story.

Thank you to Chloe Jacobs, Lisa Burstein, Rachel Harris, and Tara Fuller for keeping me sane and for being such wonderful friends. Thank you a million times over. This experience would not be nearly as fulfilling without you.

To Erica Justice, Heather Grimmett, and Tonya Johnson. I feel so blessed to call you my friends. Thank you for not laughing when I said I'd written a book and for reading it even before I knew what I was doing.

Thank you to the countless bloggers and readers out there who have shown such tremendous enthusiasm for this series. I could not be more grateful. And finally, many thanks to *you* for reading this book. I hope it is everything you wanted it to be and more.

Get tangled up in our Entangled Teen titles...

Luminosity by Stephanie Thomas

Beatrice had her first vision at the age of twelve, and now the Institution depends on her to keep the City safe from the Dreamcatchers. But Beatrice has a secret that could put everyone in danger. A secret that could kill her and everyone she loves. The enemy has been coming to her in her dreams, and she might be falling in love with him.

Greta and the Goblin King by Chloe Jacobs

Four years ago, Greta fell through a portal to a world where humans are the enemy. Now a bounty hunter, she's caught the attention of the darkly enticing young Goblin King, who invades her dreams and undermines her will to escape. But Greta's not the only one looking to get out of Mylena...

Onyx by Jennifer L. Armentrout

Thanks to his alien mojo, Daemon's determined to prove what he feels for me is more than a product of our bizarro connection. Against all common sense, I'm falling for Daemon. Hard. *No one is who they seem. And not everyone will survive the lies...*

Get tangled up in our Entangled Teen titles…

Inbetween **by Tara Fuller**

It's not easy being dead, especially for a reaper in love with Emma, a girl fate has put on his list not once, but twice. Finn will protect the girl he loves from the evil he accidentally unleashed, even if it means sacrificing the only thing he has left…his soul.

The Marked Son **by Shea Berkley**

When Dylan sees a girl in white in the woods behind his grandparents' farm, he knows he's seen her before…in his dreams. Only he can save her world from an evil lord—a world full of creatures he's only read about in horror stories. Worse, the human blood in his veins has Dylan marked for death…

My Super Sweet Sixteenth Century **by Rachel Harris**

The last thing Cat Crawford wants for her sixteenth birthday is an extravagant trip to Florence, Italy. But when her curiosity leads her to a gypsy tent, she exits . . . right into Renaissance Firenze. Cat joins up with her ancestors and soon falls for the gorgeous Lorenzo. Can she find her way back to modern times before her Italian adventure turns into an Italian forever?

Get tangled up in our Entangled Teen titles...

Conjure by Lea Nolan

Sixteen-year-old twins Emma and Jack Guthrie hope for a little summer adventure when they find an eighteenth-century message in a bottle revealing a hidden pirate treasure. Will they be able to set things right before it's too late?

Chosen Ones by Tiffany Truitt

The government, faced with humanity's extinction, created the Chosen Ones. When Tess begins work at a Chosen Ones training facility, she meets James, and the attraction is immediate in its intensity, overwhelming in its danger. Can she stand against her oppressors, even if it means giving up the only happiness in her life?

Toxic by Jus Accardo

When a Six saved Kale's life the night of Sumrun, Dez was warned there would be consequences. But she never imagined she'd lose the one thing she'd give anything to keep... Dez will have to lay it all on the line if there's any hope of proving Jade's guilt before they all end up Residents of Denazen. Or worse, dead...